Chicks Dig Time Lords

A Celebration of Doctor Who by the Women Who Love It

edited by
Lynne M. Thomas
Tara O'Shea

mad
norwegian
press

HUGO AWARD™
WINNER 2011
BEST RELATED WORK

Published by Mad Norwegian Press (www.madnorwegian.com).
Edited by Lynne M. Thomas and Tara O'Shea
Editor-in-Chief: Lars Pearson
Cover art by Katy Shuttleworth.
Jacket & interior design by Christa Dickson.

"Hugo Award" and The Hugo Award Logo are service marks of the World Science Fiction Society, an unincorporated literary society.

ISBN: 978-1935234043

Printed in Illinois. First Printing: March 2010. Second Printing: October 2011.

Also available from Mad Norwegian Press...

*Chicks Unravel Time: Women Journey Through Every Season
of Doctor Who*, edited by Deborah Stanish and LM Myles (forthcoming)

*Chicks Dig Comics: A Celebration of Comic Books
by the Women Who Love Them*,
edited by Lynne M. Thomas and Sigrid Ellis (forthcoming)

*Whedonistas: A Celebration of the Worlds of Joss Whedon by the Women
Who Love Them*, edited by Lynne M. Thomas and Deborah Stanish

*Running Through Corridors: Rob and Toby's Marathon Watch
of Doctor Who* (Vol. 1: The 60s) by Robert Shearman and Toby Hadoke

*Running Through Corridors:
Rob and Toby's Marathon Watch of Doctor Who* (Vol. 2: The 70s)
by Robert Shearman and Toby Hadoke (forthcoming)

Resurrection Code
All-new prequel to the AngeLINK novel series
by Lyda Morehouse

*Wanting to Believe: A Critical Guide to The X-Files, Millennium
and The Lone Gunmen* by Robert Shearman

Dusted: The Unauthorized Guide to Buffy the Vampire Slayer
by Lawrence Miles, Lars Pearson and Christa Dickson

Redeemed: The Unauthorized Guide to Angel (ebook forthcoming)
by Lars Pearson and Christa Dickson

AHistory: An Unauthorized History of the Doctor Who Universe
[2nd Edition now available]
by Lance Parkin

The About Time Series
by Tat Wood and Lawrence Miles
About Time 1: The Unauthorized Guide to Doctor Who (Seasons 1 to 3)
About Time 2: The Unauthorized Guide to Doctor Who (Seasons 4 to 6)
About Time 3: The Unauthorized Guide to Doctor Who
(Seasons 7 to 11) [2nd Edition now available]
About Time 4: The Unauthorized Guide to Doctor Who (Seasons 12 to 17)
About Time 5: The Unauthorized Guide to Doctor Who (Seasons 18 to 21)
About Time 6: The Unauthorized Guide to Doctor Who
(Seasons 22 to 26, the TV Movie)
About Time 7 (forthcoming)

This book is dedicated to Verity Lambert – Doctor Who's first producer (1963-1965). She was the first chick to dig Time Lords.

Table of Contents

Introduction

Tara's Story:

So this all started with a T-shirt.

When I was getting ready to attend my first Gallifrey One convention, I decided to wear a different geeky T-shirt each day, and I made up one that said "Chicks Dig Time Lords." I passed the CafePress link on to friends, and with each convention I attended, saw a number of other women in the shirt – including Christa Dickson, who designed this book. She even wore the shirt during pledge drives for *Doctor Who* on Iowa Public Television, ensuring the T-shirt was viewed by, at the very least, a fair amount of PBS-viewing Iowans.

Christa and I have teamed up for a series of "squee" panels at both Chicago TARDIS and Gallifrey One over the last five years, leading discussions about what drew women to the programme and the fandom. Before that very first panel, we braced for controversy. Segments of diehard (i.e. male) *Doctor Who* fandom had been grumbling online about the droves of new female fans that were coming into their clubhouse with their "squee" and fan fiction; we were genuinely concerned that we'd be spending an hour dodging rotten vegetables and angry accusations that we simply didn't understand the Doctor or the series itself.

What we discovered instead was a group of fans of all types – men and women – who were quite happy to listen to us ramble about both the original series and the revamped series currently airing, and what had drawn us to both. Over several years, the number of panelists and size of our audiences grew, and our topics shifted from "There are girls in fandom! No, really!" to general discussions of women in the series, women working behind the scenes and the differences of fannish behavior between the sexes.

Rather than an all-out Battle of the Sexes (which we had been dreading), instead we had a half-dozen really amazing discussions about the diversity in fandom, and the differences and similarities in male and female *Doctor Who* fandom. I had an idea that what had begun at convention panels – plus online in forums such as LiveJournal and Outpost Gallifrey – could be repacked and presented in a way that would not only appeal to female fans (longstanding or brand new), but would be a slim volume male fans would buy not just for themselves, but for their daughters and mothers and wives and girlfriends. So I pitched the idea to Christa and her husband – Lars Pearson, the publisher of Mad Norwegian Press – as a book project.

Lynne's Story:

I first heard the phrase "Chicks Dig Time Lords" when I saw it on my friend Christa Dickson's T-shirt at Chicago TARDIS 2007.

I wanted that shirt. It encompassed, in four little words, exactly how I felt about the series and its fandom. It was sassy and a little sexy, but not too much. It had a sense of humor about itself, but that didn't mean that it wasn't absolutely sincere. This forthright, fun statement about the presence of women in *Doctor Who* fandom had a real point behind it, along with lots of room for interpretation.

Christa told me that Tara O'Shea had designed the T-shirt. I had met Tara at the previous year's Chicago TARDIS. Funnily enough, she and my husband Michael had attended college together, lost touch and re-connected a decade later through *Doctor Who*.

On the "squee" panel, and the adults-only alt.sexuality panel at that convention (yes, there was liquor involved), Christa, Tara and I talked about all of the different things that we loved about *Doctor Who*, particularly the relationships between the characters. What made those conversations interesting was that each of us had quite different takes on different aspects of the show, even though we all identified as individual "squee" fans.

In the spring of 2008, once I finished co-authoring a book about rare books and special collections librarianship for my day job, I was brought into the project as co-editor. I was thrilled to be asked to participate.

The "Chicks Dig Time Lords" Story:

Together we sat down and worked out what this book could be, and what we thought this book *should* be. *Chicks Dig Time Lords*, named after that T-shirt, isn't about "us vs. them," or "boy fandom vs. girl fandom." It celebrates the shared, yet quite diverse, experiences of female *Doctor Who* fans.

Chicks Dig Time Lords brings together an amazing collection of women from three different continents with one thing in common: *Doctor Who*. This group of authors, actors, creators and members of the fan community wrote original essays just for this volume, showcasing as many different ways of being a *Doctor Who* fan as possible. They touch on every era of the program, every Doctor, and many distinct fan experiences – from fan fiction to costuming, from writing tie-in novels to running conventions, from vidding to academic critique.

Our contributors demonstrate that there is no one right way to be a *Doctor Who* fan.

Yet each of us has imagined stepping into that unassuming blue box and being whisked across the universe for an adventure, just once.

Did we mention that it travels in time?

We'll Make Great Pets

Elizabeth Bear is one of the most prolific and acclaimed science fiction and fantasy authors of the last decade, and happens to share a birthday with Bilbo and Frodo Baggins. In the last five years, she has published 12 novels, two short story collections and a novella. Bear won the John W. Campbell Award for Best New Writer in 2005 and the Locus Award for Best First Novel for her Jenny Casey trilogy in 2006. Her short story "Tideline" won both the Hugo Award for Best Short Story and The Theodore Sturgeon Memorial Award for best short science fiction in 2008. In 2009, her novelette "Shoggoths in Bloom" earned her a second Hugo. Her recent novels include *By the Mountain Bound* from Tor Books and *Chill* from Bantam Spectra. She lives in Connecticut with a Presumptuous Cat and a Giant Ridiculous Dogge. http://www.elizabethbear.com/

In 1978, I was seven years old and sitting on the black tile floor of my grandparents' living room, watching an inexplicable PBS program on which a clunky stop-motion Loch Ness monster was terrorizing a bunch of strange-looking people in a Scottish hunting lodge. The segments were short, choppily edited and broken up frequently by title sequences and what sounded like wailing theremins – not that I knew yet what a theremin might be. The strange-looking people seemed to spend a lot of time running and screaming, except for the curly-haired one with the fantastical scarf, who seemed almost supernaturally blasé and who *didn't* seem to have a proper name. At least, nobody called him by one: he was just *the Doctor*.

Of course, it was the PBS broadcast of "Terror of the Zygons," and the curly-haired man was Tom Baker.

I was in love.

For one thing, to my seven-year-old heart, very little was more entrancing than the Loch Ness monster. I was the sort of kid who collected books about Nessie – and cryptozoology in general. I knew what a squonk was before I was ten. I read my paperback copy of *The Book of Imaginary Beings* until the cover fell off. I really, really wanted dragons to be real.

For another, though, I was totally hooked on the Doctor. He was the perfect grownup. A little like Willy Wonka – in those days, Willy Wonka was Gene Wilder in a purple velvet morning coat – adventurous, playful, whimsical. He seemed to me the quintessential ideal of a timeless wanderer, quirky and arbitrary in all the right ways, as if we would somehow understand his motivations if only we were not mere flashes in the pan to him, briefly-lived pets like hamsters or mice. And he seemed, inexplicably, *comforting*.

Why anyone would find a hyperkinetic, crabby space alien with a pocket full of jelly babies comforting is beyond me, but apparently I am not unique in this response. Maybe it's early childhood training: the Doctor holds hands, so he must be your buddy. Maybe it's that Four is so quizzical and childlike, always full of wonder and a sense of adventure. Maybe it's his air of always knowing what to do, even if the right thing to do is simply, "*Run!*"

(I've often thought that the Doctor and his companions have a very physically demanding job, with all that hustling to and fro. I hope the TARDIS has a good gym: you'd need to keep your wind up.)

It was a long time ago, and I don't recall if PBS was running several episodes back to back, or if it was some kind of one-a-day thing. I do recall camping on the floor for hours, captivated by the silliness – and the Daleks and Cybermen, which were sufficiently horrifying for a kid. It was low-budget and tacky even by the standards of a kid who watched *Star Trek* in syndication and ate up *Battlestar Galactica* and *Buck Rogers*. And I loved it.

I never got as heavily into *Doctor Who* fandom as many of my friends did, in part because I never successfully made the transition to another Doctor. None of the others had Four's verve or *joie de vivre*. None of them made me feel safe. I kept watching the Tom Baker serials whenever I found them, though, and the soughing like a theremin could still send a thrill of anticipation up my spine.

But I think the Doctor (along with Roger Zelazny) has had a profound influence on my work. I remain, to this day, fascinated by the idea of stories examining the plight of an immortal being moving among brief lives. That idea intrigues me so.

What must we look like, to the Doctor? He picks us up and sets us aside, leaving us irrevocably changed in his wake but carrying on, himself, unaltered. Even in his profoundest change – regeneration, where he literally becomes a new person – he still remains the Doctor. It's a fascinating idea, that someone so mercurial – so *inconstant* – can also be the most constant thing in the universe.

And yet despite that, it is a kind of irony that there was only one Doctor for me.

So when the new series came along, I didn't greet the news of a new Doctor with the same enthusiasm – or trepidation – that many of my friends did. I wasn't all that familiar with Christopher Eccleston or his work, but I figured he would turn out to be just another Doctor who never quite hit me where I lived. But that wouldn't destroy the franchise for me, because I was content with My Doctor.

Boy, did I have it backwards. Because the instant he appeared, I felt the old familiar joy. That unexpected sense of combined adventure and comfort, the paradox of the Doctor – like an easy chair with wings.

Or like a police box that can fly.

I learned something else from Nine about why Four had always meant so much to me. Because Four was irascible, curmudgeonly, manic and sharp – but he was also profoundly benevolent and generous of spirit, and it seemed to me that Nine captured those elements as well, and so it was love all over again.

My love for the Doctor never required cohesive scripting or airtight plots. After all, my first introduction involved a giant papier-mâché sea monster rampaging across the North Sea oil refineries, a manifestation later followed by killer garbage cans with plungers on the front, and that never troubled me at all. In the person of Nine, Eccleston proved to me that I still adored the Doctor, and moreover he proved that what sells me on the character is the charisma of the actor, his manic energy and sense of fun, and – perhaps most fundamentally – the banter and snark.

The special effects were better, and the Daleks could fly, but the core *sense* of the character was still there – world-weary, but possessing, and *possessed* by, a love of adventure and novelty that can never be slaked. But there's another element, too, and one that I think is at the core of the Doctor's appeal.

He's the proof that somebody out there cares. Somebody up there loves us. In the narrative of *Doctor Who*, the universe may be cold and indifferent, but there are powers that defend life, that hold it sacred, and arrive at the last instant to pull our fat out of the fire.

It's just darned encouraging.

My friend Sarah Monette, who is both a fantasy author and a literary critic, has floated the idea that there's a binary opposition in literature to the (in)famous noir sensibility, which she refers to as "clair." In a noir universe, the world is debased and sinful, and a hero of some moral compass moves through it without changing its essential nature; his victories are at best insignificant and at worst pyrrhic. In a *clair* universe, by contrast, the world may also be debased and unfair (or it may be essentially just), but the moral compass of the protagonist is capable of effecting larger change for the good.

Doctor Who flirts with noir occasionally – it brings us apocalypses and terrible errors and tremendous suffering – but it's a primary tenet of the Doctor's existence that good *can* be done, that the universe can be changed for the better, and that no matter how bad things get or how badly we err, there is always something we can do to make it better. It is essentially a clair sensibility, in other words: the narrative supports the actions of good characters, and we know that no matter how bad things get, in the end, the Doctor will be there to haul it out.

For clarity's sake, I'm moved to compare another classic Brit SF serial, *Sapphire & Steel*, of which I am also a fan. It also concerns the activities of demigod-like alien entities who take an interest in healing the damaged time-stream of planet Earth.

However, unlike the Doctor, Steel is entirely without compassion for (or interest in) human foibles or even human existence. His colleague, Sapphire, is more humane, but even she is quite willing to sacrifice individual lives in the service of something greater. The Doctor at his most ruthless probably approaches Sapphire's attitude on a typical day. Sapphire and Steel do not keep human pets or companions, and honestly wouldn't know what to do with them if they did. If the Doctor is the crazy cat lady of time-traveling immortals, Steel is the mean old man on the corner with the BB gun, taking potshots at the little bastards to keep them from crapping in his flower beds.

Where *Doctor Who* exploits the clair end of the spectrum, *Sapphire & Steel* is unabashedly noir. And I think it's significant that the cult following for *Sapphire & Steel* is smaller than that of the good Doctor. In terms of narrative, clair is a more appealing world-view to a wider variety of people. It's nice to think that somebody out there will come play savior when we screw up really badly, and that he'll forgive us our errors because really, we're just babies on his scale.

And it's nice to think that he'll take us with him. That we'll get to experience the universe as he does, however briefly. Hanging around with the Doctor is sort of a perpetual Best Day Ever, and even if the narrative of the more recent series goes out of its way to undermine that trope, it seems to me as if the writers don't actually believe it. Sure, it has to end eventually – mere humans can't keep up the Doctor's pace eternally. We get old and we get frail; we need our silly monkey emotions validated; we want a place to put our feet up and catch a bit of a nap.

A dragon (or a Time Lord) lives forever, but mortal flesh is weak.

But in the meantime, what a glorious ride! Do you skip the chocolate cake because after you've eaten it, you won't still have cake?

So we accept that to the Doctor, we'll never be much more than pets, beloved companions despite – or perhaps because of – the fact that we need things explained in small words and short sentences. Creatures so far beneath him that it's not just that he won't explain: he actively can't, even when he tries his hardest. The best he can make us do is understand that some things are beneficial and some are harmful, that some are encouraged and some are forbidden, and we're just never going to be smart enough to understand why.

The funny thing is, that's comforting, too. It's that parental authority thing: it's nice to think that maybe somebody actually understands this mess we're living in and has a plan to deal with it, even if the best they can do to explain is spread their hands and say, "You'll understand when your species is older."

And the Doctor is just so *delighted* by us, it's hard not to love him back. He'll throw that damned ball as long as we keep bringing it over, and he'll keep coming up with new challenges for us, and being there to lend a helping hand if we get in over our heads.

I have a confession to make, though. I never wanted to be a companion. I wanted to be the Doctor. I suspect I'd be good at it, honestly; most of the things that defeat me in life are the mundanities of parking regulations and getting the paperwork filed and the bills paid on time, and if you have a TARDIS and psychic paper, those difficulties tend to resolve themselves without incident. I already take in strays; I've got that bit covered. Two hearts is a little harder, but I could figure something out, given time...

And there's something about New *Who* that I must admit doesn't charm me as much. Because it's so evident, in so many ways, that the narrative sets the Doctor above and apart from humanity. We can't even aspire to be like him, and in our worst times of crisis – even when they're largely his fault to begin with – our best course of action is to pray for outside intervention and wait for the Doctor to come save us.

I prefer to think that we can learn from him, grow up, take responsibility for ourselves.

I understand why the Doctor likes human beings – ridiculous tail-less monkeys that we are – so much. Because when we are our best selves, we're very much like him: ingenious, adventurous, lucky, energetic, damn-the-torpedoes, humane.

And aspiring to be more.

Time is Relative

Carole E. Barrowman is an English professor at Alverno College in Milwaukee, Wisconsin, where she teaches courses on film, writing and the art of the mystery. She often contributes *to The Milwaukee Journal Sentinel* and *The Minneapolis Star Tribune.* John Barrowman (Captain Jack Harkness) is her little brother. She and John co-wrote his autobiography *Anything Goes* and the comic strip "Captain Jack and the Selkie" (*Torchwood Magazine* #14). John and Carole have also released a follow-up to *Anything Goes* called *I Am What I Am,* published by Michael O'Mara Books Ltd. http://www.carolebarrowman.com/

When my baby brother John was born, the Doctor was in his second regeneration, Jamie was the Doctor's companion and the TARDIS still had that new time capsule smell to it. I was scared of Daleks, terrified of the Cybermen and the new baby in the Barrowman house was driving me mad. He cried constantly. Even after packing his mouth full of salt 'n vinegar chips in an attempt to silence the alien creature, he still managed regularly to disturb the peace of my childhood universe.

When the Doctor was in his third regeneration, ditzy Jo was his companion, I was still afraid of Daleks, and a bit creeped out by the Master, but the baby brother was growing on me. In fact, so much so that while shopping in Glasgow one Saturday morning, I insisted – and when I say "insisted," I mean forced with my arms clamped tightly around his chest – he stand outside a department store window for two or three minutes to make sure the mannequins weren't really Autons and that they were not poised to crash out of the display and follow us home. They were not and they did not, but baby brother checked his back the entire trip.

When the Doctor was in his fourth regeneration, Sarah Jane and K-9 were his loyal companions, Davros emerged from suspended animation with only minor injuries and John and I were finding our place in a new world. It was the late 70s, and my family had recently emigrated from Scotland to the United States. John and I spent many Sunday evenings watching the Doctor's exploits on WTTW in Chicago, relishing in the campiness of this particular Doctor's persona and, at least for me, in the curiosity of journalist Sarah Jane. Next to Bob Woodward and his cohorts, I'm convinced Sarah Jane influenced my initial career choice. Problem was, in my world no newsrooms were offering time travel as a perk. Two years ago in Cardiff Bay, John and I ran into Elisabeth Sladen (a.k.a. Sarah Jane). I mumbled incoherently when John introduced us (let me add here that I behaved in a similar fashion the first time I met David Tennant, only with more gushing and giggling on my part).

Despite my advancing age when the Doctor was in his fourth incarnation (19-ish), I remained skittish of Daleks and John continued to be terribly traumatized from his incident with the Autons in Glasgow. Although my family settled into our new lives in the US fairly smoothly, those Sunday nights held a certain nostalgia for John and me. We could almost taste the Doctor's jelly babies.

When the Doctor was in his fifth regeneration, well, honestly, I couldn't take him seriously as a Time Lord. This Doctor reminded me far too much of Dorothy Sayer's foppish detective Lord Peter Wimsey. Plus, around this time I was watching reruns of *All Creatures Great and Small* and all I could see in this Doctor was Tristan Farnon – adorable vet. I expected that at any moment, he'd do a flea and tick check on K-9. This Doctor's companion was Tegan, an "airline hostess" (it was the 80s), and later Peri, short for Perpugilliam (the writers had to be on drugs), who I seem to recall spent a lot of time dressed in shorts the width of a valance and skin-tight leotards. As young Americans, John and I loved that Peri was the Doctor's first American companion – and she would remain the only American companion until the entire series regenerated in 2005 and Captain Jack Harkness (a.k.a. my baby brother) and his Chula ship landed on the Whovian landscape.

During much of the fifth Doctor's exploits, I was in graduate school at Northern Illinois University studying the history of the novel, the Covenanters, John Milton and the Protestant Revolution. John was finishing high school, performing in amateur productions and high school musicals and reveling in the exploits of the Carringtons on *Dynasty*. The Doctor receded in our shifting universes, but John and I were known, on occasion, to begin phone conversations to each other humming the trademark electronic melody: "Bungalung, bungalung, woo hoo!"

During the Doctor's six through eighth regenerations I got married, got tenure and had children; therefore, I've very little memory of my own activities – never mind knowing the defining moments of those particular Doctors or their trusty companions. I did, however, continue to nurse a deep dread of Daleks. In fact, I remember waking up in a cold sweat one night when my son's Darth Vader toy started rasping from under his blankets. I was convinced I was about to be exterminated.

"Kill Davros!" I shrieked at my husband before I'd let him back into bed.

Despite John's dabbling in the Lucas universe in the 70s and 80s, and my developing passion for Mulder and his X-Files, John and I remained steadfast fans of the Doctor. It was during these final regenerations of the classic Doctor that John walked into a theater in London's West End for an open audition for a revival of Cole Porter's *Anything Goes* and walked out with one of the lead roles. He went on to star in Andrew Lloyd Webber and Cameron Mackintosh's biggest musicals, sang Sondheim at The Kennedy Center, played Broadway with Carol Burnett, performed in a number of TV shows both in the UK and the US and released a variety of CDs. Although his star was rising in the celebrity firmament, he still quickened his pace whenever he walked past mannequins in a department store window.

The Doctor's ninth manifestation may have been a short-lived one, but it dramatically altered our sibling universe when, nine episodes into the season, Captain Jack conned his way onto the TARDIS and into the hearts of fans everywhere. This Doctor's significant companion was Rose Tyler, and, although his persona was more brooding than playful, his regeneration kick-started the franchise anew and sent *Who* fans like me into our Dalek lunch boxes, or to the back of our basements in search of our sonic screwdriver pens and wind-up K-9s (one sits on my desk to this day).

As wonderful as it was to have the Doctor active in our universe again, this incarnation was traumatic on a personal level. To my complete horror in the final episode of the series, "The Parting of the Ways," the Daleks back my baby brother into a corner and kill him. Bam! Just like that. I was gobsmacked. I stared at my husband for a beat, paused the television, leapt from the couch and grabbed for the phone. Within minutes of seeing my childhood fear realized and my unshakable paranoia vindicated, I tracked John down in London and interrogated him fully. What's your middle name? Mum's maiden name? My middle name? I had to be sure there was no permanent damage.

Given our shared history with the Doctor, I reveled in John's stories about life in the TARDIS (of course it's real). In fact, when John first read the script that intimated Captain Jack was the Face of Boe, he immediately called Russell T Davies to make sure he'd read correctly. Then, disregarding the time difference between the UK and the US, he called me. It was 4 a.m., and you don't want to know what my husband said before I could get back into bed.

"Kill Davros!" pales in comparison.

John had to keep this delicious detail a secret, but he was bursting with Whovian geekiness and he knew even if the Sontarans tortured me, the secret would be safe. John also knew no one else in the family would appreciate the sheer enormity and the utter brilliance of Russell's story arc. This cool revelation about Captain Jack notwithstanding, it's actually the single line mantra from Jack's debut episode that still sends John and I into a laughing jag.

At the groom's dinner the night before my wedding, John managed to convince the bartender that he and my soon-to-be-brother-in-law were indeed old enough to taste a martini or two (they were not). Minutes before we were to be seated for dinner, I discovered John and soon-to-be-brother-in-law giggling like idiots at the bar. Naturally, I reamed John out in the classic manner of Big Sisters everywhere. He listened stoically, and then, as I marched away, he yelled across the bar in broad Glaswegian, "Carole, you're not my mother!"

"Are you my Mummy?"

Respond loudly and in Scottish please: "No, Carole! You're not my mother!"

In the Doctor's tenth regeneration, his companions were Rose Tyler, Martha Jones and Donna Noble – a mature companion with sass and sarcasm who reminded me of my own female friends. During this Doctor's tenure, Captain Jack was living and dying (and dying again) at Torchwood, the Daleks stopped off in Manhattan (yikes!) before battling for universal supremacy (again), and, in one of my favorite episodes of all time, the Doctor battled his wits with the Bard in "The Shakespeare Code." This Doctor's regeneration saw my children celebrate graduation and birthday milestones, John and his long-time partner Scott celebrate their civil union, and – at the height of this Doctor's escapades – after all these years, I finally set foot on the TARDIS.

John and I were collaborating on his autobiography, *Anything Goes*, and I was shadowing him on the *Torchwood* set for six weeks. On my first day, John decided to give me a personal tour of the set, which is spread across an industrial complex in Cardiff. The Torchwood Hub shares the same warehouse area as the interior set for the TARDIS. This means to get to the Hub, John and I had to walk directly in front of this hallowed space.

Up to this point in my tour, John had been the consummate professional and polite baby brother. He introduced me to the *Torchwood* cast and crew, pointed out where to find lunch or dinner and how important it was to get to the food before Gareth David-Lloyd, and then he escorted me to a building at the rear of the complex. Inside, it was full of the flotsam and jetsam of years of scary monsters and fabulous aliens.

"Wait here a minute," John said, disappearing behind a heavy black safety curtain.

I waited and waited and when I began to worry that baby brother had left me there so he could beat me and Gareth to the food wagon, I yanked aside the black curtain.

A full size Dalek charged at me. "Exterminate her! Exterminate her!"

My heart went into tachycardia. I think I may have peed my pants.

John leapt out from behind the Dalek, laughing hysterically and chanting, "Payback!"

Later on our way to the Hub, John and I stepped up onto the TARDIS. Its circular console loomed in front of us, the marks of generations visible all over its detailed surface. I reverently touched a few of the controls. I may have giggled.

"We're ready for you, John," called one of the *Torchwood* assistants.

John and I stared at each other for a couple of beats as if our childhood, our own evolving companionship, was displayed in front of us. Then we high-fived each other and burst into a resounding chorus of "Bungalung, bungalung, woo hoo!"

Being Jackie Jenkins: Memoirs from a Parallel Universe

Jackie Jenkins wrote the column "The Life and Times of Jackie Jenkins" for *Doctor Who Magazine*.

1997, March-ish

"Have you ever heard of Bridget Jones?"

It was Gary Gillatt, editor of *Doctor Who Magazine*. I hadn't. It was before the film (BZ – "Before Zellweger"). At the time, Bridget Jones was a fictional diary that ran in *The Independent* newspaper. Its writer, Helen Fielding, had just turned the idea into a novel. Bridget is insecure and neurotic and makes a mess of social situations. The book's dust jacket introduces the novel as follows: "A dazzling urban satire of modern urban relations? An ironic tragic insight into the demise of the nuclear family? Or the confused ramblings of a pissed thirtysomething?"

"I'm looking to do a *Doctor Who* version of that," said Gary, "and I thought of you." Charming. I wasn't even 30.

Gary wasn't in the habit of phoning me up.

"I got your number from Directory Enquiries."

I'd met him a few times at *Doctor Who* conventions, and he was kind about some pieces I'd written for fanzines. At the time I was working for a local paper, on the Entertainments' section. I used to go down to the theatre to interview whoever was on, and if they'd been in *Doctor Who*, the questions would move onto that. The paper wasn't really interested in that material, but I kept it for myself, and at another convention I ran a number of names past Gary, to see if he was interested in using any of them. Most had been through the magazine a dozen times but one caught his attention. "That would go with an Archive we're running. 1000 words, ASAP?"

"Great," he said when he read it. Honestly, I thought? I had totally overestimated the *Who* material and had to pad like hell.

"I enjoyed your interview," a friend said later. He then started to quote some of it back to me. Oh God, I thought, that's one of the bits I made up...

Anyway, the Bridget idea was one of many attempts to push *Doctor*

Who Magazine in a different direction. The American TV Movie had come and gone. No one was making *Doctor Who* again.

"I want our character to be trendy," Gary was saying. "I want every fan-boy to fall in love with her." On the trendy issue, he said, "When our character and her friends talk about 'Underworld,' they don't just think about the 1978 Tom Baker story, they think about the band as well."

"There's a band called Underworld?" I said.

"Yeh. You've not heard of them?"

"No."

"Oh."

Gary's advice was that I get myself a copy of Fielding's book, as that was the template of what he wanted. I read it over two evenings and put it down feeling slightly depressed. Funny what people get excited about, I thought.

April 1997

The thing about Jackie Jenkins was that she wasn't all that made up. The name was. That was Gary's. I'd gone for Bethany James. Bethany sounded breathy and therefore sexy, but I think that was vetoed because it sounded too similar to Fielding's creation. But the character, especially Jackie's knack of getting into embarrassing situations – accidental or pre-meditated – well, that wasn't too wide of the mark. A year or so after the column had finished, Jackie's name cropped up in an editorial where then-*DWM* editor Alan Barnes added that she was just a *DWM* invention. But that's not how it felt. Gary e-mailed me to say how sad he was to see Jackie so easily dismissed and I thought the same. You see, Jackie-type things happen to me all the time. A few years before *Doctor Who* came back, I was invited to a party by one of the writers of the BBC *Doctor Who* novels (and now the series) who had just moved to the area. Arriving late with a carrier bag of cans was television script-writer Steven Moffat, the most successful person in the room bar none. Introduced to him, I wanted to say how much I admired his early 1990s sit-com *Joking Apart*. As I did this, I found myself rating it with his other comedies, *Chalk* and *Coupling*, and making a little hand gesture that clearly indicated a first, second and third place.

"So what you're saying," he said, "is that I'm slowly getting worse."

It was one of those "ground, swallow me up" moments.

Later, I resigned myself to the fact that I probably wouldn't have to think about Steven much in future. And now look what's happened.

May 1997

The first "The Life and Times of Jackie Jenkins" was published in *DWM* #250.

"I read your piece," a friend said. "To be honest, I didn't think much of it." To be honest, neither did I. The first "Jackie Jenkins" was never meant to be seen in the form that it was. Initially Gary had only asked for a rough draft. It was far too long but that didn't matter, he just wanted to see how the idea was going. In the end, though, he ran with it anyway, editing it himself. My problem was that it felt like a pointless ramble. It needed a plot, or to make an observation of some sort. It was also full of Bridget-isms. Bridget Jones would mark down her vices and concerns in curt opening paragraphs:

Saturday 11th November
Weight 9 stone 2 (from where?)
Alcohol units 7 (bad)
Correct lottery numbers 2 (vg)

So Jackie would say:

"Resisted buying old 'Loch Ness Monster' novelisation in charity shop, even though in much better condition than my two other copies – you've got to draw the line somewhere."
"Times I've pretended my pen was the Sonic Screwdriver – 9 (vg)."
"Positive thoughts about 'Time and the Rani'- 1 (poor)."

As an impression it was OK as far as it went, but I just didn't really like the style that much. If there were *DWM* readers that only ever read the first "Jackie Jenkins," then I don't blame them.

1997, June/July

"We're getting letters," Gary said.

Oh God, here come the complaints, I thought. I opened the relevant *DWM* at the letters page to find a picture of Jackie with a heart drawn round it. I should say at this point that the girl in the picture isn't me. Gary wanted Jackie's true identity to be a secret, so the face of Jackie Jenkins became a girl who worked in Marvel's distribution department, and even she was always photographed half hidden behind a copy of *DWM*. As the heart picture implied, the comments were positive, but I knew not everyone thought like that. I was at a convention a week or two later when a usually enthusiastic acquaintance came up to me with a stony face.

"Please don't tell me you're Jackie Jenkins..."

It was like I'd died.

For me, Jackie Jenkins started to come good about three or four issues in. Bridget Jones may have been Gary's inspiration, but the more I thought about it, the less relevant she became. Jackie Jenkins wasn't Helen Fielding, she was Nick Hornby. Her column wasn't really a diary, it was *Fever Pitch* and *High Fidelity*, in as much as those books aren't really about football and record collecting, but about being a massive fan of something. Jackie was designed to be cool, but I don't think she retained that very long, because cool isn't funny, and being a fan is. Both "ha ha" and peculiar. *High Fidelity* starts with a list – how *Doctor Who* fan is that? – and *Fever Pitch* with the author daydreaming about an Arsenal match within 15 minutes of waking up.

Gary never questioned the change, although he must have noticed it, as all the Bridget-isms, all the "v good," "two positive thoughts" stuff had disappeared. In the beginning, Gary would want to be in on the subjects Jackie would be discussing.

"What about something on the McGann film?", I asked.

"Perhaps not," he said. "We're trying to move away from that at the moment. What about Terry Nation?"

Nation had just died and fans would be re-evaluating his work.

"What about a Top Ten of Pertwee's velvet jackets?" I said.

"Fine."

"Or who Denys Fisher's Tom Baker doll really looks like?"

"Even better..."

After a while the discussions stopped and he would just ask: "So what's in the next one?"

The original line-up for "Jackie Jenkins" was Jackie, Chas and Nigel. Chas was a dyed-in-the-wool fan and Nigel was more ambivalent. Both were real people to the point that, as Nigel's ambivalence grew, he drifted away a bit and pretty much out of the column altogether. Nigel had got a girlfriend – the dreadful, stick-thin Nicky Parrot in the column. She was the type of person that wouldn't understand why adults would even want to watch *Doctor Who*, let alone discuss incidental music or if the Doctors were Spice Girls, which ones would they be. In real life, Nicky wasn't so thin, but Nigel still threw most of his *Doctor Who* stuff away when they moved into a flat together.

At one point Gary suggested Jackie should have a boyfriend, so I invented Patrick. In the column, Jackie adored him, but I had made him so good and polite I found him boring, so I chucked him after about five issues. I'm only guessing here, but I think the boyfriend idea might have been Gary's attempt to make those who liked Jackie a little bit jealous. That sounds like I'm overestimating peoples' interest. In most cases, if people read the column, they did so for amusement, but there was a small minority who took it more literally. I know this because *DWM* would get letters addressed to Jackie personally, which they would then forward to me. Almost all of them were looking for a relationship.

The boyfriend idea, however, had mileage. So a few issues after Patrick, I came up with Darren Barry. In fact, he wasn't a boyfriend – he was a lover. How saucy does that sound? Just writing it makes me gasp at how extraordinary *DWM* was back then, and just what the column got away with. There's the comic strip, there's an Andrew Pixley Archive on *The Faceless Ones*, and there's Jackie Jenkins talking about the Past Doctor novels and having casual sex under a pile of coats at a party...

Darren wore black and was the Master to Jackie's Doctor. They were at school together, where they spent most of their time trying to get the other into trouble. As adults, they weren't much different, except they now fancied each other rotten, and most of their spats usually ended in sex. Although obviously such moments were alluded to rather than stated as bluntly as that.

I think I enjoyed the Jackie/Darren installments the most. He became quite an important character in Jackie's life, always turning up at the moment of some life-changing decision. Most of the altercations played out like parodies of great Doctor/Master confrontations. The end of "Logopolis" was one, with a mobile phone and an important text message taking the place of the radio-telescope and the Master's "People of the Universe" speech. When the column came to an end, as I knew that it eventually would, I felt that Darren would have to be part of it, taunting Jackie to the very last.

November 1997

"How do you feel about Jackie guest hosting the Shelf Life review section for an issue?"

It was Gary, offering more Jackie exposure. Jackie was a bundle of fan obsessions and observations. It was silly and conversational, and not analytical in the way reviews needed to be.

"Do you think that would work?"

"I'm sure you'll manage."

I often thought that Gary was Jackie's biggest fan and this was just a means of getting more of her in the magazine. To be truthful, I don't think I did manage it that well. I incorporated some of Chas and Nigel's comments, which muddied the water a bit, and my attempt to bring Jackie's humour to bear on the products only made them feel like they weren't getting their proper attention. I know that one of the novels I dealt with is considered as quite important and something of a classic, but you wouldn't have picked that up from the review. Sadly, the whole experience turned quickly sour a few days after publication. Despite my belief that Jackie's style had blunted the reviews' effectiveness, one of the authors of that month's crop of books took massive exception to something I'd said. There was a huge stink on the Internet, where the author called for me and Gary to be sacked. Everything went a bit mad for 24 hours. It wasn't exactly Daleks and Thals, but it was certainly unpleasant. I still think the initial reaction was childish and bullying.

January 1999, Our Price

"That's £19.99 please."

BBC Video had just reissued "Revenge of the Cybermen," this time with all its episode endings and title sequences intact.

"Oh, if you like that, you might also be interested in this." The sales assistant turns round and comes back with a CD of the music from *Queer as Folk*. Somebody had clearly been watching the Channel 4 series. Vince, one of the show's gay characters, loved *Doctor Who*. Funny. You buy one Cyberman video and the world has you down as a lesbian. I meant to put that incident in the column but never got round to it.

July 1999

"The Life and Times of Jackie Jenkins" came to an end in *DWM* #280. I was sad to see her go, but it was just about the right time. Jackie and friends had mused over just about everything. They had gone to book signings, visited exhibitions, obsessed over telesnaps and had BBC novel proposals rejected. Jackie had gone on holiday, fell out with her work colleague and Nigel had walked. There had been dream sequences and parodies. Jackie had become Bridget Jones, Nick Hornby and – in the last six months or so – the lead in some weird kind of *Doctor Who* referencing sit-com. I love the sit-com ones. Moffat's *Joking Apart* was definitely an influence, and so was *Friends*. Now, of course, there's a whole new series to play with, but back then, it was good that Jackie wasn't allowed to go stale.

Three linked instalments ending in a cliffhanger was how Gary saw it. So Darren Barry was back, flashing a job posting to America and asking Jackie to come with him and leave her friends and UK fan life behind. The moment really called for a regeneration, but that couldn't happen, although there was a flashback sequence and a feeling that Jackie was about to get lost in the Vortex.

Jackie was definitely a product of *Doctor Who*'s wilderness years, and there's no way the column could strike the same notes now as it did then. She was a *Doctor Who* fan when the rest of the world wasn't. She was an outsider in her TV tastes, part of the party faithful. Much of her attitude came from a feeling that *Doctor Who* was a guilty pleasure that no one else much knew about. A love that daren't speak its name.

DWM recently ran a column called "You Are Not Alone" that retread a lot of Jackie's old obsessions and thoughts about the show, but in an era when *Doctor Who* garners an average audience of over eight million, it's difficult to make a title and idea like that resonate any more. In the 90s, if you asked anyone if they could remember any *Doctor Who* companions, they'd say K-9 and "that girl in the skins." Now they give you the names of the entire Tyler family and a strong opinion on Donna Noble. Jackie would have to be different because I'm different, and my view of the series has changed. If Jackie was writing now, an early instalment would have to deal with how much I love the new series but how I also feel annoyed by it because my love for the new has made me quite critical of the old. I'm wrestling with those feelings of betrayal all the time. Tom's my favourite Doctor, but he was brilliant in a narrower field of material, and he never had stories like "The Girl in the Fireplace," "Human Nature" or "Midnight" to shine in. And that's another thing. You couldn't write a column saying something like that and expect everyone to take it on face value. Some would see it cynically as an attempt to suck up to BBC Wales, or worse, think it was written on their request. Modern Jackie would have to address how it feels to find that your favourite thing is now everyone else's. There would be an inevitable air of smugness about it too. I suspect a number of columns would be easy to paraphrase with a simple "I told you it was brilliant."

December 2004

Issue #280 wasn't quite Jackie's last appearance. When *DWM* hit its 350th issue, she popped up again as one of a number of features that were revived as part of the celebrations. The new series was about eight months away and Jackie was in the position that a lot of old fans found themselves at the time – wanting the show to come back but fearing for it as well. It would have been helpful if there was more information about when I wrote it, as apart from Christopher Eccleston and Billie Piper's casting – and the news that the Doctor was wearing a leather jacket – there wasn't much to play off. What had happened to Jackie in the interim I left vague, but she was at home and clearly hadn't seen Darren Barry for a long time. Naturally he turned up and with an even greater temptation than before. That job of his had now taken him to Cardiff.

My Fandom Regenerates

Deborah Stanish is a Philadelphia-area writer and freelance journalist. She is a frequent contributor to *Enlightenment*, the fanzine of Canada's Doctor Who Information Network (www.dwin.org). Some of her essays will appear in *Time, Unincorporated*, Mad Norwegian's fanzine archive series.

A few years ago I was on the elliptical machine at the gym, trying desperately not to call out to Jesus to take me home, when one of those annoying chatty types climbed onto the machine next to me. We'd been "smile and nod" gym buddies for a while, but up to that point I'd been safe from idle conversation. I knew my number was up when he gestured towards my T-shirt.

"Who are The Regenerates?"

"The Regenerates?" I asked, puzzled.

He nodded to my shirt, a faded staff shirt from Writercon 2006 with "My Fandom Regenerates" printed on the front.

"What kind of music do they play?" he asked, taking a swig of water and cranking the incline up to nine.

"It's not a band, it's a television show," I responded. "*Doctor Who?*"

He rolled his eyes, put on his earbuds and with that I was dismissed.

Now to give this story some perspective, the water bottle he was drinking out of was emblazoned with the Philadelphia Eagles logo. He had an Eagles gym bag, an Eagles sweat towel, an Eagles license plate cover and an Eagles flag flying from his SUV's window. I would bet money that he was a season ticket holder and a face painter to boot. But I, wearing my slightly referential fannish T-shirt, was the weird one in the room.

The incident reminded me that a sort-of social hierarchy still existed when it came to "fandoms," and within that hierarchy sports would always be at the top of the pile while media fandom would be regarded as slightly suspect by the mainstream. There's nothing odd at all about flying a team flag in front of your house, but can you imagine your neighbor's reaction if you hoisted up the iconic *Doctor Who* logo?

While *Doctor Who* has risen in stateside cachet thanks to the new series' prominence on the Sci-Fi Channel and the incredible popularity of *Torchwood* on BBC America, it had a long way to go to rise in American SF esteem. My first exposure to *Doctor Who* was similar to most Americans. It was that strange thing you bumped into on Saturday afternoons, populated with bubblewrap monsters and only living on PBS. My not-so generous assessment was that it was the weird British series that was admired by those kids at the very bottom of the geek hierarchy.

First, let's get the terminology straight. The word "geek" has come a long way in the past decades, and I'm referring to the dark ages of geek – the pre-Internet days when the term wasn't synonymous with "cool tech kid," "Bill Gates" or "Future IT god who will pwn your soul." Back in my day, geek was the undesirable caste, the untouchables who could be counted on to wheel in the A.V. equipment or provide comic relief at lunch.

Being a late bloomer, I didn't come into my geek until later in life. But even though I didn't run with that crowd, I was aware of the geek hierarchy. After all, this was the *Star Wars* era (the cool movies, not the later ones with Jar Jar Binks). Everyone had a smattering of SF knowledge.

In those dark years, before you could download that hottest manga hours after its release a half a world away, the SF world was a little more narrow. If you Google "geek hierarchy" today, you'll get a couple of hundred hits for variations of an amusing flow chart which proves that no matter how odd you think you are, there is always someone just a little further down the chart. This means that there is always someone a little higher on the flow chart as well, but that's the law of the jungle, right? Of course, anyone from the outside looking in thinks the whole thing is a hot mess of weird and usually wanders off to check out *The Huffington Post* or the scores on ESPN. For the rest of us, it's a glimpse at just how far we've come in regards to accessibility and connections.

During those years when access to content was limited to what you could catch on network television, at the box office or in the local comic shop, there was a very clear geek hierarchy. At the very top, at the peak of Mount Olympus, was *Star Wars*. *Star Wars* was a phenomenon. You absolutely couldn't catch geek cooties for enjoying a social phenomenon. If you wore your Luke Skywalker T-shirt to school for three months straight, well, let's just say there was a line and it could be crossed. Falling below *Star Wars* – crossing the line into definitive geek territory – was *Star Trek*. There were no acronyms like "TOS" or "TNG," because there was only one *Star Trek*. Again, there were lines. The occasional Spock fingers were tolerated, but wearing Spock ears or carrying a mock phaser pushed you firmly into the untouchable caste.

Then there were the minor SF fandoms: a few holdouts from *Battlestar Galactica* (the one with Dirk Benedict, not the cool one), and, god help us all, *Buck Rogers*. And below that, so far below it was practically in the basement, was *Doctor Who*.

Like I said, *Doctor Who* was weird. First of all, it was British, which made it slightly suspect. It wasn't cool Brit like the Sex Pistols or vintage Bowie, but weird Brit with bad teeth and laughable special effects. Second, it only aired on public television stations which, at that point in PBS history, were as dry and dusty as the "Planet of the Dead." At a time when American television was working to bring their SF offerings up to Industrial Light & Magic standards, *Doctor Who*'s production values were still a bit on the dodgy side, relying on clay monsters and tinfoil. It was not appointment television by any stretch.

The irony of those generalizations and misconceptions are not lost on me today.

Discovering fandom later in life is both a bane and a blessing. You're definitely way behind on the learning curve of fannish behavior, lingo and history, but you also have a clearer sense of your own identity. When you find something that clicks, it's because it touches you in a way that transcends traditional group behavior. There is a feeling of finding your "tribe" that's less a sense of wanting to fit in and more a sense of joy that you can share this amazing thing with other people who understand the obsession. From an adult point of view, the whole concept of a fandom hierarchy seems irrelevant and a little silly. Once you've taken that step into fandom, you find a sense of solidarity that transcends fandom borders.

Then you meet some idiot at the gym and you realize that no matter how comfortable you are in your own skin, you're still going to get the stink eye when you come out of the fannish closet.

Doctor Who wasn't my first fandom, but it was my first traditionally male-oriented fandom. My first fandom experience was the world of Joss Whedon, and it was primarily a girl thing. All of a sudden I went from spinning in the dark to a place filled with bright and articulate women who debated fiercely and created with abandon. I had found my tribe and it was a heady experience. When that tribe started talking about the relaunch of *Doctor Who*, I could feel my eyes rolling. Apparently, I hadn't completely let go of the old perceptions. When the chatter grew and finally turned into a dull roar, I started to pay attention. Maybe I was missing something, and since there is a level of trust that develops within a fandom, I decided to give it a go.

And I was lost.

I could tell you the exact moment it went from a pleasant diversion to full-on headtilt. While struggling with the Autons, the ninth Doctor says: "That's not true. I should know. I was there. I fought in the war. It wasn't my fault. I couldn't save your world. I couldn't save any of them." Well, *hello* there, unexpected depth and intrigue.

With a few years of prior fandom experience under my belt, I entered the fray. I'd learned that you don't rush in, you tread lightly. You poke around forums and communities, learn the landscape before you commit to your public space.

What I discovered was that fandom was giddy. After years of being consigned to the periphery, clinging to life in the form of books and audio plays, when even the die-hard fan had given up hope of ever seeing their show come back to life, watching it blaze forth on their television screens filled them with euphoria. Sure, there was grumbling in some corners about characterization and accusations of "sexing up the TARDIS," but for the most part the joy of having their fandom regenerate created good will to spare. It was into this fannish environment that I dipped my toes. And it was good.

Barely a year later, I was approached by a fannish friend, the former editor of the fanzine *Enlightenment*. The current editor was looking for a new columnist and would I be interested? I'd like to say I gave it some thoughtful consideration, but the truth is I jumped at the chance. Here was an opportunity to blather on about something which I loved to an audience outside of my cozy fandom circle. It had taken some time, but I had found my niche within *Doctor Who* fandom and the chance to explore other fannish circles was enticing.

The editor, the wonderful Graeme Burk, was looking for someone to bring a girl perspective to the fanzine. This was the new *Who*, and the girls were storming the castle. Producer Russell T Davies had brought *Doctor Who* back to life with a new sensibility that firmly embraced female viewing tastes. The show introduced a strong female lead as the gateway character into a dense world with over 40 years of backstory, tossed in a bit of romantic subtext and intriguing stories, and topped it all off with a few spectacular explosions. It was a recipe for success, and *Enlightenment* wanted to explore the emerging girl fan culture.

Of course, there had always been women in *Doctor Who* fandom. The girls weren't rare mystical creatures brought forth on the nebula of Christopher Eccleston's rugged sensuality or David Tennant's quicksilver charm and fantastic hair. The girls were always there, just off to the left. Being a relatively new fan, I'd only heard second-hand stories from the days of the classic series, but it seemed *Doctor Who* fandom always carried the whiff of Old Boys Club and in the hierarchy of *Who*, the girl fans hovered near the bottom. Is this perception correct? It depends on who you talk to and where they fell in that hierarchy. I've met girls who swam through the waters brilliantly and girls who ended up creating their own niches and formed their own hierarchies within the larger fandom. Perception is a tricky thing, but in terms of fandom power, influence and control, it was primarily a man's world.

The sudden influx of new fans to any fandom can be disconcerting to long-time members; the sudden influx of girl fans to a traditionally male fandom even more so. The girls had a different toolbox and they had it packed before they entered the door. Words like "unresolved sexual tension" and "emotional arcs" went from being the noise in the background to topics posted on the forums of Outpost Gallifrey. It wasn't that those topics never existed, it was that they had rarely been acknowledged – but now they reached tsunami proportions. With that tsunami came stereotypes: if you were a girl fan, you must be a shipper; if you were a girl fan, it must because you were a fan of Rose rather than the Doctor; if you were a girl fan, it was because you were looking for a soap wrapped up in SF paper. Sweeping generalizations on both sides created an environment of misconceptions.

Being aware of these misconceptions, entering the metaphorical locker room of a traditional fanzine wasn't as big a deal as I'd imagined it would be. As a female in a traditionally male fandom, I expected a bit of resistance. While there have been a few experiences akin to being the odd lump in the corner that's poked at curiously, the entré into boy fandom has been anticlimactic. There were no fireworks or beating down the glass ceiling. It's been more an experience of existing in intersecting circles rather than forming a great fandom melting pot. There is often a sense of talking at entrenched fandom rather than engaging in any real dialogue. I wondered if it was because the boys had already established hierarchies and continued on as if nothing had changed.

After a few years, the fandom cracks began to show and the euphoria seemed to wane. It was business as usual – which in any fandom means ideological debates, canon battles, ship wars and n00bs v. establishment. There were debates on what classified a "real fan" as opposed to a poseur opportunist. Hierarchies were summarily judged and found lacking. Established fans found themselves in the position of being casually dismissed by the new order. There was an element that declared classic *Who* was dull and plodding, while simultaneously vowing loyalty to RTD and all that he espoused. They ignored cries that they were "doing it wrong" and embraced the new sensibility. Sola scriptura mixed with a healthy dose of authorial intent became their new canon.

Was this only a girl thing? Depends on where you decided to hang your fannish hat. On LiveJournal, a new hierarchy of girl fandom was evolving. In this new hierarchy, your place was determined by to which tenant (no pun intended) you swore your allegiance. The giddy homogenous nature of early New *Who* fandom quickly splintered. In traditional male fandom, allegiances were often based on which Doctor or era you preferred. In the fandom culture of LiveJournal, lines were quickly drawn based on which companion you preferred. The new series was calculated to catch the attention of the girls and a large faction took that one step further by choosing to make the companion the focal point of their fannish interactions. As fandom evolved the fissures increased, splintering the hierarchy even further. Your appreciation of the classic series, position on racial interpretations and how you approached class issues created more subsets on the metaphorical hierarchy diagram.

For the most part, the male counterpart was bemused. Comments on my columns during this time period were filled with head scratching. They simply didn't understand what all the racket and fuss was about. It was vastly different yet pedestrianly similar to the arguments over the JN-T years and whether or not the eighth Doctor was canon. The moves were the same, it was only the language that was different. It wasn't a battle of the sexes, it was a battle of comprehension.

There are lots of places to discuss, debate and rhapsodize over *Doctor Who*; where you choose to hang your hat often colors your perspective of fandom. LiveJournal is social, interactive and immediate. It's also insular and you begin to think that your corner of fandom is the norm, the top of the fandom hierarchy. Stepping outside of that insular bubble can be jarring or refreshing depending on your expectations. Interacting with fandom at large, particularly in forums that are not focused on the emotional story, which are more likely to be populated with female fans, offers the opportunity to see fandom in a broader perspective. You have a clearer picture as to how your hierarchy fits within the greater whole. The emotional story may be the initial draw for some girl fans, and a percentage may be content to move no further. But for many, the emotional story was the gateway. Just as the character of Rose was a deliberate plot device created to draw new viewers into the world of *Doctor Who*, the new series, as a whole, acts as a device to draw new viewers into the dense catalog of the Whoverse.

Does this mean the traditional hierarchies are shifting? Perhaps. The concept of separate but equal has never been particularly successful and the girls are bringing a lot to the fandom table: creativity, intelligence and a new worldview. Sweeping generalizations are easy, but we are more alike than we are different. Our focus and interests may vary, or not, but to dismiss something as less relevant is a missed opportunity.

Adventures in Ocean-Crossing, Margin-Skating and Feminist-Engagement with *Doctor Who*

Helen Kang is a feminist cultural studies scholar and a doctoral candidate at a major university on the west coast of Canada. In her spare time, she blogs, beads, writes and watches endless hours of television, all in the name of cultural research.

I. Television baby who went into hiding

I am a child of television. Some of my earliest and dearest memories of childhood involve the idiot box. Obsessively following a Japanese animation of *Anne of Green Gables*. Memorizing and singing the intro to the latest cartoon series. Repeating after words and numbers on *Sesame Street* with my younger sister. Trying to stay awake to watch late-night movies on satellite American channels intended for American GIs.

Aside from my family, television was a constant that bridged my journey from South Korea to Canada at the age of eight. I didn't need to fully understand English to appreciate the quick-paced humor of colorful cartoons after school. After English as Second Language sessions in the morning, and time spent sitting quiet, scared and confused among my classmates, Disney and Warner Bros. felt more familiar than too salty foods, snow in November and the artificial brightness of supermarkets.

Once in a while during our channel surfing after school, my sister and I would encounter shows that seemed too odd to be on the air during peak children viewing hours. I remember seeing the psychedelic blues and reds and hearing the outlandish sounds that crystallized into words in white letters: *Doctor Who*.

Click.

My sister and I weren't interested in live action shows during our after-school hours, much less a show flooded with words we could not understand and a strangely dressed man speaking British English. We preferred "educational" shows for children much younger than my age, and cartoons with upbeat songs that we could sing to.

Much of North American pop culture and not-so-popular culture eluded me for years. I listened to Korean pop music when my friends were listening to the new American hip-hop and many bands that I discovered much later for the first time at parties under the "retro" playlist. I devoured books about child detectives (not *Nancy Drew* or *The Hardy Boys*, because they were too difficult to read at the time) while my friends swooned over *The Baby-Sitters Club* and *Sweet Valley High*. I embraced my tomboy-hood and secretly yearned to be a part of the world of boys, full of adventure like in *The Goonies*, a movie that was my Bible during childhood. I was content to be a loner among my girlfriends in that respect. At that age, the world still felt small and contained.

My adolescent years changed everything. It's a time when knowing the rules of coolness is of the utmost importance. I didn't know the rules. I had always wandered in the margins with my detective books and Romantic literature. But suddenly, after one summer, I knew the rules of coolness were important. For fear of becoming a social outcast, I armed myself with vigilance and pretense. I learned how to hide my lack of knowledge of popular culture at the same time that I would hide the fact that I didn't know certain English words.

"Not knowing" was a no-no in my book and being discovered for not knowing was even worse. It was like being caught naked in the changing room, my early pubescent body exposed to eyes that were ready to laugh at any sign of weakness or shame. I struggled hard to maintain the pretense of being in the know; at the drop of a name of a famous television show, song or celebrity, my sense of social stability, which I had so painstakingly built, came tumbling down. Early sci-fi "geeks" – the steadfast ones who braved the turbulent era before geeks became cool – at times lament being pushed to the margins as social outcasts. Well, I couldn't even tell you the difference between the center and the margin, what was "in" and what was "out." I was, and am still, an outsider to the majority of pop culture references and jokes. For me this was all part of "becoming" Canadian – an identity I could officiate with citizenship papers and various education degrees, but which I could never fully attain.

II. Crossroads

I have always been partial to fantasy. I was well-versed in *The NeverEnding Story*, *The Last Unicorn* and *Labyrinth* by age 12. I watched *The Goonies*, *Indiana Jones* and *Star Wars* before I learned to speak English. I read Ray Bradbury in grade seven, but found "real" science fiction too dry in comparison. But like anything else in life that is new, timing is important and you need someone to show you the ropes, point you to the good stuff right away and in proper sequence.

In my early 20s, several events came together in unexpected and exciting ways: I discovered feminist and queer politics, I befriended a life-long *Doctor Who* fan, and my television-watching was transformed by DVDs. Through feminist politics, I began to understand and come to terms with my own gendered social history. I embraced queerness and transgressive sexuality. For the first time, I truly understood what being on the margins meant, and that it had the potential to be a powerful and empowering space.

My feminist politics took shape in relation to popular culture. I learned how to "read" for cultural codes of gender, race, class and (dis) ability in Hollywood movies, independent videos, novels, comics, music and, of course, television. I dissected imagery, gestures and language and I found myself in command of the thing that at once allured me and scared me throughout my teens. I found tremendous pleasure in being able to talk back to cultural texts, to formulate my own readings, to excavate sub-text and to weave alternative narratives. Contrary to the common accusation of feminists being angry all the time and hating everything that culture has to offer, feminism is a positive force in my life, providing me with a way to critically engage with popular culture in ways that I never could before.

I took a renewed interest in sci-fi and fantasy, which I had mostly abandoned during my teenage years. My first real dip into sci-fi as an adult was a double-dip into *Doctor Who*, introduced by a close friend and lifelong fan, Robert Smith?. The psychedelic blues and reds jumped from the television screen like a memory so distant it felt like someone else's. Indeed, for Robert, *Doctor Who* was a significant and indispensable part of his childhood and identity. Although I didn't immediately take to the original *Doctor Who* as he would have liked, nevertheless that night became my entry into sci-fi and fandom. Robert also introduced me to J.R.R. Tolkien and I began to proudly claim the labels of "fan" and "geek." By the time I reached my mid-20s, I was writing class papers on *Lara Croft: Tomb Raider* and *Crouching Tiger, Hidden Dragon*. The hours of sitting in front of the television after school as a child, despite parental threats of punishment, started to pay off. I became what media scholars such as Henry Jenkins call an "aca-fan," or an academic who identifies as a fan.

After completing my undergraduate and Master's degrees, I moved out to the West Coast to begin my PhD. At the same time that I began a new life in a new city, more and more television shows became available on DVD, changing the way I watch television. I am a ruthless channel surfer – recall the after-school cartoon sessions with my sister – and I don't have the patience or loyalty to follow a show week by week. I filled my spare time – and I had a lot of it, being a student and not knowing a lot of people in town – with television on DVD. I watched *Firefly* in a matter of a day or two and caught up on *Battlestar Galactica* and *Lost* over a matter of a few weeks. With the influence of my sister, who was by then working as a story artist for a major animation studio, I also acquired an appreciation for good storytelling and character development.

It was into this ripe moment where television on DVD and feminist politics and analysis intersected in my life that I did a triple take at *Doctor Who*. Robert told me about the new *Doctor Who* series re-imagined by Russell T Davies, creator of *Queer As Folk*. By this time, my sensibilities and preferences for television had changed and our friendship had significantly deepened during those five-plus years. I wanted to be a part of Robert's fandom, too.

III. Doctors and Companions

I practically devoured the first season and was left thirsty for more until the second season aired. I was delighted by the history of the show that lurked behind the brooding yet impossibly comical ninth Doctor in black leather jacket, so convincingly brought to life by Christopher Eccleston, whom I knew as the creepy corpse-sawing introvert in *Shallow Grave*. I relished the campiness brought by Captain Jack Harkness, which has sadly diminished so greatly in subsequent series of the new *Doctor Who*.

I was devastated when Eccleston regenerated into the tenth Doctor but immediately grew fond of David Tennant. I followed his growth, both as a character and as an actor, and could relate to him more than I could with Billie Piper or Freema Agyeman. I found Rose endearing and Martha quick and daring, but both felt juvenile as characters. Sure, the show is rated and ultimately made for a children's audience, but does this mean that girls and young women are to always see themselves as wide-eyed groupies or the romantic interest of the leading man or the leading Time Lord? Despite their individual moments of strengths and surprise, Rose was the Doctor's wannabe sweetheart and Martha couldn't shake off the label of "rebound."

Don't get me wrong. I cried my eyes out when Rose and the Doctor got separated at the end of Series Two. Break-ups are sad, no matter the circumstance. But I was equally happy to see Martha reject the exciting journeys with the Doctor at the end of Series Three. To her, the Doctor was like a bad boyfriend: the boyfriend who still dwells on his ex, whom you have to bail out of trouble (i.e. from shriveling up in a cage in the Master's lair) and who makes you hurt your family. Well, that's a pretty good lesson for girls and young women: ditch the loser, even if he is shiny. But ultimately, Rose and Martha reinforce the unspoken hetero-sexual myth that women will always relate to powerful men in romantic ways and that in a deeply fundamental way women will be defined in relation to men: their growth and movements, including appearances and disappearances across parallel worlds.

It wasn't until Donna materialized through the incredible skills of Catherine Tate that I felt the Doctor found his match and equal. Or at the very least, someone who could challenge him instead of relating to him in a romantic or sexual way. And I found a way to relate to the show just at the moment when I began to wonder if the show still had any-thing left for me. Unlike Rose or Martha, Donna is already "formed" by the time she meets the Doctor. She already has a strong and established sense of morality that comes with life wisdom. Perhaps this is the reason why I can relate more with Donna than I can with Martha, who is closer to me in age. When Martha meets the Doctor for the first time, she is a medical intern and not yet experienced in moral decisions as they unfold in life, messy and complicated. She is unable to deal with the losses that come with adventure, something that the Doctor has come to accept as tragic reality, especially after the decimation of his race.

On the other hand, Donna is able to both feel and confront losses and even to push the Doctor to take alternative actions. In "The Fires of Pompeii," she convinces the Doctor to "meddle" with history to save a family from a volcanic eruption. "We have to do something" is Donna's code, which is quite different from the Doctor's approach to the uni-verse: "Explore but don't meddle, except to ensure the natural course of time and to prevent the extinction of a race." The difference in their approaches may have to do with the fact that Donna is a (mortal) human and the Doctor is a Time Lord. Human lives are shorter, and our sense of time is much narrower, compared to that of a Time Lord who can feel the immensity of time and space at every point of his existence. The Doctor is more concerned with maintaining the intricate balances of the universe, while for Donna the immediate suffering of those in front of her have the highest priority.

It's not to say that, then, the Doctor is cold and ruthless. The tenth Doctor is especially sympathetic and compassionate. We have heard him utter the words, "I'm sorry. I'm so sorry" numerous times during the new series. He is an interesting mix of what we in a society with philosophical roots in Descartian dualisms call "empathy" and "rationality" that works well for his character as a Time Lord: he feels deeply and yet makes difficult moral decisions when he has to.

This doesn't then mean that Donna is somehow irrational and hyper-empathetic in comparison. Her moral insistence on going against the grain of "rationality" of written history to save one Pompeiian family, for example, is a perfectly rational decision: the Doctor has the means and the opportunity to save these people, so why not spare them from death? While Rose and Martha, too, pushed the Doctor to these decisions at moments of crises, Donna has the unusual strength to feel deeply and at the same time to persuade the Doctor to act. What is interesting and exciting about the difference between the moral instincts of the Doctor and those of Donna is that both are valid and make perfect sense. Of course you can't meddle with time as a time traveler. Of course you can't let someone die when you can save them.

Like any really good science fiction, this particular episode of *Doctor Who* pushes the limits of our understanding. The differences between the Doctor and Donna go beyond Descartian dualisms of male / female, mind / body and rationality / emotions that saturate many levels of thought and action in Western societies. Morality as it unfolds in everyday life situations is messy, amorphous, and uncertain and is much more complex than neat dualisms, which have been ceaselessly refuted by feminist and other critical thinkers. Right / Wrong is tough to differentiate at times and we are compelled to make decisions that we continually return to in our minds to wonder: "Was I right?"

The tension between the moral impulses of Donna and the Doctor also affects their relationship as characters. Unlike Doctor / Rose, Doctor / Jack, Doctor / Sarah and Doctor / Martha combinations that exude various degrees of romantic / sexual subtext, the Doctor / Donna combo feels more like two adult siblings: they genuinely like one another and enjoy each other's company, but still bicker and fight like when they were kids. This relationship has a much greater potential for intricate power struggles, yet also a strong intimacy between the Doctor and his companion. One of the primary examples of this is in "Planet of the Ood," when the Doctor and Donna discover container tanks full of enslaved Ood. When Donna expresses her disgust at the future human race for institutionalizing slavery, the Doctor replies that slavery exists in Donna's time, too.

> The Doctor: "Who do you think made your clothes?"
> Donna: "Is that why you travel around with a human at your side? It's not so that you can show them the wonders of the universe. It's so that you can take cheap shots?"
> The Doctor: "Sorry."
> Donna: "Don't... Spaceman."

In this short conversation, we see two strong-willed individuals clash then revert to child-like play. It's a delicate dance that can easily break apart their relationship. The Doctor makes a biting social commentary of Donna's (and our) contemporary world, making an implicit reference to sweatshop labour, global circulation of capital and global inequalities. It's a comment that would have shut Rose or Martha (or any one of us fans) right up.

But Donna is unlike any of us. She points out something that I personally hadn't thought about so far. What if there's a small part deep in one of the Doctor's two hearts that enjoys pointing out how little his companions know? A semi-innocent ill will, a desire to feel superior, a "mine is bigger than yours" impulse? It's a great reminder to us, as fans of the Doctor, that he is imperfect, that he has flaws. As fans, we may be his wannabe sweethearts, best friends and unfortunate rebounds in our individual fanatic worlds of *Doctor Who*. As fans, we are his virtual companions and may tend to place him on a pedestal. He is a Time Lord, after all. He has a sonic screwdriver and a really cool time-travelling spaceship with an acronym name.

But behind the flashy exterior – and a shiny pretty one that is! – he is a person who feels happiness, anger, loss, sympathy. He has weaknesses that are not so shiny that we as fans may overlook because we like him on the high moral horse. (Seriously, who didn't like the scene in "The Girl in the Fireplace" when the Doctor crashes through a time window on a white horse to rescue Madame de Pompadour?) To recognize that he is imperfect and flawed doesn't take away from being able to enjoy the show and genuinely like the Doctor, a.k.a. Spaceman.

IV. Who Now What?

Donna ends Series Four unable to remember her adventures with the Doctor, but *we* remember them. She appeared at just the right moment for the Doctor, for David Tennant and for the fans. The Doctor was ready to be challenged in his moral decisions; Tennant was ready to elevate his acting performance; and the fans were ready to move on from being wide-eyed groupies to true companions on his journeys. Now that we are on the verge of the eleventh Doctor and the journey of a new actor into Whoverse, where will the show take its fans now?

I just hope that the new Doctor and the new writers do justice to the show thus far and are able to come up with their own voice. This means to honor the 40-plus years of the show's history and at the same time to raise the bar on sci-fi television through innovative and smart storytelling, acting and effects. This feminist aca-fan holds her breath. Can the next chapter of *Doctor Who* match the energy and intelligence of the force that was the tenth Doctor slash Donna?

For me personally (without the cape of feminist aca-fandom), Donna represents a hope for the years to come as I turn the page of another decade in my life. Donna is given a chance to live all the excitement and challenges we associate with youth as an older and more mature self. It's the fantasy of wanting to return to childhood or to teenage years, but without the insecurities that you had back then. The Doctor in his TARDIS may not be real, but the promise of adventure never ceases with age. Now, isn't that a hopeful thought?

What's A Girl To Do?

Lloyd Rose authored the very popular eighth Doctor novels *The City of the Dead* and *Camera Obscura*, along with the seventh Doctor novel *The Algebra of Ice*. She also wrote the eighth Doctor audio play "Caerdroia" for Big Finish. Along with her *Doctor Who* work, Lloyd has written for the American television series *Homicide: Life on the Streets* and *Kingpin*, and served as the theater critic for *The Washington Post*.

It's not Billie Piper's fault, all this Rose-controversy. She can act and has a natural, easy presence. It's not really the fault of Russell T Davies either, even though he created her. It's not the fault of her two leading men, Christopher Eccleston and David Tennant, both generous performers. It's not the fault of fandom, despite all the hormonal and jealous squeaking. It's not even, exactly, the fault of sex.

Let's blame it on television.

For 33 years, the Doctor was chaste as a Grail knight. Though many of his avatars attracted interest from fans that wasn't entirely cerebral, he wasn't cast with sex in mind until Paul McGann was given the role in the 1996 television movie. This was a co-American production, and that meant sex: not only McGann, with his angelic good looks, but Daphne Ashbrook with her large, well-displayed breasts – a second Peri, only with a medical degree. With McGann in the role, it was impossible not to think of the Doctor as an erotic object. But, even with that historic Doctor's First Kiss moment, he was a remote one. McGann's remarkable eyes often seemed fixed on some inner vision slightly more interesting than whoever was admiring him. And certainly he was made to be admired – a passive beauty, like a male odalisque, ironically aware he wasn't going to have to lift a finger to have lovers flock to him.

There were hopes the movie would be the pilot for an ongoing show, and as far as can be judged from one outing, this ongoing show would have featured an action-adventure hero in the ordinary romantic mode, probably falling in love with a new woman each week, with lots of kissing and some implied off-screen sex. Kind of like Captain Kirk, but with an English accent and better manners. There's a built-in problem with this sort of television set-up – almost as much as celibacy, it robs the hero of the possibility of romance. Sure, Kirk had Edith Keeler. He also had babe after alien babe, some of them with alarmingly big hair. After a few weeks of this, you couldn't take his heartbreak seriously, and his amorous exploits became increasingly more of a joke. This would have happened to the eighth Doctor too – stuck in his flashy American television program with motorcycles and exploding special effects and bosoms, he would have ended up as a shallow playboy. Not exactly what you want for the Doctor. It wouldn't have been McGann's failure. The trap comes with the territory, and it always snaps shut. Acting talent, good writing, smart directing – all the skills of television production – are helpless against the demands of a multi-part narrative featuring a new adventure each week.

None of Russell T Davies' considerable sophistication in dramatizing sex and its discontents for television was of any use to him when he came to *Doctor Who*. Aside from its being a children's show (not a limitation for the series anticipated by the televison movie), there was the fact that the Doctor was an alien whose historical interest in these matters was contradictory when not opaque. Interestingly, Davies didn't try to clear things up. The Doctor is clearly a sexual as well as a sexy being, but beyond that the situation is cloudy. Christopher Eccleston's Nine flirted with a tree-lady and was amusingly jealous of Rose's young male admirers, while David Tennant was capable of gasping after a kiss is planted on him, "Yep, still got it." Steven Moffat had Nine put off dancing with Rose because he was too busy trying to resonate concrete, but let Ten be drawn offstage by the enchanting Madame de Pompadour for some dancing of her own devising. Yet it was impossible to quite pin either man down. Nine didn't really have long enough as a character; Ten had four years in which he was alternately adorably flirtatious and blankly indifferent – pretty much, as far as I can tell, depending on the scriptwriter. Mysterious and incomplete as the Doctor's behavior was, though, a considerable number of fans and casual viewers expressed the opinion that the character of Rose "worked" with Nine and didn't, to a greater or lesser degree depending on the critic, with Ten.

The two Doctors are very different and so, more importantly I think, are the two actors. Eccleston, though his Nine hunched inside that leather jacket as if it were a protective shell and projected a scarred wariness, is a warm actor, emotionally straight-forward and accessible. But while Ten is a more blithe and outgoing character, Tennant is cool – elusive and ultimately unreadable. Eccleston has an "ordinary guy" sexiness; he's a bloke. Tennant is a little distant, even passive – not "come-hither" passive like McGann, but hidden, as if he's a secret even he doesn't know. (His fans want to help him find out.) Part of this coolness comes from the sense he gives of self-containment. Eccleston was damaged; you felt his rawness and need. Tennant acts pain beautifully, but I never quite believe him – somewhere in there, he's satisfied just the way he is. This completeness is a shade eerie, even hermetic, and part of what has made him so perfect for the alien and incomprehensible Doctor.

But it's not a great quality in a romantic lead. For there to be any chemistry, the audience has to feel the potential partners need each other. Tennant lets off occasional emotional winces, but otherwise his surface is smooth and untroubled. Not until he decided to play desperation full-out, in his scenes with the Master at the end of Series Three, did he seem exposed and at risk – part of what charges that relationship with its romantic/sexual undercurrent. Nine, the very definition of the walking wounded, found solace in Rose, learned how to live again during his adventures with her. Eccleston and Piper were relaxed and amusing together; a good temperamental fit. All the tenth Doctor's later insistence on Rose's specialness, which too often strikes an unconvincing note, makes sense if you imagine the show's ending after the first season. It's when Rose meets Ten that the trouble starts – the trouble being that the character no longer has anything to do.

Tennant's Doctor doesn't need saving and he doesn't need a guide; his happily abstracted monologues suggest he doesn't even need anyone to listen to him. He's doing just fine by himself. Tennant and Piper have fun together, and they seem to like each other, but they don't click, either as performers or on-screen lovers. He's too seamless; she has nothing to hold on to. He strides along, dreamy-eyed and self-satisfied, and she trots after him. Piper's openness, her willingness to be (and not just act) vulnerable, is one of her best qualities as an actress, but it sinks her here. In the face of Tennant's serene complaisance, she seems needy and intrusive.

Matters weren't helped by the show's wavering on the matter of the Doctor's feelings. In "The Christmas Invasion," he wonders, with a wink at Rose, if this new incarnation is sexy. Yet Tennant has said in an interview that he sees the Doctor as a non-sexual being. So... he wears that tight suit only to inspire hopeless yearning all round? His emotional state is confusing too. In "School Reunion," he tells Rose he'll never forget her like the others (and like he happily appears to forget

Sarah Jane at the end of the episode), and yet in the very next episode, he's fallen for Madame de Pompadour and wants her to come live in the TARDIS with them. Seriously, all sniggering aside, *for what?* Ten – and Tennant – is like a child here, gathering all his toys for a tea-party. Yet after a few more episodes, we're asked to believe his hearts break like a man's, not a child's, when he loses Rose at the end of "Doomsday."

This awkwardness about how to handle Ten's romantic nature continued to bedevil the show. Davies tried to solve it by having Martha in unrequited love with the Doctor, but it was pretty much a disastrous idea – her callous, shallow treatment by the man she loved would have fit right into *Queer as Folk*, but only made the Doctor look like an intergalactic jerk. So with Donna, Davies went the opposite direction – and, perhaps significantly, Catherine Tate's affronted refusal to consider the Doctor *that way* makes her partnership with Tennant a success; they have a natural comic rhythm together, and he's more at ease with her than any of his other partners. Basically, Davies solved the problem by making it a non-issue.

If Davies had trouble when he had a free hand in casting the tenth Doctor's companions, it's hardly surprising that his handling of Rose faltered when he had to change "her" Doctor in mid-stream. In spite of various explanations and denials, it's probably safe to assume that Davies didn't cast Eccleston as the lead in a risky relaunch of a beloved TV series with the understanding that he'd only have him for a year. The muddled state of Tennant's introductory script, "The Christmas Invasion" – it feels like Christmas padding (with an out-of-action Doctor) stuffed around an aliens-threaten-Earth story – indicates a certain scrambling and hurry. Piper had been delightful in the first season; there was certainly no reason to recast her. Just as there was no way to know that she would turn out to be the wrong companion for the Doctor that Ten became.

These are the vagaries of television. Audiences react to a series as if it were a story told in chapters, one a week. We expect character and story consistency, and it's nice if the show gives the impression that someone involved knows where it's going. And producers try to provide this. But these are really the qualities of a novel – a story created by one person, worked on at leisure, and presented to the reader in finished shape. Television has, so to speak, lots and lots of moving parts. It's made on the run, and the scores of people and the amount of material involved mean that nothing can be entirely controlled. (In order to maintain the quality of *The Sopranos*, David Chase took a season off to recharge and reorganize, but only a producer with a huge hit can get away with this.) The mishaps with happy-endings become little legends – like the way the complete screw-up of trying to use carts for pursuit on the beach in *The Prisoner* (sand in the engines wrecked them) resulted in the last-minute substitution of weather balloons and the birth of the sinister and beloved Rovers. In a more recent save, the writers of *House* dealt with Kal Penn's defection to a political career by making his character a suicide, and so giving Hugh Laurie an existential crisis to be brilliant in. The deterioration of Rose as a character shows what happens when a problem comes out of nowhere and there isn't a solution.

Actually, don't blame television.

Blame reality.

An Interview with India Fisher

India Fisher has played Charley Pollard – a companion to Paul McGann's eighth Doctor, and later Colin Baker's sixth Doctor – in more than 35 Big Finish *Doctor Who* audio dramas. She has also appeared on *Dead Ringers* and *Elephants to Catch Eels*, and outside of *Doctor Who* is probably best known for narrating BBC Two's cookery program *Masterchef*.

Q. Can you tell us a little bit about your experiences with *Doctor Who* before you became a companion?

A. Like most people of my generation, I grew up with *Doctor Who* as a staple part of Saturday night viewing; my brothers and I would watch it by the fire in the kitchen whilst Mum cooked supper. Tom Baker was my Doctor, and for me, the silhouette of the hat, big hair, scarf and coat will always be *the* Doctor. I'm ashamed to admit that my view of the companions was less than good – as a child, I always wondered why they fell over so much, or were so easily kidnapped by the baddies. Such story devices, which are designed to move a plot along, can be somewhat lost on a seven year old!

Q. What have your interactions with fandom been like, and what surprised you most about those experiences?

A. I knew *Doctor Who* had a cult following, but had no idea how passionate the fans were before I came to Big Finish. My first convention was Gallifrey [One] and I was totally taken aback. For one thing, Jason [Haigh-Ellery] informed me on the plane that my stories hadn't actually come out in the US yet, so I was astounded that anyone even knew who I was. The reception I get at conventions never ceases to amaze me – it's so humbling. People took Charley to their hearts so quickly, and for that I'm eternally grateful. Cheesy as this may sound, the fans have always felt like a *Doctor Who* family – I was taken into the fold and made to feel part of that instantly, and it's still the same ten years on. I'm just waiting for people to get sick of the sight of me, to be honest!

Q. Did you do a lot of preparation to find the right tone for Charley, who is from the 1930s?

A. This is going to sound awful, but no, I didn't do any research into the 1930s before I started playing her. Alan Barnes did such an amazing job writing "Storm Warning" [Charley's intro story] that my job as an actor was made so simple. It was all there for me on the page – Charley as a character just instantly jumped out. I didn't have to worry about how I was going to play her or what she'd be like; she was already there, fully formed and real. A trained monkey could have done it; I just read the brilliant lines Alan gave me.

Q. Can you tell us what it's like to work with Big Finish, and in audio as a medium?

A. Big Finish is an utter joy for work for. Gary [Russell], Jason and Nick [Briggs]' love of *Doctor Who* was always so evident, right from the word go. It's always great to work for people who are so passionate about what they're doing. They cared, and that showed in everything – from the writing and the casting, right down to how they treated the actors and the atmosphere they created in studio.

In the early McGann days, we recorded down in Bristol, and there was a real company feel to the work. We'd record an entire "season" of audios in a week, and the plays would generally be cross-cast, meaning that everyone stayed in the same hotel – and more importantly for company morale, the bar! It was one of my first jobs, and I just felt so privileged to be working with the likes of McGann, Mark Gatiss and Simon Pegg – to name but a few! I learnt so much that has stood me in such good stead – especially from McGann, and how he worked – in those early days. He was so in control of the mic, and for that I'm extremely grateful.

Q. Do you think that Charley's relationship with the eighth Doctor, which dates back to 2001, influenced the new series at all?

A. When it was announced that Russell T Davies was bringing back *Doctor Who*, I wrote to congratulate him, and he was kind enough to reply to my e-mail saying how much he enjoyed the eighth Doctor and Charley dynamic, and that he would never have been able to create a character like Rose if it hadn't been for Charley. I was blown away by that.

Q. Now that we've seen Christopher Eccleston, Billie Piper and John Barrowman flirting with each other, the idea of a Doctor-companion relationship doesn't seem as strange as it did years ago with the eighth Doctor and Charley. To what degree was Charley's relationship with the Doctor was romantic love versus the abiding love one might have for a good friend? Do you think the two of them ever truly figured out the difference?

A. It does seem strange, now that we've had kissing in the TARDIS, that there was such a furore over Charley simply saying she loved the Doctor. I always felt it was an extremely complicated definition of love anyway. We have to remember that Charley ran away from home and joined the Doctor at a very young age, and that he became literally everything to her – her family, her best and only friend, a father figure and yes, to some extent, a crush. She'd never known any other type of love, never even had a boyfriend, and here was this charismatic, amazing man whom she was in awe of. But, I'm convinced that it was never a romantic love. I don't think Charley ever thought of it like that; it was more than a love one has for a friend.

Q. How was playing Charley opposite the sixth Doctor different from being paired with the eighth?

A. Charley grew up hugely as a character in the transition between the Doctors. C'rizz's death really affected her, and she was utterly appalled by the eighth Doctor's reaction to his passing – or rather, his lack of one. The realisation that the Doctor had traveled with a succession of companions who had come and gone, and that at some point she would be replaced too, was devastating. She had assumed that because he was the most important person in the world to her, he felt the same way; she knew then that it was time for her to stand on her own two feet. When she saw the eighth Doctor die – or so she thought – it meant that when she met up with the sixth Doctor, she wanted to protect him from information about his fate. Because she was in control, it created a shift in their power balance, and she was no longer a little girl utterly in awe of the Doctor.

Q. What do you think it is about Charley that – much like Lisa Bowerman's Bernice Summerfield – gives her such longevity as a character, and makes her a candidate for her own series? Even after she's been given two departure stories, you're scheduled to do a Companion Chronicles audio, and it'd surprise nobody if Big Finish started doing solo Charley adventures.

A. I have no idea why people have taken Charley to their hearts, but I'm eternally grateful to them for doing so. I suppose she's a likeable companion because she's game. She never shrinks from a challenge or a fight, never complains or whinges. She says what she thinks and doesn't sugarcoat anything. She's the type of person we all strive to be – open, honest, up front, happy in her own skin and with the choices she has made in life. I am very lucky to play her; she's a hero of mine.

And yes, I'm recording a Companion Chronicle – tomorrow, in fact! It's written by John Dorney, and it's brilliant. It's a return to Charley travelling with the eighth Doctor, but she's very much in control of things – hilariously so, as you'll see! And I believe that Nick Briggs has now officially said that he's thinking of writing a Charley spin-off box set. I've loved every minute of Charley, and was miserable at the thought of never playing her again, so I'm thrilled to be given yet another reprieve! As I've always said, I'd be happy playing Charley well into her eighties – the first companion with a Zimmer frame!

Q. Finally, where do you get your shoes, and does Charley have taste in shoes as marvelous as yours? (We've seen your shoes at conventions, and they are *fabulous*.)

A. Ah bless you. If you're referring to the blue pair with the T-bar I wore at Chicago [TARDIS] last year, they're from a shop called Jones the Boot Maker. It sounds flasher than it is; it's just a chain. I'm actually not that much of a shoe girl – I have a few all-purpose pairs, but I'm certainly no Imelda Marcos. I always go for something that has a sensible heel; I'd just break my neck in a pair of Manolo Blahnik's. It's also a fairly recent thing; I've got more girlie in my old age – the older you get, the more effort you have to make – and gone are the days when I would turn up to conventions in jeans and trainers. But believe me, that's what I spend the majority of my time in.

Costuming: More Productive Than Drugs, But Just as Expensive

Johanna Mead has been a science fiction fan for over thirty years, and a costumer for almost as long. She's is a bit surprised to hear that she's considered an "old school" fan of *Doctor Who*, because she didn't start watching the show until at least 1976. She lives near San Francisco with her cats, Tigger and Jack; and her sewing machines, Gertie, Romeo, Cohen, Wally and Behemoth. http://www.skaro.com/personal.html

I can't tell you how many times I've been asked: "Wearing costumes at a science fiction convention. Isn't that sort of... childish?"

"Childish." Interesting choice of words, that. Let me tell you a little bit about my childhood.

When I was of an age to play make-believe, the playground game-of-choice was *Star Wars*. It wasn't the greatest game if you were a girl, as you were generally stuck with arguing about which of you got to be Princess Leia, and which of you got relegated to the nameless ranks of the Stormtroopers. I thought Princess Leia was a bit soppy – an unpopular opinion, I know – and so I learned how to make laser-gun noises with the rest of the gang. There weren't any alternatives. If you were a girl, you were the princess or a Stormtrooper, because that was all a girl was allowed by her peers to be. The 1970s schoolyard: bastion of conservative thought.

But then I suggested that we play *my* favorite show: *Doctor Who*. Brilliant!

There was some resistance at first, despite the occasional use of laser guns and an absolute plethora of strange planets in need of exploration. But I got the girls on my side. Why be a Stormtrooper or some silly princess in need of rescue when you could be a journalist, or a knife-wielding savage or even a Time Lord? That got my friends' attention. Some of them were *particularly* keen on playing Leela, now that I remember it...

The playground soon became the boundless realm of all of time and space. Wrongs were righted, shattered histories restored and surprisingly intense debates about just *how* Daleks could conquer the universe when they couldn't tackle a set of stairs occurred. Sure, the boys claimed the role of the Doctor, but the *girls* picked him. After all, we weren't going to run around time and space with a wally, were we? Of course not. Instead of re-enacting stories we'd seen on television, we made our own.

Fun abounded until the release of *Return of the Jedi*, and I knew I was beaten. My pals didn't see much contest between Nyssa with her unfortunate tulle skirts and Princess Leia in a metal bikini – even if Leia, once again, had to be rescued by the boys.

A Brief Flirtation With *Star Trek*, but Seduced by New *Who*...

In my late teens, I drifted away from *Doctor Who* and science fiction fandom, only to return to it once I'd gotten over that dreary *I'm too cynical for wobbly sets* stage that a lot of fans seem to go through in their early 20s or so. That period didn't stop me from getting a tattoo of the Seal of Rassilon in the meantime, but "How *Doctor Who* Made Me The Person I Am Today" is fodder for another day.

Star Trek fandom lured me in for a time, mostly by the simple fact that most of my friends were active in it. I joined a club, worked a few cons and even made a costume or two. Sewing has been a hobby in my family for several generations – my grandmother was a professional seamstress – and it was inevitable that I'd make costumes to accompany my participation in *Trek* fandom. But *Trek* palled – for which I'm a little relieved, given how it's all turned out – and I found myself in a rather strange position. I was a fan without a fandom.

Fortunately, it didn't last long. PBS lured me back to *Doctor Who* with Sunday night reruns. The show's charms prevailed against half a decade of entrenched cynicism, and I shamefacedly admitted that I had treated it unkindly. Then a friend convinced me to visit Gallifrey One, a *Doctor Who* convention in Los Angeles, whereupon I learned that the fandom still thrived. *Hello*, thought I. *Maybe there's still some fun to be had, here.* And, *unlike* certain other fandoms, the fact that I was female seemed quite incidental.

It wasn't until the new show that I fell head-over-heels in love with it, again. Up until that point, my affection was more of that held for a favorite, but slightly embarrassing, cousin. But as soon as I saw "Rose" – and it took my friends nearly a year to convince me that the BBC hadn't ruined my childhood memories – I was smitten again. Foolishly, embarrassingly, *15 years old and waiting for the phone to ring* smitten. It was quite nice, really – a contrast to the pedestrian circumstances of everyday life.

I returned to the conventions and re-connected with friends who asked why I wasn't making any costumes for my newly re-discovered love. Many of the intervening years had been filled up by live-action RPGs and, almost incidentally, I'd applied my costuming habit to *that* and so had improved my sewing skills to the point where I didn't bring home no-way-stretch fabric thinking it would make a decent Bajoran uniform (which, for the record, it emphatically *doesn't*).

The notion of costuming *Doctor Who* made a lot of sense, and I felt a little silly for not thinking of it earlier than I did. I had somehow forgotten the appeal of picking anything from time and space and saying, "I think I'll be *that*, today." Despite my infatuation with the new series, however, I looked to the old school for inspiration. One of the tricks of successful costuming is knowing your limits. Donna Noble and the return of Sarah Jane Smith were still a few years away, and a lithe 20-something I am *not*. Know your limits – but don't balk at challenging them, occasionally – and play to your strengths.

Inevitably, I identified costumes I wanted to tackle: the Rani, most of Romana I's wardrobe, a few of Jo Grant's more flamboyant ensembles. The list has long since outstripped the time I have available to sew, and each new season is good for a couple of ideas, too. It's great to have such a variety of items to choose from, depending on my mood, my budget, what mad group concept my friends might be coming up with for the next convention.

"But what's the *point* of wearing a costume?"

Fans and non-fans alike have asked me this. There's the usual reason: it's a focused outlet for a broader talent. I'd rather use my sewing skills to make costumes, not quilts, especially as a costume can provide the opportunity to learn new sewing techniques. I learned more about the vagaries of piping and trimming a coat whilst tackling Romana's purple "The Androids of Tara" monstrosity than I ever wanted to. Also, costumes are simply *fun* to wear, a change from the daily grind.

And there are the less-obvious reasons...

Clarity of purpose. If I'm in costume at a convention, there is no way that I'll be mistaken for some long-suffering partner dragged against her will to the event. Don't deny it, my friends, the assumption that any woman at a sci-fi media con simply can't be there of her own volition remains sadly persistent at times, despite an improving trend.

But if I'm traipsing about in my best Romana rig, there's no doubt that I'm not only there by my choice, but that I'm having a hell of a good time. Naturally, I look forward to the day when I don't have to rely on any such devices, and the awful assumption seems to be breathing its last – especially in Whovian circles, with the advent of the new series.

Vanity. I'll never make a costume I don't believe I'll look good in. Not just good, but damn good. I'm currently in the midst of re-creating Mercy Hartigan's swathes-of-red Victorian dress not out of some masochistic compulsion to pleat a couple dozen yards of organza ribbon (trust me, that's not something costumers do for fun), but because I know it's going to look absolutely stunning once it's done.

A little vanity can be good for the soul, but a woman who admits to such motives risks... let's call it *criticism*, in certain circles. But conventions tend to be safe – or *safer* – spaces for a person (female or otherwise) to show off a little and say "Look at me!" In fact, I must admit that hollering for attention – whilst somewhat armored by the costume of another character – was my primary motivation for costuming at conventions until quite recently. I'll explain what has recently supplanted my vanity in just a moment. Meanwhile...

Few things are more fun than creating your own canon. Fanon is the term the kids[1] are using today, isn't it? And that's how costumes such as the one I've nicknamed "Femmy Ten" were born.

I loved the tenth Doctor's brown suit, but there was no way I could get away with a suit cut for his build as I'm more hobbit than elf. So I created a version of his costume which I described as "the Doctor, following an unfortunate accident when he reversed the polarity of the neutron flow one time too many." I think the Doctor looked rather smashing in a pinstripe corset and a short skirt, but don't ask what happened to Rose. She won't leave the TARDIS.

That's not canon, you say? Who cares! If the show's producers aren't lying awake at night thinking about continuity – and Russell T Davies has made it clear that they aren't – then I'm not going to, either.

Crossplay. This simply means that you dress up as a character of a gender other than your own. Think of the number of Captain Jack Harknesses[2] you saw the last time you were at a convention. How many of them were women? Most of them, I bet.

Jack Harkness is an outwardly confident, internally vulnerable and

---

1. If you'd told me, even five years ago, that I'd be identifying as an "old school" fan of *anything*, I wouldn't have believed you. To me, "old school" *Doctor Who* fans are those who started watching it in the 1960s.

2. Is "Harknesses" the correct plural for "Harkness"? Pray we never have to find out. The world really isn't ready for more than one of him.

complex character with a past of doing pretty much as – or who – he pleased, and nothing too dire in the way of consequences (unless you want to count the paperwork at Torchwood as some sort of punishment detail). Who *wouldn't* want to be Jack, at least for a little while? Crossplay isn't my thing – I'd rather flatter my curves than *flatten* them – but the popularity of Jack amongst female cosplayers makes sense to me. In fact, it made so much sense that I was a little puzzled when I heard other fans query the point. "Why do they want to dress up as men?" they'd ask, with varying degrees of confusion or contempt.

There's no single answer, but here's the one I like: with Jack Harkness and Captain John Hart, there's an implication that the only characters in the Whoniverse who can get away with sexual confidence, brains and beauty are *male*. If the setting won't provide a female equivalent, then female cosplayers will take the male character and make it their own. There has been some brilliant discussion about Jack's popularity amongst the crossplayers, and I couldn't hope to do it justice here. Suffice it to say, I think it's great. Fans are having fun, and that's what matters over all else.

"Femmy Ten" and Captain "Kat" Smith

When I started writing this piece – and gave my costuming motivations the first hard examination they'd had in a very long time – I was a little horrified to realize that my first response to the question "Why costume?" boiled down to "because it's pretty," complete with an implied giggle at the end.

Alarm bells clanged and feminist guilt rumbled. Wait a moment? Feminist guilt? Where the hell did *that* come from?

Stomach sinking, I reconsidered the "Femmy Ten" costume. On the one hand, it's a silly little joke. On the other hand, I'd neatly suggested that a female Doctor would be completely useless. Have you ever tried running down a corridor in a tightly laced corset whilst wearing heels? I have (I was late for a panel), and it nearly crippled me. There'd be no racing to save the day in *that* ensemble. All I had considered, initially, was that I look good in a corset (plus, I wanted the challenge of making one with pinstripes). I can get away with a short skirt, and for heaven's sake, you don't wear *flats* with a skirt above the knee. Much, much later, I realized that, as a woman who has long ranted about fashion as a conspiracy to weaken women, I'd shot myself in the foot.

Just as I was about to brand myself The Betrayer of Female Fandom and second-guess every costuming decision I've ever made, I remembered Captain Katherine "Kat" Smith. She's another costume borne of a combination of mischief and knowing what I can and can't get away with in a costume. I love the concept of the Time Agency – not just Jack Harkness or John Hart alone, but the whole, wonderfully unexplained notion of 51st-century humans getting up to some probably shady shenanigans in time. Any workforce that features a murder rehab program is going to elicit my curiosity. As I don't like to crossplay, that meant creating my own canon, once again.

The costume that became Kat Smith had an inauspicious beginning. Retro-military style top, jeans, riding boots, a gunbelt from my *Firefly* wardrobe and a T-shirt with *Bite Me or Kiss Me* emblazoned on the front, chosen more because I thought that something that obnoxious would give it a little oomph. I referred to the ensemble as "Girly Time Agent," and wore it to a convention or two.

It was my first disappointment, although I couldn't quite put my finger on *why*. Granted, it was a costume that required a bit of explanation – the vortex manipulator on my wrist being the only clue – but even then, I had this vague feeling of unease when I walked the halls. I changed the designation from "girly" to "generic," thinking the problem might have been that the adjective was trite and dismissive. It was, but even after the change, the dissatisfaction remained.

Finally, I put it down to violating my recently adopted rule of "no more costumes that are inside-jokes requiring five minutes' explanation"[3] and quietly put it away.

The dissatisfaction finally crystallized as I put together a "no reason" project. (My husband: "In heaven's name, why are you making a red and black patchwork leather corset?" Me: "I just wanted to see if I could." A lot of my projects start that way.) But I came to realize that it *did* have a reason – that reason being homage to truly wretched 1980s militaria chic. And what else could a Whovian do with 1980s-militaria garb *except* integrate it into a Time Agent's rig? What I'd really wanted to do all this time, and had unconsciously been working toward, was to create an original Time Agent persona, with her own name, history and attitude, not some pallid and nameless "generic."

It's one of the few costumes I'll actively *cosplay* – assuming a character, as well as the clothes – because I want to make a point of being an unequivocally female character, with that cheerfully 51st century atti-

---

3. A rule that I dropped almost as soon as I took it on board. Ask me about the Lucy!Master costume I made for Gallifrey One in 2009. On second thoughts, don't. It'll take *far* too long to explain.

tude towards interpersonal (or interspecies) relations and the devil take my critics.

I'm *much* happier with the costume now. "Kat" is a character in her own right, and I'm much happier for it.

Thirty years on, I'm playing make-believe again, and I wouldn't give it up for the world.

Girl Genius: Nyssa of Traken

Francesca Coppa is Director of Film Studies and Associate Professor of English at Muhlenberg College. She is also a founding member of the Organization For Transformative Works, a non-profit organization established by fans to provide access to, and preserve the history of, fanworks and culture. She has recently been writing about fan-vidding, both as a feminist art form and as a fair use of copyrighted works.

I saw my first episode of *Doctor Who* on a 13-inch black and white TV with rabbit ear antennae. It was broadcast on PBS, but not on New York's main station, Channel 13 (WNET). No, you had to use your television's mysterious *second* dial, and find it on Channel 21 (WLIU), somewhere between the Spanish language stations and the strange, downmarket educational programming. Just tuning in to one of those mysterious, staticky UHF stations felt like science fiction in itself; you certainly knew you were watching something outside the mainstream. (That impression was only exacerbated by WLIW's fundraising telethons, which were staffed by fans wearing floppy hats and long multicolored scarves.)

There was, of course, only one Doctor. Oh, all right: we all knew he was technically the *fourth* Doctor, but Tom Baker was the only Doctor most Americans knew in 1982. PBS started broadcasting Tom Baker's seasons of *Doctor Who* in the late 1970s, and by time I saw my first episodes, the fourth Doctor had solidified his hold on American fans' imaginations as *the* Doctor. Sarah Jane Smith (Lis Sladen) was more or less *the* companion, having been in the majority of episodes broadcast in the USA. By the time I began watching *Doctor Who*, "the Doctor and Sarah Jane" had achieved iconic status as a duo in zines, in fan art, and in cosplay at cons.

But the fourth Doctor isn't *my* Doctor, mainly because Sarah Jane isn't *my* companion. I know that many people love Sarah Jane (and I'll bet there's at least one essay in this book explaining why) but for me, she was always too much of a damsel. Looking back, I can see how Sarah Jane represented feminist values circa 1973: she was a professional woman, a journalist, and "spunky" – a time-traveling version of her non-genre counterpart, Mary Richards of *The Mary Tyler Moore Show*. But Sarah Jane wasn't a compelling identification point for me – I was a serious, bookish, scientifically-minded girl; a member of the math team, a lover of puzzles, a reader of science fiction.

So my companion, then and now, is Nyssa of Traken, who was introduced to us both as an alien aristocrat and a brilliant scientist specializing in bioelectronics. My favorite episodes are those of the fifth Doctor's early years, when he was traveling with Nyssa, Adric and Tegan Jovanka. Alas, this is not a popular set of companions: in a 2007 post on the *Guardian's* TV and radio blog, Daniel Martin lists the Doctor's five best and worst companions, and rates Nyssa as the 4th worst, Adric as 2nd worst.[1] But the reasons behind the ratings are interesting. Martin's panning of Adric begins with "Everyone hates a boy genius," and he subsequently refers to Nyssa as "[a]nother bloody genius and noblewoman." Martin assumes that everyone shares his dislike of teen geniuses, but representations of teenage genius, particularly *female* genius, particularly female *scientific* genius, weren't and aren't all that common on TV. And from my perspective, Nyssa's fairy-tale looks and aristocratic cool were extra-special assets. I loved her cloud of curly hair and her lovely clothes and her tiara, but she's also brainy and a really convincing scientist, not a nerd or a joke. I'm sure that Daniel Martin dislikes Nyssa precisely because he thinks she's the sort of character a teenage girl *would* like, but speaking as someone who was a teenage girl during the fifth Doctor's run, I can testify how important it was to me to see someone like Nyssa on my TV screen.

We first meet Nyssa in "The Keeper of Traken" (1981), but she properly joins the team a bit later, in the back-to-back stories "Logopolis" (1981, Tom Baker's last adventure) and "Castrovalva" (1982, Peter Davison's first). From the start, Nyssa's era of companionship featured a couple of elements that were crucially important to me as a teenage girl, even though I couldn't have articulated them at the time:

1) Most of Nyssa's episodes pass the Bechdel test. The Bechdel test, formulated by feminist cartoonist Alison Bechdel, articulates principles similar to those Virginia Woolf articulated for women's literature in *A*

---

1. Daniel Martin, "*Doctor Who*: the five best and worst companions," guardian.co.uk, Culture: TV and radio blog, 28 March 2007. Accessed July 4, 2009. [http://www.guardian.co.uk/culture/tvandradioblog/2007/mar/28/doctorwhothefivebestandw]

Room of One's Own: that books should feature women who like each other and work well together. Bechdel's criteria are a little bit more specific than Woolf's; a story passes the Bechdel test if it:

a) Has at least two women in it,
b) who talk to each other,
c) about something besides a man.[2]

Sadly, there are numerous blogs and websites devoted to bemoaning how many mainstream novels, films, and television shows continue to fail this simple test. (Genre fiction, alas, is particularly bad: *Star Wars*, *Raiders of the Lost Ark* and *Lord of the Rings* all fail.) But because Nyssa joins the Doctor's crew at the same time as Tegan, her episodes routinely pass with flying colors; in fact, it is not an overstatement to say that Nyssa and Tegan, working together, are often the show's heroes. In "Castrovalva," the fifth Doctor is incapacitated by his regeneration and Adric has been kidnapped by the Master, leaving Nyssa and Tegan to help the Doctor into the recuperative space of the Zero Room, fly the TARDIS to Castrovalva (albeit with help from Adric, as we eventually learn), build a Zero Cabinet and then physically carry that cabinet – with the Doctor inside – for miles over rough terrain. (Okay, we're told the Doctor is levitating inside the cabinet, but still!) Then the women have to climb a rocky cliff to get to the Dwellings of Simplicity. Nyssa and Tegan's camaraderie and heroism dominate the episode, and I realize now how much it affected me to see them working together and saving the Doctor with their wits and strength.

While Christopher H. Bidmead wrote "Castrovalva," it's worth noting that the story was directed by Fiona Cumming, one of only five female directors – out of 73 total – to work on the show. In fact, more episodes of the fifth Doctor's seasons were directed by women than any other. Cumming, who had worked as an assistant floor manager and a production assistant for *Doctor Who* since its creation in 1963, went on to direct three additional stories ("Snakedance" and "Enlightenment," both 1983; and "Planet of Fire," 1984), while Mary Ridge directed Nyssa's last story, "Terminus" (1983).

---

2. This test was first articulated in "The Rule," an episode of Bechdel's ongoing comic series, *Dykes to Watch Out For*. The strip is reprinted at Bechdel's blog: [http://dykestowatchoutfor.com/the-rule]. Accessed July 4, 2009.

2) While special, Nyssa is not unique. Actually, there are many ways in which Nyssa is literally unique – not the least of which being that she's the only survivor of her home planet of Traken. But, in ways that I found emotionally important as a teenager, Nyssa is *not* unique: she is neither "the girl" (because Tegan is present), nor "the alien" (both the Doctor and Adric are from planets other than Earth), nor "the teenager" (Adric is about her age), nor "the genius" (Adric never let you forget his genius, mathematical excellence badge and all). In other words, Nyssa had many foils and mirrors in the series, which was terrific; it saved her from being perceived as freakish. It also allowed her to have many kinds of peers: of her own age, of her own gender, and of her own genius. I have already written about how much I liked Nyssa and Tegan together, but I also liked Nyssa with Adric, not because I wanted them to date (well, okay; not primarily!), but because they had this strange chemistry as teen alien scientists. It meant that Nyssa wasn't alone in the universe: she was smart and different, but being smart and different could be *normal* in a place like the TARDIS. There were others like you. (There were maybe even boys like you!) That was something I really needed to know when I was 13, and boys seemed – well, even less comprehensible than aliens!

3) The structure of Nyssa's time with the fifth Doctor allows us to imagine numerous other stories and what-ifs. For a significant but indeterminate amount of off-screen time – between the end of Season Nineteen and the start of Season Twenty – Nyssa was the fifth Doctor's sole companion. Numerous professionally made novels, audio plays, and short stories are set during this time (which some *Who* chroniclers have called "Season Nineteen-B"[3]), as well as reams of fan fiction. Season Nineteen-B allowed fans and pro-writers alike to develop the one-on-one relationship between the Doctor and Nyssa, a relationship that couldn't always be explored in very much depth because of all the companions competing for screen time (and the Doctor's attention). But in these *other* stories, we got to explore other aspects of Nyssa's personality, including her personal serenity (Traken was a planet dedicated to peace and harmony) and her psychic abilities (which are exacerbated when she is around other psychics, though they apparently make her particularly susceptible to mental influence).

In televised canon, we last see Nyssa in "Terminus," in which she

---

3. http://www.whoniverse.org/biography/timeline05.php

chooses to remain behind at a leper colony to apply her scientific skills for good; she wants to develop a vaccine to cure Lazars' disease. (When Tegan tearily protests that Nyssa will die if she stays, Nyssa hugs her tightly and says, "Not easily, Tegan. Like you, I'm indestructible.") But in the novel *Asylum* (2001), Peter Darvill-Evans tells us that after years of time-traveling and roaming the galaxy fighting against war and disease, Nyssa went on to become an academic at a university on an unspecified planet – a technographer whose dissertation was on the 13th-century philosopher Roger Bacon. *Asylum* gives us a Nyssa in spiritual crisis, torn between continuing to fight the good fight at her politically charged university in 3488 and retreating into a life of pure scholarly contemplation in medieval Oxford, which reminds her of Traken. In the end, she returns to her professorship with a renewed commitment to life's worthier struggles.

Then in the Big Finish audio play "Circular Time" (2007), Nyssa – seen during her travels with the Doctor – writes a novel and has her first serious relationship (with a graduate student, of course). In a later section, set in the future (and after events in *Asylum*, it seems), she is married and has children but still manages to connect with the Doctor and save his life, this time through a shared dream. In one notable speech, Nyssa explains to her scientist-husband that her time with the Doctor turned her from someone who followed "science as a sort of art, as a hobby" to "someone who wanted to change things" – an arc that parallels the Doctor's own. In fact, as an alien who tends to approach life from a point of view that's part humanistic empathy and part scientific curiosity, Nyssa is perhaps most like the Doctor himself.

So even as we have both grown older, Nyssa has remained a good role model for me. Like her, I became an academic, though my areas of specialization are a little more modern; as I edge closer to 40, I well understand the desire to leave social activism to the next generation and just settle back with a good book. Nyssa was an unusual representation of a teenage girl, and now she's an even rarer thing: a grown woman whose primary conflicts are philosophical rather than romantic. (As one *Asylum* reviewer noted, "One thing I appreciated is that Peter Darvill-Evans didn't go for the cheap trick of killing her husband, dooming her to a life of misery on an alien planet or any of the other gimmicks we've seen used to bring a little drama to other returning companions in the novels... instead he gives Nyssa a successful and pleasant life after leaving the TARDIS, which pleased me and was particularly surprising given the grimness of 'Terminus'."[4] Or, as another reviewer put it, "We get actual character exploration!... This older Nyssa is a great character, mixing world weariness and fears for her safety in a dangerous universe with much of the innocence that defined the character on TV."[5])

So here's to Nyssa of Traken: alien aristocrat, scientific genius, university professor, freedom fighter and woman of ideas. May she continue to inspire all her chroniclers, fan and pro-writers alike!

---

4. "A Review" by Finn Clark 12/8/01, located at The Doctor Who Ratings Guide: By Fans, For Fans. [http://pagefillers.com/DWrg/asylum.html] Accessed July 4, 2009.
5. "Quite Charming" by Robert Smith? 2/10/01, ibid.

An Interview with Sophie Aldred

Sophie Aldred played Ace, a companion to Sylvester McCoy's seventh Doctor, on *Doctor Who* from 1987-1989, and has revived the role in numerous audio plays. Through the years, Sophie has consistently worked as a children's television presenter and actress on shows such as *Corners*, *Words and Pictures*, *ZZZap!* and *Melvin and Maureen's Musicagrams*.

Q. Prior to your auditioning for Ace, how familiar were you with *Doctor Who*?

A. I wasn't actually a fan, as I now understand fans to be. But because *Doctor Who* was such an immense part of British culture, I of course watched the show when I was growing up and became a huge follower of it. But I wouldn't say that I knew every episode – as with all children my age, it was a natural part of growing up. It was what everybody did on a Saturday night.

My first Doctor was Jon Pertwee – that much, I can remember. And I have vivid memories – not of particular episodes, but of my childhood being flavoured by that presence of Jon Pertwee and *Doctor Who*. And of the assistants as well, like Sarah Jane Smith and Jo Grant. They had a big impact on me as a child.

Q. What were your strongest memories of the Doctor's companions?

A. I really loved Jo's character. She was really sweet and vulnerable, and I remember her kind of "girlyness," her femininity – which I wasn't very into at all at the time, because I was a tomboy. So, while I liked watching Jo, she didn't strike me as much as Lis Sladen. I was a little bit older when Lis came along, and I identified more with her character – her need to question, that she was a journalist. It gave her a little added bonus, that she absolutely had a profession. She was probably a stronger female than Jo, though I loved them both.

Q. What were your thoughts about Ace when you were playing the role?

A. I didn't really have any idea what it would be like, or any kind of preconceptions. Looking back, I was very sort of bowled over, so shocked to get the job in the first place because it just seemed like such an amazing dream. I'd never done any TV before, and never even stepped in a TV studio. It was all so new and so exciting and thrilling, I didn't really get a chance to think about that sort of thing. Developing the character had more to do with my relationship with Sylvester, I think – we hit it off straight away and were such good friends.

But to be honest, I was just sort of living in the moment, going from script to script. There were certainly times when I would see "Oh, yeah, we're really progressing with this story!" When I first got the script for "The Curse of Fenric," I thought, "Wow, this is really exciting, because Ace is being made to confront some demons here, and she's learning a lot, and she's growing a lot." I recognized that it was a fabulous chance for me to develop as an actress as well. And then I'd get a script like "Battlefield," in which Ace was much more like she originally was in "Dragonfire" – rushing about and chucking bombs around and shouting "Wicked!" Those adventures definitely had their place as well; it really differed from story to story.

Of course, the beauty of a show like *Doctor Who* is that there's no time frame – "Battlefield" may have taken place years before "The Curse of Fenric," we don't quite know. We were also filming them out of order as well, so that was another thing to consider – there was no kind of linear progression in *Doctor Who*. It doesn't really matter.

Q. What was it like the first time you saw "Dragonfire," your intro story, with all the performances edited together with all the music and sound effects?

A. I watched it in a funny old little flat that I was living in with flatmates I'd had for ages, and they kept my feet firmly on the ground. I remembered it was just so weird – there was I, on the screen! We sat in our living room there and watched it, and I thought "Gosh, is that really me?" It was really a very strange feeling. I know some people don't like watching themselves on screen – I don't quite know why that is, maybe they just get embarrassed. Sylvester doesn't like watching himself. But I've always looked upon it as a really fantastic opportunity to change, to develop, to grow to applaud what I like, and to think, "Oh, maybe I could have done that better."

It's very odd because it doesn't seem to be *me* that's on the screen, even when I'm doing presenting work – which is ostensibly much more "me" than Ace was. I think it's because you're one step removed from yourself even with presenting – I'm playing "Sophie Aldred," and that's not actually really what I'm like. Even when I'm on stage at a *Doctor Who* convention, that's not the "me" that my friends see.

Q. How did you react when to Ace being resurrected for audio, loosely for BBV, and then more officially for the Big Finish audios?

A. We did our first audio dramas pretty soon after the cancellation of the show. [BBV producer] Bill Baggs was producing his own original material, and I remember that Sylvester and I got asked to do a story based on *The Tempest* [named *Island of Lost Souls*]. It was written by Mark Gatiss, who has gone on to become such an amazing figure in British television, and *Doctor Who* in particular. Bill did his stories, and then we were also doing video stuff with Keith Barnfather [director of *Mindgame*, etc], and then we started doing the *Doctor Who* audio dramas when Big Finish started up. So it's been a very natural progression, and wonderful to be still playing that same character for all those years.

Q. Does your take on playing Ace now differ from your time on the TV series?

A. I don't think I approach playing Ace now differently than I did in *Doctor Who*. I still work from the script as it is, which I've always done. I'm very much in the moment with my work, and I really relish doing work fresh. I always like my first takes, but I've learned to develop stamina and hold back a bit, so I can repeat performances take after take. It's the same with the audio scripts, in a way. What brings it to life for me is to be in the studio with Sylvester and the other actors – to be sparring and interacting with them. Now that we have Philip Olivier playing Hex in the audios, we've got this fantastic banter between the characters; I've really relished that, and the character change Hex's arrival has brought about for Ace. So, I do my work when I'm actually in the studio; I will read a script and familiarize myself with a story, but I try and save something for when I'm with the other actors, bouncing off them.

Q. How do you feel about the way audiences have responded to Ace over time, and what about their response makes you the most proud?

A. At first, I was surprised that people were actually watching me... it was such a big change in my life, living in this funny little flat and then suddenly having the papers wanting to talk to me. It was strange, but I also felt it was a real opportunity for me to help people. I recognized that from the very beginning – when Ian Briggs wrote "Dragonfire," he based Ace's character on several girls that he knew from working in a youth theatre group. He invited a few of them to the studio to meet me, and it was very odd, because there they were, about ten years younger than me. But it very useful for me to interact with them, and they – the people who the character was based on – became the first ones to give me that encouragement and say, "This is what we're like. This is what we do, and how we are." It was amazing to have that feedback so quickly.

Later, when I started getting letters from young girls who were so relieved to see a realistic, strong female character on British TV, it just felt really good to give people something real that affected them. There weren't that many characters – and certainly, not many 16-year-old girl characters – like that on British TV at the time. *Eastenders*, which had quite recently started up, has a strong young character played by Susan Tully. But your normal, everyday programs just didn't have that many young, strong female characters who were reflecting society. Nowadays, they seem to be everywhere. But it's funny to think back to when there was a dearth of such roles.

Q. Did you have any preconception of what the conventions would be like, before attending your first one?

A. I had no idea. I went to my very first convention at Imperial College in London, and thought it would be a few people in a room who maybe wanted to shake my hand. I had no idea it would be hundreds of people in this lecture theatre. And there was Jon Pertwee and all the guys from UNIT, so I was trembling to meet *my* Doctor Who. I was totally unprepared for the size of the event.

But having said that, I'm quite extroverted and really love meeting people. For me, conventions are a fascinating view of life, a chance to see how other people live, to see what makes them tick. That was especially true when I started getting invited to America and then Australia – what an amazing opportunity. It was just brilliant to go; not so much for the travel, because I never particularly wanted to travel. But I think I'm just wired to love people. I love finding out about the world through other people – all the different nationalities, populations, what people do for a living. I'm very nosy. And at a *Doctor Who* convention, I have carte blanche to turn the tables on all the people asking me questions, and ask them about their lives.

Another huge joy of conventions is meeting the other men and women who have worked on the program through the years. When I first got the part, somebody said to me, "Welcome to the family," I thought, "Oh yeah, right. How weird." But it's so true, it's become a real family. I've been able to develop friendships with people like Anneke Wills, who is another fascinating, amazing woman, and who has become a great friend. We share this extraordinary thing, that we were "Doctor Who Girls." Having worked on the show is like being in a club – I know I could ring up any of them, and we'd have a lovely chat.

Q. What do you think it is about Ace, a TV creation of the 1980s, that remains relevant even today?

A. The great thing about Ace is that she's totally blunt, honest, says exactly what she thinks and doesn't edit what she's saying. I think people really like that about her. She's also flawed, but people always love a flawed character. And she's vulnerable in her own way as well. I think they just recognize something in her: she's a troubled soul, she's not all happy all the time, she's not one-dimensional. She's a well-rounded character, and her relationship with the Doctor has a great strength to it.

I think that with the new series, the relationship between Rose and the Doctor possibly had some of its roots in Ace and her Doctor. I'd love to talk to Russell T Davies one day, and find out whether, consciously or not, Ace contributed to some of the ideas he had for Rose.

Q. What do you think children take away from *Doctor Who*, in terms of what the program says about the potential of women?

A. It's very important that children see the strength in female characters. Now that I teach as part of my work, I can clearly see that around the ages of seven, eight and nine, the girls go to one side of the classroom, the boys go to the other. It's so marked, almost like a natural part of child development. The boys are invariably very good at maths and sports, and the girls are invariably very good at painting, drawing, reading and writing. It's so interesting, like it's a part of their biology and brain wiring.

But when the boys come out and play cricket during break time, I am constantly trying to get the girls involved. Having played football and cricket myself as a child, and having been a tomboy, I can see that some girls find it very important to join in with the cricket, while others are very happy if they never pick up a cricket bat in their lives. On the other hand, it's very important for the boys to see that girls and women can be strong.

Q. What are some of the best memories that you have from your time on *Doctor Who*?

A. *Doctor Who* was such a vivid, amazing time for me – in which I went from the back row of the chorus in *Fiddler on the Roof* to suddenly having national fame on one of the nation's best-loved television programs – that I was drinking it all in and trying to remember as much as I possibly could. I don't just remember amazing things, I recall little details like the catering on location. There were these big tables groaning with food, and John Nathan-Turner would say, "It's time for a tea and a tart," in a sing-song voice. I remember events at conventions, like performing at Visions in Chicago with Jon Pertwee doing a scene from *The Navy Lark*. There's things I never in a million years would have imagined I would be doing – I can still feel the sort of tingling I got when I smacked the Dalek with that baseball bat and it reverberated up my arm. And, of course, I remember working with Sylvester – sharing that amazing time together, feeling very happily fond of each other and knowing we were doing a good job.

Rutle-ing The Doctor: My Long Life in *Doctor Who* Fandom

Jennifer Adams Kelley is a fixture in the American *Doctor Who* fan community. She was one of the contributors to The Federation series of *Doctor Who* original fanvids and served as the stage manager and Masquerade head at every HME Visions convention (Chicago's former giant *Doctor Who*/ media convention). She is currently the head of programming and publicity for Chicago TARDIS, an annual *Doctor Who* convention. She is also one of the directors of the *Doctor Who* forum Gallifrey Base. She blogs sporadically about her fannish experiences, both past and present, at www.blogforgallifrey.com.

I caught the wave of American *Doctor Who* fandom early in the 1980s, as the show's cult popularity swept through the country engulfing high school and college students especially in a warm, wet pool of delight. Living in Chicago – the epicenter of US fandom – I had easy access to conventions, gatherings, fan clubs and merchandising. Most importantly, there was a different *Doctor Who* story every Sunday night at 11 p.m. on the local PBS station. I wrote fan fiction, made fan art, recreated companion costumes, crocheted 17-foot-long scarves, met various *DW* actors and production people, befriended fellow fans both locally and nationally, and joined national and regional fan clubs. Yep, you guessed it: I was an obsessed teenager!

By the summer of 1983, I had only one thing left to try in fandom. I absolutely, positively *had* to make my own *Doctor Who* film.

See, I was in film school at the time. I wanted to make films (and television shows) because I loved the medium so much, and had gotten so much pleasure from it as a child. My *Doctor Who* passion compelled me to make my own *DW* film, but I didn't want to make a serious story – the BBC was already doing a brilliant job of that. I wanted to spoof the show gently, using absurdity and humor to lovingly highlight both its foibles and successes, in the SF equivalent of *All You Need Is Cash*. In other words, I wanted to Rutle the Doctor.

I had a problem, though. I didn't have *time* to make a *DW* film during the school year, when I had access to equipment and people. And when my schedule opened up in the summer, I didn't have equipment or people access. What I needed was a group of like-minded individuals who could pool resources together to make home-grown *Who*.

My dream group barged into my life one humid Saturday in June.

I had recently joined the UNIT Irregulars, a local fan club so huge it needed several "divisions" in order to accommodate everyone at meetings. I was assigned to the newly-minted Deerfield division, and toddled along to a meeting. The other members weren't the bon vivants I had anticipated, so I found myself bored by most of the proceedings. About 450 years into the meeting, though, the crew from the Libertyville division arrived, headed by a fellow named Chris. Along with his fellow divisionites, Chris showed up with a purpose: to announce that UNIT would be making a video that summer that would spoof the entire history of *Doctor Who*, entitled "The Five Faces of Doctor Booh" (the title derived from the BBC2 repeat season in 1981, which was called "The Five Faces of Doctor Who"). Chris laid the plot (such as it was) on us, then had those who were interested fill out a questionnaire specifying interests both in front of and behind the camera.

Ooh, I couldn't *believe* it! I would have squeed, had I not been trying to appear cool. I filled out the questionnaire, mentioning that I was a film major and thus had cinematography experience – and that, oh yes, I also had Sarah, Leela and Romana costumes. I gave the form back to Chris, and chatted with him for a minute or two about the project before wandering off. I absolutely didn't want to geek out about the project, because I wanted to be part of it so desperately.

Chris called me up a week or three later. Apparently I was the only person in the club with any experience in running a camera (let alone making a film), so I was totally in as cinematographer. And, oh yeah, I could play Sarah, too. *Squee!* Filming would be the last weekend in July.

We had to report for a full read-through the Friday evening before filming. I arrived at Chris' basement just in time to hear him say, "Where's Jennifer when you need her?" "Right here," I replied as I finished descending the stairs. I showed him where he had gone wrong with the camera set-up in less than ten seconds, thus impressing both him and everyone else already gathered.

As we got down to the nitty-gritty of the read-through, I quickly realized that, yeah, they were a group of crap actors. Being of dubious ability myself, though, I felt right at home. That feeling extended into that Sunday, where we went from early in the morning straight through to mid-evening with no real break. Having already proven I knew where the "on" button and focus ring were, I was given pretty much complete scene-staging control. Chris busied himself with getting the next segment set-up for filming, and things went slowly but smoothly.

The following month, we premiered "The Five Faces of Doctor Booh" at US 20, a local convention where the club worked security in exchange for being able to have Nicholas Courtney and Ian Marter in the room when we screened the film. The actors treated it (and us) kindly; the club members all congratulated Chris on a job well done.

Well! As it turns out, *no one* took the spotlight from a certain high-ranking member of the UNIT Irregulars – who shall go nameless – like that. Soon after the con, Chris was kicked out of UNIT. The rest of the Libertyville branch quit, as did those of us from other divisions who had big parts in "Booh." We reshot bits of "The Five Faces" to edit out the person who had ejected Chris from the group (and to make it *au courant* by putting in the as-yet-not-even-having-filmed-their-first-stories sixth Doctor and Peri), and created "The Five Doctors Booh." On the true 20th anniversary of *Doctor Who*, we gathered in costume in Chris' basement to watch both the re-edited film *and* the world premiere of "The Five Doctors" on our local PBS station. (Yes, that's right, Chicago saw it before the UK did!)

On that fateful day, a new organization was founded – not a club with a strict power hierarchy, but a fan co-operative, banded together because of common interests and the desire to prove we could be a different kind of organization... one that served all the group members and the television shows we were interested in, not individual egos. We called ourselves... The Federation.

Oh, don't roll your eyes like that – yes, we were *that* earnest, as only young adults can be.

We sailed along nicely for several years. Sure, cliques existed within the group, but it pretty much boiled down to "the usual gang of idiots," "people who came to meetings but didn't quite fit in" and "those who subscribed to our newsletter and got our videos and lived way far away in places like Minnesota." Our main activities – other than watching spanking new *Doctor Who* stories that in those days only took six to eight weeks to reach us – all centered around making films. Sometimes we would venture forth into a costume contest or skit competition or just some silly cosplay in convention hallways. (We attended many a convention, not only the huge local Spirit of Light ones, but smaller ones in Ohio, Florida, Louisiana, Wisconsin, Minnesota and Missouri.)

It was filmmaking, though, that really kept us together. In a five-year period, we made 21 different pieces, all of them send-ups. We combined *Doctor Who* with *All Creatures Great and Small*, *Monty Python and the Holy Grail*, *Willy Wonka and the Chocolate Factory*, *The Man From U.N.C.L.E.*, and all sorts of 60s-80s tv shows. We also took the piss out of *Blake's 7* twice, and made fun of spy shows, *The Monkees* and *Doctor Who* conventions. (We even produced two convention parodies, which had us playing the guests as well as the con staff.) Our most famous production from the era, "S-A-V-E-W-H-O," mocked pledge drives and the documentaries usually shown during them, tracing an absurd version of *Doctor Who* history even as the "actors" pleaded for more dosh to keep the tradition going.

Ah, what great times those were! I got to write and direct my favorite television show, after a fashion. I also had continuous inspiration for my next costuming project. "Oh, I'm playing Peri again? I'll need a new outfit for that..." We brought our films with us to conventions wherever we went, screening them in our hotel room if we couldn't get a spot in the video room. We became a "known" fan group.

We made most of our films between 1984 and 1987, with the creation of the "Video'zine" partially driving the need to keep turning out fresh product. The "Video'zine" was an every-so-often compilation of interviews and other *Doctor Who* extras we didn't get to see in the States, interspersed with American-made fan films. Since it was a Federation project, we all felt strongly that every issue should have a new Federation production in it, along with the ongoing soap opera spoof "Thirteen Lives to Live" and, of course, Federation-produced bumpers introducing each segment.

Chris always organized things, whether it be a meeting or a filming or a convention trip. His non-fan life fell apart in 1987, though, forcing him to step back from the club. None of us had a problem with that, since several of us had been doing a lot of the writing, production, and post-production work on the various films, and everyone else was willing to carry on the same as it was before it was.

With Chris no longer in the picture, I took over running the club newsletter and scheduling meetings and the like. Someone else took over the "Video'zine," and a third person did a lot of newsletter writing and fanzine compiling. The three of us worked so well together, we decided we'd write the next production – another compilation spoof entitled "Reign of Turner" that laughed at the entire John Nathan-Turner era of the show. We three would create and film it without anyone else's input. The other club members would be actors only, and would be required to spend most of their weekends in the sweltering summer of 1988 making the film.

Hoo-boy, not the smartest of things, in retrospect.

Factions formed, in-fighting began. The three of us who wrote "Reign of Turner" became the "We" – and the other faction the "Not-We" – in conversations. (The other faction reversed the nicknames, naturally.) What was once a good time and great camaraderie stopped being fun. By the time filming wrapped some seven months later, none of us really wanted much to do with the Federation or fandom in general. Just as well, because *Doctor Who* entered its 16-year hiatus with the airing of "Survival." Other clubs had similar issues and fell apart as well. *Doctor Who* fandom in the States collapsed and died.

Or... did it? You certainly couldn't tell by the attendance at Visions! A thousand-plus fans every year couldn't be wrong, could they?

I first heard about Visions as The Federation was breaking apart. Those involved managed to be civil to each other during an evening answering phones for a pledge drive at the local PBS station. In the station's break room, I ran across Bob McLaughlin, whom I knew from various conventions. He talked up a con idea he had, something along the lines of the huge Spirit of Light ones, but fan-run. He made vague noises about me maybe running the Masquerade; I made vague noises that I'd be interested, and we left it at that.

Sometime later I ran into Gene Smith, a dealer with whom I was friendly. Gene was co-chairing the con with Bob, and said they definitely wanted me to run the Masquerade. I liked the idea, as I had competed in so many competitions, I knew a thing or two about how the event should be run.

No one bothered to tell me about staff meetings, though, so I showed up to run the competition the weekend of the convention and had to basically beg and plead for supplies, set-up help, etc. The Masquerade came off successfully despite the last-minute scrambling, so I was asked to continue, and was actually told when and where the meetings were going to be held. Before long, I had amassed more responsibility. By the last Visions in 1998, I ran opening and closing ceremonies, the Masquerade, the variety show, and supervised the main programming room during the day.

Visions served as my only real connection to *Doctor Who* fandom in the 1990s. Truly, I needed a break from all the back-biting and bitchiness that followed the collapse of real organized fandom in the States. Also, I didn't particularly care for the original *Doctor Who* novels that Virgin (and, later, the BBC) was publishing. Thus, I mostly moved on.

I dabbled in several other fandoms, teaming with my dearest girl-friend to publish fanzines and anger people with TV reviews posted to mailing lists. I also got married, and landed one of those awful "real" jobs that required long hours and longer commutes. The Paul McGann TV movie aired while I was pregnant; soon I had too much on my real-life plate to do anything fannish other than Visions. While the first wave of Internet fandom exploded with rec.arts.drwho, egroups mailing lists, and Web 1.0 sites, I hid safely behind the bunker of being a newly-hatched stay-at-home mom.

Visions went out on a high note – it was a smoothly run event that everyone enjoyed. And as Visions took its bow, The Federation came back out of hibernation. We had been quasi-friendly for several years; enough time and tide had passed that we thought we might like working together again – with a twist. Since the series wasn't in production, why not make a *serious* story? Fan filmmaking was coming back in vogue, thanks to people talking up their productions on the Internet. It might be worth our while to see what we could do.

We had filmed "Realitywarp," a sixth Doctor/ Peri adventure, in the summer of 1998, and premiered it at the last Visions. We made "Traumaturge" in November 1999, figuring that since we didn't have a convention to go to/ run, we might as well make a movie Thanksgiving weekend. We also came up with the idea of "The Six-Minute Movie," a website that would host fan films in RealVideo format that were just six minutes long. We made several shorts for the website; other people latched onto the idea, too, and we ended up hosting a dozen films. (YouTube has, of course, eliminated the need for such a site.) In 2002, we filmed "Shadowcast," our most recent (and ambitious) production.

Word about things tend to get around, of course, and the We found out about a new convention called Chicago TARDIS, organized by Gene Smith. (Gene had left the Visions con committee after the first year, but was eager to fill the void Visions left.) The We cruised over to Gene's store both separately and together, to discuss the convention over the course of 2000. Gene had a guest list, but he was vague about what would actually be going on at the convention. About six weeks before the event, I wheedled out of him that there would be a dealers room, autograph sessions, photograph sessions, and an hour-long panel with the guests each day. I wondered what else; he looked sheepish. "It's like a Creation con, you know," I pointed out. "You really need some other programming, panels and stuff, for when the guests aren't on stage...."

"Okay," he said, "Come up with some."

And, with the help of my e-mail address book, I did. Chicago TARDIS has been growing ever since. Our latest event – held in 2009 – had three programming tracks and 900 people in attendance. It's now the second-largest convention devoted to *Doctor Who* in the United States, after Gallifrey in Los Angeles.

I've now run so many conventions that they tend to blur together, although I can usually recall whether something happened at Visions or Chicago TARDIS. I get great satisfaction from putting together a convention schedule that people seem to enjoy year after year. I find there's nothing better than having a fellow fan tell me they've had a fantastic time. It makes the hours of hard work worth it.

When I'm not promoting or preparing for Chicago TARDIS, I spend most of my fannish time these days supervising the day-to-day workings of the popular online forum Gallifrey Base. (The We formed the not-for-profit corporation that manages the forum.) The Federation is in pre-pre-production for our first long-form spoof in 20 years. (Hey, with *Doctor Who* back in production, there's no need, as far as we're concerned, to make *serious* fan stories!) We're also contemplating how to celebrate the 25th anniversary of "S-A-V-E-W-H-O," and working to get our classic productions available in 21st century formats.

So, yeah, I've been around *Doctor Who* fandom for longer than incoming Doctor Matt Smith has been alive. *Plus ça change, plus c'est la même chose.* Fans still watch the show; still argue over plotlines and characters; still make costume recreations, fan art and fan films; still write fan fiction; still over-analyze the underlying text; still flame each other over petty differences of opinion... only the names change. We all keep gathering together virtually and physically to share our love for *Doctor Who* and all the people involved with it. I continue – as I have since the dawn of time, seemingly – to share my love for the show in my own way, using both my creative and managerial talents. Otherwise, I keep watching the wheels of fandom go round and round. I really love to watch them roll. If I didn't, I wouldn't still be here. *Allons-y!*

Marrying Into the TARDIS Tribe

Lynne M. Thomas is the Head of Rare Books and Special Collections at Northern Illinois University, where she is responsible for archiving popular culture materials that include science fiction and fantasy literature, comic books, dime novels and historical children's literature. She has published articles about cross-dressing in dime novels, as well as articles on science fiction archiving for the Hugo-nominated fanzine *Argentus* and the Nebula Awards blog. She is the co-author of *Special Collections 2.0*, a book about web 2.0 technologies and special collections in libraries with Beth Whittaker of Ohio State University, published by Libraries Unlimited in 2009.

I am a convert to fandom. I became active in organized fandom less than ten years ago, and *Doctor Who* fandom since 2001. Before that, I had never been to a convention. I had never participated in a fandom community. I had never had a love for a show, a book, a movie or a comic that made me want to bounce up and down with enthusiasm and then talk to other people about it at length. *Dirty Dancing* and *The Phantom of the Opera* came close when I was a teenager, but the experience wasn't quite the same.

And then I fell in love with a *Doctor Who* fan.

Michael had his work cut out for him – I didn't even know what that meant, to be a fan, in the active fandom sense of the word. He slowly introduced me into media properties that had fandoms that we could enjoy together, like *Xena: Warrior Princess*. Later, we added *Buffy*, *Angel*, *Firefly* and *The Avengers*, along with *Doctor Who*.

My first pro-run convention was a *Xena* convention, during our honeymoon. When the late Kevin Smith, who played Ares on the series, winked at me as he signed my glossy (and I struggled to stay upright and not make squeaking noises), I was hooked on the "getting to meet celebrities on my show" experience. A "squee girl" was born – despite my not having yet heard the term.

The rest of that convention, though, left me a bit disappointed and restless. Michael assured me that fan-run conventions were *different*, and that I would like them better. I didn't feel like I knew enough – or *felt* strongly enough – about *Doctor Who* to attend one, though.

So Michael continued my education. I was introduced to different classic Doctors. I thoroughly enjoyed much of Tom Baker and Peter Davison, and surprised myself with my admiration for Patrick Troughton (I still think "The Mind Robber" is brilliant). I developed affection for Sarah Jane, Leela, Liz Shaw and Nyssa, and enjoyed Kate O'Mara's Rani and Roger Delgado's Master more than I probably should have. As Michael's collection grew, so did my affection for the series.

But I didn't become a *real* fan, not really, until I saw Ace take on a Dalek with a souped-up baseball bat in "Remembrance of the Daleks." Because traveling with the Doctor may be hard, frustrating, and dangerous, but it sure beats the hell out of being a waitress in an intergalactic malt shop. At that moment, something clicked in my brain, saying YES. THIS. *I get it.* Ace became *my* companion, and Sylvester McCoy became my favorite Doctor.

I was ready for a *Who* convention.

In 2000, I attended United Fan Con and Chicago TARDIS. In my excitement, I kept starting conversations with guests and fans while standing in line, in the dealer's room, in hallways, and at parties and what we like to call BarCon. In 2001 at United Fan Con, we met Bill Baggs (who made *Who*-related audios and videos during the Wilderness Years as the owner of BBV), Paul Ebbs (a *Doctor Who* novelist that has written for Big Finish, BBV and British television), and Steve Johnson (an artist who did lots of work for BBV and Mad Norwegian Press). We all loved the show to death, and yet most of our conversations had very little to do with *Doctor Who*. We talked about other cult television, politics, you name it. We got on well enough that when they were in our local area, we went out for pizza. Since they had been visiting the Beinecke Library's exhibits on the Yale campus (where I worked at the time), we talked about rare books. They were flabbergasted when I joked that the 1623 First Folio of Shakespeare's *Works* isn't considered to be all *that* rare in the United States. In that moment of cultural exchange, I learned that there are more copies of that book at the Folger Shakespeare Library than there are in the UK, period.

After they left town, there were continuing conversations on the Internet, Christmas cards exchanged, and just general getting to know each other. To this day, we have a standing sushi date with Bill and Steve every year at Chicago TARDIS.

Bill introduced us to Sylvester McCoy the year that he was a guest at

TARDIS. The two of them then proceeded to beat Michael and me at pool. Actually, it was a close game until Michael's final shot, when Sylv leaned over and whispered into Michael's ear "you're going to lose," using his best Doctor voice. Michael then (rather understandably) flubbed the shot, losing the game. Bill also introduced us to Ruth Ann Stern, a member of the TARDIS staff and a longtime friend of his. She introduced us to Sophie Aldred at that same TARDIS – where I was rather speechless, and Michael was roped into installing car seats for Sophie's kids. At these conventions, we re-connected with old friends like Tara O'Shea (whom Michael had met years before in college), and built friendships with Lars Pearson and Christa Dickson of Mad Norwegian Press, as well as a host of other people too numerous to name individually, many of whom had some hand in this anthology.

I had found my tribe. These were my people.

For the first time in my adult life, I felt as though I truly *belonged*. In a fandom for a show that, in 2000, *wasn't currently on the air*. Upon reflection, this seems to fit; I'm a professional rare books librarian, after all.

Change, my dear...

In 2002, I became pregnant with our daughter, Caitlin. Through the entire pregnancy, we watched the classic series in order, one episode each night before bed. Caitlin has literally been a *Who* fan from the womb; she kicked along to the theme song.

The Doctor traveled from place to place, making hard choices, fixing problems, and slipping away quietly when his work was done. Even when he was frightened, he got the job done, which we found deeply reassuring. He regenerated again and again, learning from each previous version of himself and moving forward. Change, being different, did not mean the end of the world. It simply meant making adjustments.

Our life changed when Caitlin was born, as the lives of parents always do, but our changes were a bit more challenging. Caitlin is special. She has a rare congenital disorder called Aicardi syndrome. We needed to make *lots* of adjustments, and our life suddenly looked very different than we had planned, rather like all of those years in which the Doctor was unable to control the TARDIS.

Our fandom is used to change, though (even when we critique it to within an inch of its life). Our friends in fandom adjusted right along with us, and our convention experiences were tweaked to fit Caitlin right in. At Caitlin's very first convention, United Fan Con 2003, Peter

Davison and Katy Manning both insisted upon holding her for photos, treating her as any other child, despite her visible differences. Friends new and old made a point of asking after us, and offering what help they could.

Change came again to our household in 2004. When Caitlin was just over a year old, my experiences in the *Doctor Who* community and general SF fandom opened the door to my dream job and a move to Illinois. I now go to science fiction conventions all over the Midwest as part of my job, which involves archiving SF literature. My *Doctor Who* fandom led me to an even larger community of friends that made us feel welcome and loved in our new life. We began to build a life in Illinois, creating a community of care for Caitlin that helped her to excel, and giving Michael the opportunity to begin working on his own writing career.

And then *Doctor Who* came back on the air.

... Did I mention that it travels in time?

While Michael and I hold some fundamental differences in how we approach the series (we may never resolve the argument between us about the nature of the relationships between the Doctor and his companions), we both agreed that we'd rather see no new televised *Who* at all than *Who* done badly. Like the rest of fandom, we approached the new series with great trepidation.

Doctor Who had changed again. *And it was awesome.* We ate up every episode, eagerly awaiting the next one. Michael was giddy to see updated versions of his favorite monsters, references to continuity from the classic series (you should have seen his face when the Macra turned up in "Gridlock"), and nods to the New Adventures novels. I was fascinated by Eccleston's clearly traumatized, broken Doctor, and how knowing Rose made him better. I never thought that I'd care so much about a Dalek that its death could make me cry. I thrilled to meet Captain Jack Harkness, the first omnisexual superhero, who swept Rose off her feet. Captain Jack was brash, over-the-top, flirtatious, brave and wonderful. He was also overtly sexual in a way that highlighted the Doctor's loneliness. I was thrilled when he got his own series, and am a die-hard *Torchwood* fan for a long list of reasons – but that's another essay for another time.

The new series has it all, in spades: action, adventure, romance, silly monsters, humor, heroics, scientific gobbledygook, deep emotion and, most importantly, that implacable optimism intrinsic to the series. No matter how bad the situation is, the Doctor makes adjustments, changes, and goes on to win. Even when winning is just, well, going on.

"Everybody lives, Rose. Just this once! Everybody lives!" indeed.

Just as I got comfortable with the new Doctor, change came to the show once again, and Christopher Eccleston regenerated into David Tennant. In that moment, my answer to "who is *your* Doctor?" changed forever.

David Tennant has become *my* Doctor. His interpretation of the Doctor hits my brain in such a way that my instinctual reaction is "*that* is the person I'd travel through time and space with, oh yes" (with all of the implications thereof).

Tennant is also *my* Doctor because *he is one of us*, a lifelong fan of the show. It's not just a really neat acting job in a long line of neat acting jobs. He is part of our tribe. He *knows* what it means to have the chance to take the TARDIS for a spin, and he has never taken it lightly, on-screen or off. I love knowing that deep down, there's an eight-year-old boy inside *him that jumps up and down with glee* every time he steps through those blue doors.

After all, I fell in love with a *Doctor Who* fan.

I'll miss David as the Doctor, but change is part of how the Doctor's world (and ours) works. I'll adjust. I'll make room in my heart for Matt Smith. I promise.

Unlimited Rice Pudding...

One of the beautiful things about *Doctor Who* and its fandom is that there's room enough for everyone. We don't have to agree on our favorite Doctor, our favorite companion or our favorite episode. Instead, we all agree that we love this show (and bicker good-naturedly about the details). In a universe that doesn't always change for the better, despite our best efforts, we love a show about embracing change, making adjustments, and moving on. Whether that requires the assistance of Torchwood, Sarah Jane, UNIT, Shakespeare or K-9 is really up to each of us.

Raising a special kid often requires those same ideas. In the nearly seven years since Caitlin was born, *Doctor Who* has become a talisman, a touchstone for our family as we continue to build a community of friends and acquaintances that share our love for the series. This fandom community has become our solace, our support, and our occasional escape from the difficulties inherent in raising Caitlin. They know us not just as Caitlin's parents, but as fans and as people, and they let us be all of those things at once. Our fandom community has acted as the Doctor does, accepting change and committing acts of kindness for which we are deeply grateful, which help us to keep going.

Fan volunteers at conventions, unasked, waved our daughter to the front of the line for photographs and autographs with *Who* celebrities at her first Chicago TARDIS last year. The folks waiting in line encouraged it. Convention staff made sure that getting Cait's wheelchair into position for photos, which is sometimes awkward, was seamless on both occasions. Another fan dedicated funds from *Buffy* fandom fundraisers to supporting our daughter's Make-A-Wish trip. Vendors in the dealer's room gave her gifts, just because. Our daughter was queen for a day, because *Doctor Who* fandom just does that.

And it's not just the fans.

Elisabeth Sladen and Colin Baker were the main guests at that same convention. Lis called Cait "sweetiepop," held her hand for the photo, and commented that she must be at least nine, since she looked such a lady. Caitlin grinned, and preened, and generally was really excited to meet Lis (she's also a big fan of *The Sarah Jane Adventures*). When we got Lis's autograph, I happily paid for a glossy, but she insisted that Caitlin pick out a second one, gratis, from Father Christmas, and signed both photos extra with kisses on them just for her. Lis also went out of her way to say goodbye to Caitlin as she was checking out of the hotel while we were in the lobby.

Colin called her "twinkle" during photos and was also exceedingly nice. He made sure to wave hello to her when Michael pointed him out walking along the hall, saying "Look Caitlin, it's the Doctor!" Caitlin squealed with delight, because we had just finished watching some of Colin's stories in preparation for the convention. In the dealer's room at the Big Finish table, Lisa Bowerman, Nick Briggs and Jason Haigh-Ellery were also super nice, and Caitlin now has a signed Nick Briggs badge. Lis didn't have to give Caitlin an extra glossy. The nice guys running the autograph lines didn't have to let us jump the line. Colin didn't have to wave, and Lisa, Nick, and Jason didn't have to spend ten minutes talking to our daughter, even if she has listened to her fair share of Big Finish audios.

They could have all remained professional and kind, but disinterested. But that's not how this community works.

Because, you see, our fandom is truly bigger on the inside.

Tammy Garrison and **Katy Shuttleworth** are the creators of the fancomic *Torchwood Babiez*. In their day jobs, Tammy is a librarian and Katy is a storyboard artist/animator. http://tw-babiez.livejournal.com/

IT WAS A TAD SURREAL. WE WERE NEW TO DOCTOR WHO FANDOM, AND HERE WERE PEOPLE THAT **WE** RECOGNIZED FROM VARIOUS LIVEJOURNAL COMMUNITIES...

...RECOGNIZING US AND GUSHING OVER OUR STUFF, THE WAY WE GUSHED OVER THEIRS!

ANYHOW, ANOTHER YEAR PASSED, TWO MORE ISSUES OF BABIEZ WERE POSTED.

NEXT THING YOU KNOW, IT'S TIME FOR CHICAGO TARDIS AGAIN. AND THIS TIME, EVEN **MORE** PEOPLE KNEW US!

"WE SKIPPED THE DOCTOR WHO NOVELS PANEL TO HANG OUT IN THE LOBBY."

"AS SOON AS IT LET OUT, WE WERE BOMBARDED BY OUR FRIENDS, TELLING US BABIEZ WAS BROUGHT UP IN THE *ONE* PANEL WE DECIDED NOT TO GO TO!"

OMG!

YOU SHOULD HAVE BEEN THERE!

THEY WERE SINGING SONGS ABOUT IT!

APPARENTLY, THEY WERE TALKING ABOUT INTRODUCING DIFFERENT READING LEVELS FOR DOCTOR WHO AND TORCHWOOD NOVELS.

BABIEZ WAS NOMINATED FOR A KIDS' LEVEL TORCHWOOD BOOK!

BOTH PAUL CORNELL AND GARY RUSSELL AGREED AND SAID THEY LOVED THE COMIC!

WE'RE GENUINELY AMAZED AND HUMBLED BY THE OVERALL RESPONSE FROM EVERYONE.

PEOPLE HAVE MADE T-SHIRTS, ICONS, FANVIDS, DRAWN FANART, KNIT DOLLS...

THE LIST GOES ON!

I WAS EVEN RECOGNIZED AT THE 2009 NEW YORK COMIC CON!

"I WAS WAITING IN LINE FOR A PANEL WITH EVE MYLES AND DIRECTOR EUROS LYN WHEN SOMEONE ASKED ABOUT A PIN ON MY BAG THAT I HAD DESIGNED."

YOU DON'T HAPPEN TO WORK ON TORCHWOOD BABIEZ, DO YOU?

THE PIN IN QUESTION HAD ABSOLUTELY NOTHING TO DO WITH BABIEZ, BUT THE STYLE WAS SIMILAR.

AND I WENT TO THE 2009 GALLIFREY ONE, I GOT TONS OF LOVE, INCLUDING FROM SOME KIDS WHO WANT TO COSPLAY THE BABIEZ NEXT YEAR!

"EVEN GARY RUSSELL ASKED WHEN THE NEXT PART OF BABIEZ WAS COMING OUT!"

"WE WERE EVEN ASKED TO BE ON A DOCTOR WHO COMICS PANEL WITH TONY LEE AT HURRICANE WHO!"

The Digging Chick

Lisa Bowerman trained at the Bristol Old Vic Theatre School, and is an actress who has appeared in numerous UK television shows including *Eastenders, Grange Hill, Bad Girls, Casualty* (playing a series regular, para-medic Sandra Mute), *Spooks* and *Doctors*. She notably played the role of Cheetah woman Karra in the *Doctor Who* story "Survival." She has also worked extensively in theatre and radio. Lisa is perhaps best known for her work playing Bernice Summerfield, who was originally created by Paul Cornell as a seventh Doctor companion in the Virgin New Adventures novels. Big Finish launched the Bernice Summerfield audio adventures in 1998; to date, Lisa has appeared as Bernice in ten seasons of audio plays (47 stories in total). She also played Bernice alongside Sylvester McCoy and Sophie Aldred in two *Doctor Who* audio plays, and alongside Paul McGann in the audio "The Company of Friends." She began directing for Big Finish four years ago, working on many plays across ranges that include *Sapphire & Steel, The Tomorrow People, The Companion Chronicles, Warhammer* and the monthly *Doctor Who* series. Lisa is also a professional photographer – for more than 20 years, she's been established with *The Spotlight*, a UK directory of actors and actresses. (In such a role, she took some black and white photos of a short-haired Matt Smith, which turned up in several articles when he was announced as the Doctor.) She also serves as the House Committee Chairman of Denville Hall (the retirement home for the acting profession) and as a trustee of The Actors' Charitable Trust.

My involvement with the *Doctor Who* world started in 1989, when I appeared as Karra in the final classic *Doctor Who* storyline "Survival." Even then, I think I realised that science fiction as a genre, although associated with many negative stereotypes, has always served women pretty well in terms of their portrayal in a dramatic context. There are the odd exceptions of fantasy figures – but more often than not they're in command, or at least in parity with their male counterparts. Rona Munroe, who later became a very well respected playwright, wrote the script for "Survival" – and regardless of its final implementation (the well-documented area of the Cheetah People's make-up!), it was unbelievably strongly written for the female characters.

It's easy to dismiss sci-fi as a niche market, but it seems to me as a non-expert, non-fan outsider, that it's capable of encompassing great stories that are resonant and relevant to everyone – because it can deal with them in allegory. Some seemingly bizarre locations, aliens or planets can reflect more of the way we live our lives today than some people might expect.

Of course, I'm now involved in sci-fi in a way that I would never have expected, having played Professor Bernice Summerfield in audio form now for more than ten years, as well as directing audios for Big Finish in the *Doctor Who*, *Sapphire & Steel* and *Tomorrow People* ranges. And from my perspective as an actress, television drama (especially in the UK at present) presents very little of what I recognise as a woman in the 21st century. It's easy to have a moan about the fact that women (especially of a "certain age") are portrayed as either single mums or executive ball breakers. Science fiction presents us with very different perspectives, and a whole gallery of strong female role models. I'm not talking here about overtly feminist tracts; above all, I hate polemic writing with a vengeance, and it serves nobody's cause well. What I'm talking about are well-rounded, human beings that respond in a complex and recognisably human way.

You could argue that the likes of Lara Croft are little more than male fantasies, but I suppose I've been luckier than most in the fact that Bernice is a woman of a very different cut. She's resourceful and instinctively brave, but she has weaknesses and a sense of humour. That's what makes her so good to play. Essentially, she's a moral creature passionately believing in what is right and wrong. The fact that she is confronted by dilemmas that might not be so black and white is what makes her interesting.

What's struck me is the amazing impact Bernice has had on people who have read her from the very beginning, back in the days of The New Adventures. It's been documented before, but when I first heard I was auditioning for the part (and yes – that *was* in Nick Brigg's flat with a microphone strapped to an uplighter!), my friend Stephen Fewell (who subsequently played Jason Kane) asked if I was going to play Bernice Summerfield. I have to confess that I had completely forgotten her name, and said that it was likely I would. He announced that I *had* to play her, because... "she's a complete icon"!

It was always going to be difficult to know how to approach playing "an icon" so close to the readers' hearts, all of them imagining Benny in their own way: how she looked, how she sounded. Coming to it with no previous knowledge of her was probably a good thing, and what struck me at the audition – where I read from the script to the slightly surreal audio "Oh No It Isn't!" – was that Benny just leapt off the page. Jacqueline Rayner's adaptation of the book of the same name by Paul Cornell was excellent; witty, and very easy to read. The fact was, Bernice was just a great character... and, although it sounds flippant, very easy to play.

Over the years I've always been aware that Bernice appeals to both men and women – which is very gratifying. It has, of course, been down to the writing – at the end of the day, everything comes down to that. Some authors have caught Benny brilliantly, some have tended to go for the obvious – and I'm always at pains to tell the producers (whoever they are at the time!) that I really hate it when she's over-flippant and over-written. Yes, she uses humour in times of stress, but not *all* the time – there's moments when even *I* want to give her a slap!

After 11 years of Bernice (in audio form, at least), it's important to keep the audience interested, and to keep things fresh. The writers and producers have done a great job. Her journey really has encompassed everything over the decade, and she's certainly come a long way. She hasn't just stayed the same old character, although her humor is still there. Everything has been tempered by what's gone before; it would have been ridiculous if we'd been trotting out the same old stuff for all these years – and I think the audience would have deserted us a long time ago! I have to say, though, that it still irks me when some fans dismiss The New Adventures altogether as "not proper *Doctor Who*" – particularly when they read a book with Benny in it, fail to like it, and just dismiss her out of hand. She's come *so* far since those days, and I feel passionately that she has survived in her own right, and proven that she's a strong enough character to stand apart from the *Doctor Who* universe. Then again, I *would* say that, wouldn't I?!

I've had some very interesting correspondence from fans over the years, and what has struck me is what an amazingly positive role model Bernice has been, especially for teen girls. There's very little concession for her being girly – she has human frailties, but is very focused and gets on with things. Bernice, and all she represents, in some cases has given people strength to do things they might not have done. You could argue that building any decisions on a fictional character is odd, but when no others around you seem to hold out any hope, you grab onto the nearest thing possible. Paul Cornell has created a great character.

I've watched with interest (if not a little frustration) that more characters in Bernice's mould have been turning up on the new wave of fantasy and sci-fi shows on television. Not least the archaeologists on both ITV's *Primeval* and *Doctor Who* (River Who?!) – but I'm not bitter! I so hope that Bernice herself gets a wider audience... I read somewhere that she is (both in print and audio) one of the longest running sci-fi characters out there, and yet has stayed very much in her niche. I love it when I hear that someone has discovered her through recommendation – so, readers: no pressure then!

This particular chick is off to dig up a few artifacts...

The Tea Lady

Tara O'Shea does mysterious things with PhotoShop and HTML for fun and profit. The child of a British expatriate and an American schoolteacher, she cannot spell, has an unplaceable accent and owns ten free-standing bookcases of everything from nonfiction about the founding of the OSS to all of Edgar Rice Burrough's *Tarzan* pulp novels. She has been a supermarket check-out girl, a founder in a commercial airline, a freelance journalist and a calendar girl. She can whistle almost any tune, and is very good at introducing people to other people. She currently lives in Chicago, and has no intention of ever leaving. And someday, she will (probably) learn how to drive a car. Maybe.

My first *Doctor Who* convention was a multi-fandom show called Visions back in 1990, with guests from *Who, Blake's 7* and *Robin of Sherwood*. I was there as a *Robin* fan, but during opening ceremonies, I struck up a conversation a *Who* fan named Fred – he was wearing a fourth Doctor scarf his mum had knitted for him, complete with frock coat and hat – who was sitting behind me in the main ballroom. I decided afterward that a show that inspired such loyalty and passion had to have something going for it. Intrigued, I started watching on my local PBS broadcasts of the show, and peppered Fred with questions during lengthy phone conversations that caused my parents a lot of grief the first time we received a $200 long-distance bill.

I started reading everything I could get my hands on about *Doctor Who*, learning not just about the stories, but about the stories of the people behind the stories. I bought Peter Haining's oversized *Doctor Who* books and began collecting the Target novelisations and back issues of *Doctor Who Magazine*. For a young girl who gobbled up speculative fiction, learning that the series had originally been produced by a woman was a revelation. The SF clubhouse didn't *have* to include only boys such as Gene Roddenberry, George Lucas, Rod Serling and Terry Nation. Verity Lambert wasn't just the youngest producer at the BBC, she was the *only* female producer working there in 1963 when the series was conceived, and was an *equal partner* in creating a franchise that endures almost half a century later.

By the time the Doctor regenerated into Peter Davison, I'd fallen in love. The fifth Doctor was *my* Doctor, and Tegan quickly became my favorite companion. Then I went away to university, and other fandoms beckoned like bright shiny toys. I still attended local media and comics conventions, but primarily to socialize; *Doctor Who* became simply a sweet memory from childhood. Then in 2005, I watched "Rose" out of nostalgia and curiosity. By the final scene of "The End of the World" – as the Doctor tells Rose how his planet had burned – I was completely won over. By "Dalek", I had gone from being a dabbler to being a hardcore fan. I dove headfirst into online *Doctor Who* fandom, writing short stories and joining discussion communities on LiveJournal.

I knew that there was a local *Doctor Who* convention, Chicago TARDIS, because I'd worked as a gofer at Visions. Many of the TARDIS staff were former Visions staffers, and when I contacted Jennifer Adams Kelley in 2005 to tell her I wanted to attend the con but was too broke to afford a ticket, she told me the show needed someone to look after the green room. In case you don't know, the green room is a lounge with drinks and food, where the guests can relax between panels and autograph and photograph sessions. Green rooms are ideally located close enough to the convention space so the guests won't be late for their obligations; this is particularly important for some of the actors, who try to maintain a very high energy level onstage.

The thing that struck me immediately on walking through the lobby doors of the hotel was the intense sense of *community*. I was incredibly fortunate that the very person in *Doctor Who* fandom that I met after my decade-long hiatus was Shaun Lyon, the head of programming for Gallifrey One, the largest and longest running *Doctor Who* con in America. I felt welcomed, like a long-lost relative now found and cherished. I met Rob Shearman late Sunday night at the convention, and ended up taking a day off work to show him around Chicago; we hunted for secondhand books and DVDs in Lakeview. I went to my first Gallifrey One convention a few months later, and with each show I've attended, the *Doctor Who* fandom family here in the US and in the UK have blossomed into genuine friendships.

When I went with mates to the UK last year, I had a chance to visit with "my crazy *Doctor Who* friends" (as my family's come to know them). Simon Guerrier made me scrambled eggs on toast in his and his wife's flat, and showed me the "monsters" at the Crystal Palace. I rambled around Oxford's ancient buildings, led by the much-smarter-than-me Caroline Symcox. Rob Shearman crawled all over the Embankment with us, and took us through the National Portrait Gallery, pointing out where he wrote bits of "Dalek." (Rob does a lot of writing, it seems, when he's wandering about museums and such.) I traded fonts with Lee Thompson (we're both graphic designers; it's in our blood), and he took us for dinner at Tattershall Castle. I had Italian food with Restoration Team-member Steve Roberts and Sue Cowley one night. In Cardiff another evening. longtime fans Jon and Carolyn Arnold let me play with their infant and watch an episode of *The Sarah Jane Adventures* in their living room while we ate fish and chips from the local chippie. Afterward, Carolyn delighted in showing me her scrapbooks of photos from cons going back to the 1980s, and I got to see lovely embarrassing photos of folks like Paul Cornell, when he was but a youth with a disreputable haircut. He had the same mad grin, though, that he wears in all our Gally pics on Facebook.

We all met through *Doctor Who*, but real friendships are formed during the wee hours in a convention hotel lobby, when someone sneaks in coolers of beer after last call. If you're lucky, they're the lasting sort of relationships that are aided by Skype and e-mail and the ever-present Facebook and Twitter feeds. Instead of having friends I only see a week out of the year, I now log in each morning to see what everyone's been up to while my hemisphere sleeps, or folks in the United States go off to their day jobs at schools, offices and government facilities. We're close-knit thanks to technology, now – a vast extended family the spans the globe.

Since my first Chicago TARDIS, I've learnt a lot running the green room there – but it's all very specialized knowledge.

For example, Colin Baker is allergic to cheese, and can sign autographs forever if he has enough Red Bull. If you give Laura Doddington peanut butter, you will win a friend for life. Lis Sladen loves salt and vinegar crisps. Occasionally, you will have to chase Rob Shearman with sandwiches. Everyone loves fresh-brewed coffee, but having the electric kettle so people can have a cuppa is essential. When I introduce myself to new guests as "the tea lady," it's only half in jest. The one thing American hotels never ever get right is the bit where tea requires boiling water.

India Fisher loves pumpkin pie. Nigel Fairs will try at least one wasabi pea per day, each time expecting a different result (bless him). Hummous and veggies are always a good idea, as are Dove dark chocolates, especially with Gary Russell around. Nick Briggs doesn't drink caffeine. Comic book-writer Tony Lee can consume vast quantities of Mountain Dew. Eric Roberts will call you "doll," and Eastern European film sets do not have hummous. Los Angeles agents do not know what HobNobs are, and will have to be educated. You can never have too much bottled water. Ever.

Tiny emergencies are inevitable. One of the first Doctor's companions mistook the paper coffee filters for bowls the year I brought lentil soup. One actor actually took a gofer to task on the mainstage when she brought black tea instead of green tea. Mini fridges kill fresh produce dead, usually by freezing it solid. One hotel never cleaned the room from one day to the next, so I learnt to always keep a supply of kitchen wipes. Chairs will mysteriously disappear and reappear. Some crockpots, on the other hand, never return. And the less said about the year I thought salads would be a good idea, the better. Avocados? Never a good idea.

Bananas are the perfect convention food: they're portable, keep without being refrigerated and are actually good for you. Eating one makes you feel so health-conscious and adult, you can reward yourself with a plate of crisps and some chocolates afterward. No, really.

Minions are important. Someone has to be there all day to make sure fresh coffee gets brewed, and we don't run out of anything. I kidnapped two of my best friends to dogsbody for me after the first two years of trying to handle shopping, transportation, set-up and tear-down myself. Now, my friend Liz flies over from Scotland days before the show, and she and Becca and I do the shopping at the small local stores, where I buy everything from gluten-free biscuits to Marmite to fresh-made spinach and cheese pies. One year when Becca (and her car) weren't available, this involved liberating a shopping trolley from the nearby Target store and jumping curbs to bring it right up to the hotel front door, where I kidnapped a bellhop and a luggage cart to bring it to the green room.

It may seem glamorous to outsiders, spending the week-end hobnobbing with the guests. But the truth is, while I enjoy catching up with friends like Rob, Paul and Gary Russell – or watching mesmerized as Nick Briggs shows us photos of his new baby on his laptop – I'm not actually there to socialize. I'm there to do a job and to not infringe on guests' privacy. The green room has to be a safe space where people can recharge, without feeling they have to always be performing.

I love it, even when it means I'm up at 7 a.m. on a Friday morning only four hours after tumbling into bed. I love having an important job to do, and while I can't control anything that happens outside the green room, one thing I can do is make sure that people have a quiet place to come and sit between being "on" as a paid performer. There's a really simple reason for this: if the guests are relaxed and happy, they have a good convention. If they have nutritious food to eat instead of just soda and sweets, they're less likely to crash and crash hard from the sugar high at 4 p.m. in the afternoon, when they've still hours of photos to take and autographs to sign. Also, if the guests enjoy their time at the convention and feel properly looked after, they'll recommend the event to their friends and co-workers. Then I get to feed *new* people – some of them people who've played my childhood heroes.

Hopelessly Devoted to *Who*

Jody Lynn Nye is a best-selling science fiction and fantasy author with over 35 published books and over 100 published short stories. Her science fiction and fantasy novel series include *Mythology*, *Taylor's Ark* and *The Dreamland*. She has also co-authored four novels with Anne McCaffrey (*The Death of Sleep, Crisis On Doona, Treaty At Doona* and *The Ship Who Won*) and the non-fiction guidebook *The Dragonlover's Guide to Pern*. In recent years, Jody has collaborated with Robert Asprin on seven novels in the *Myth Adventures* series. Tor Books released her most recent novel, *A Forthcoming Wizard*, in 2009. http://www.sff.net/people/JodyNye/

I have always been exactly in the age demographic at which *Doctor Who* was aimed. When it first aired, I was six years old. I was not fortunate enough to have seen it then. Still, having always enjoyed the escape provided by fantasy and science fiction, I was ready for it when I did eventually see it in my early 20s.

About 1979 (the exact date has faded into the mists of time), Barbara, the friend who introduced me to the concept of science fiction and media fandom in the first place, invited me to watch the program with her. My own local PBS station, WTTW in Chicago, didn't broadcast the show. (It later did, though on a distressingly random basis until dropping the show altogether when Lionheart Productions – the BBC's US distributor at the time – raised its rates. WTTW was dependent upon pleasing its arts-conscious subscribers, who weren't willing to pay for a cult television show aimed at children but was broadcast at a time slot – the middle of a weekend night – more suited to socially maladroit geeks who might otherwise be watching the cheap horror movie on another channel.)

I felt a little as though I was being inducted into a secret society. A longtime Anglophile, I had discovered British humor on my own (*Monty Python*, et al), and the actors whose *Tiger Beat* photos had graced my walls in my pre-teenage had all been British as well. I understand colloquial English without the need for subtitles, and I liked the subtle, self-deprecating style and humor of UK media. I was hungry for more

SF television programming. So, I hung my disbelief from a handy suspender and sat down to enjoy myself.

I came in during the middle of a scene, without a clue as to what was going on. On screen, a child with short, dark hair and a heart-shaped face wearing colorful overalls was scrambling over rocks trying to get away from a monster that looked as if it had been made up of spare parts. The episode was "The Brain of Morbius," and the little girl in overalls was actually a grown woman – the fearless and resourceful Sarah Jane Smith – who quickly became my first and favorite companion. Not long thereafter, a tall man with a mop of brown curls, blue eyes and a mouthful of prominent white teeth – not classically handsome but appealing nonetheless – appeared and saved the day. This was the fourth incarnation of *the* Doctor, who quickly became *my* Doctor.

I loved it. Really. It hit my funny bone. I loved the absurdity of a space-time machine that looked like a phone booth but was dimensionally transcendent and sounded like a Xerox machine with asthma. The special effects and costumes were cheap in comparison to programs made in Hollywood, but they clothed a quality program. The plot was well-constructed. The action was exciting and had good pacing. The dialogue was good. The acting was far and away better than I would have expected for a show aimed at children. I adored the actors. The characters were well enough drawn to understand and care about. The villain was suitably evil but had a touch of pathos; a space-going Beast to Sarah Jane's Beauty. I was eager for more.

The show was not aired regularly, nor was it broadcast in my area at the beginning. I was dependent upon friends to tape it for me on videocassette. Young fans with access to YouTube and easily shared electronic files will be horrified to find out that videocassette tapes once cost as much as $30 each; the most that you could cram onto each one was six hours, all of which had to be recorded in real time. The SLP setting sacrificed quality for length, but it was the only way to get your money's worth. Copies were cloned for friends, and each successive generation was noticeably worse. The first part of the signal to drop out was the color burst. After that, the picture deteriorated until you were watching Peter Max silhouettes that you were pretty sure were the Doctor and his current companion/s, with a guess for what the monster of the week looked like. Fortunately, the audio, though scratchy, was good enough that you could almost tell what was going on. Yes, we were that devoted. Yes, that deranged. Yes, that desperate. Yes, I still have my tapes. (No, I haven't looked at them in a long time.)

In September 1980, my friend Barbara took me to my first science fiction convention: WorldCon in Boston, Massachusetts. Most conventions are a few dozen to a few hundred people, but a WorldCon can have many thousands. This one was attended by six thousand fans.

Until you have been to a convention, you wouldn't know that each tends to have its own distinct subculture; they're not just a weekend get-together of oddballs. Fandom also has its own vocabulary, and is more accepting of a wider range of people than almost any other subgroup I have ever met. All genders, races, body types, political parties and religions are welcome (or at least tolerated), under the "do unto others as you would have others do unto you" mantra. Since many, if not most, of the attendees have been ostracized in their ordinary environments, they work hard not to reject others. On convention weekends, you can be the person that you want to be. Almost all of the attendees have above average intelligence, are enthusiastic and possess the hunger to look for an alternate reality or an alternate future. Many scientists, including ones who work for NASA, attend SF conventions.

Having become interested in *Doctor Who*, I wanted more than just the stories I could see on television. So I was pleased to discover a lot of *Who* books for sale, and asked the convention dealers for a recommendation of a good one. They were amused by the question. The Target books, all imported from Great Britain, turned out to be novelizations of episodes – much like the *Star Trek* episodes committed to print by James Blish. Original, non-canonical stories were not written or even countenanced for many years.

At the time, *Doctor Who* was a much smaller fandom than *Star Trek* or *Star Wars*, but it was not difficult to find a few *Who* fans at a convention. Most of the *Who* fans I met were women, but there were a number of men as well. My boyfriend at the time, a deeply devoted fan of the show, was a would-be documentarian and magazine editor. Still, the preponderance of *Who* aficionados I met were female, every age, shape and marital status. I knew a mother-daughter pair who were firm fans. The mother's husband built them a full-sized TARDIS that lived in their family room for years.

Who fans tended to congregate around the tables of hucksters who sold *Who* zines (more on them anon), imported toys and packets of jelly babies. We discussed our favorite episodes, traded trivia and gossip, and gathered around those fans who had some inside knowledge of what was coming next. Tom Baker was still the Doctor at the time, but he had newer companions than the ones I was currently watching. John

Nathan-Turner, newly anointed producer of *Doctor Who*, was considered to be "evil" based upon rumors that he was trying to kill the show. And we would gather in the hotel room of anyone who had lugged their videocassette player with them to watch tapes. The most desirable were new episodes, transferred (usually poorly) from the PAL scan system used in Great Britain to the North American NTSC signal. There was some cheerful rivalry as to who had the best collection of tapes, who knew the most gossip, who had met the actors, who had made the most accurate replica of the TARDIS, K-9 or the sonic screwdriver, and so on.

The passion of a creative mind hooked on a universe it loves is that once it enjoys all the episodes/issues provided by the producers or writers of the series, movies, television, or literary, it wants more. Fans expanded the repertoire of "canonical" stories on their own, some of which were as well regarded as the professional publications.[1] *Star Trek* was the first media "universe" that had given rise to tribute stories from devoted followers, but it was not the first storyline to provoke pastiche. That honor almost certainly belongs to Sherlock Holmes, whose readers were moved to write their own, both straightforward further adventures and sometimes biting parodies, among them Isaac Asimov and Rex Stout, the creator of the sedentary detective Nero Wolfe. In a way, the much-honored collections such as *The Misadventures of Sherlock Holmes* edited by Ellery Queen might be considered professionally produced fanzines.

As this was pre-Internet and just at the dawn of the plain-paper copier, all of these digests were laboriously typed and set out by their amateur editors. Some were cut onto mimeo stencils, others taken to offset printers. Hand-drawn/lettered covers were the norm. Because of their production costs, zines could not be produced as cheaply as books, so the cover prices were high. Editors struggled to break even, let alone make money. Issues ranged in price from about three dollars for single story issues to 15 or so for a fat digest. A few looked almost as good as a literary magazine off the shelf, but the majority did not. Hungry fans were undiscerning and forgiving of weak material.

An offshoot of the fannish philosophy that advocates being your own person included trying out one's budding talents at publishing. There was room in zine publication for wannabe writers, editors, artists, layout people and sales representatives. Fanzine contributors were paid in

---

1. And some of which became professionally published, such as *Ishmael*, a crossover *Star Trek/Here Come the Brides* novel written by Barbara Hambly and bought by Pocket Books in the frenzy that followed the publication of the first *Trek* novels.

copies (generally a single copy from the limited print run), not cash. It was difficult to make money doing this, but editing or writing for a zine was more about getting one's imaginings into print, for the satisfaction of oneself and the pleasure of others. Fanzines could explore themes that the producers never thought of, or shied away from. We extrapolated further adventures from favorite episodes. Some were successful; others less so. Like the writing, the quality of artwork ranged from dreadful to amazingly good. Some fans were professional quality artists. A few were actively pros, others bided their time until they had reached the quality or confidence level to become pros, and some were content never to be more than amateurs.

It was hard not to get interested in participating. A good friend of mine (who also became a professional author) set up her own fanzine and asked me to contribute. I was delighted to. Not only did my writing appear in two issues, but I hand-lettered the title logo, which appeared at the top of the cover of each issue. Over time, I wrote perhaps ten or 12 fan stories, about half of them *Doctor Who* – a piker's output compared with most fans, whose work overspilled dealers' tables at conventions.

A brief perusal of my small zine collection revealed that women were the driving force behind *Doctor Who* amateur publications. All but one were edited by women. A majority of the writers were female, as were all of the artists but one. True, there might have been more men out there; I don't have a very comprehensive collection, but most of the devoted fans I knew were female.

What was the appeal of the show for me? Granted, it was a program created for children. Adults could see how cheesy the special effects were, and the costume budget was very small. Sometimes the costumes were new, designed specifically for a story arc, but so many had the air of having been resurrected from a historical costume drama, or made up from a retired fire curtain and a couple of feather boas. Often, the most expensive things on the set were the vehicles for filming (such as the Whomobile, which Jon Pertwee had bought himself).

But it was the skeleton clothed by these sad rags to which I responded. I was always more attracted to intelligence and character than muscle; the Doctor was a geek hero who used brains instead of brawn. The kind of fan who would later be attracted to Daniel Jackson instead of Col. Jack O'Neill in *Stargate SG-1* wanted the brainy, cute guy who could solve the problem but never pick up a weapon. Most of the Doctors were charismatic, brilliant, empathetic, but just far enough removed from humanity to act as a good foil for it.

Many fans accepted *Doctor Who* as their secondary fandom, coming to it from *Battlestar Galactica* (the original series starring Lorne Greene, that is), *Star Wars* or *Star Trek*, but a few of us had *Doctor Who* as our primary or sole favorite. Those of us who were mainly *Who* fans were not comfortable being part of a military or quasi-military organization. Consultant, yes – we could be consultants, but without having to answer to superior officers with rigid command structures and tightly-controlled haircuts. Doctor Four and his wild curls was a symbol of nonconformity and free thought. I liked that. I liked *Star Wars* and *Star Trek* and many of the others, but I loved *Doctor Who*.

The companions were more than just sidekicks. They had a share in the perils and pleasures of time travel and the responsibility in making sure they survived the adventure. As a girl who grew up to believe in equality and empowerment, I identified with Sarah Jane, an independent reporter who had lied her way into a scientific conference where she met the third Doctor, an incarnation I also came to adore. She was forthright, brave and liberated, and willing to fight for herself – not a girl who had to be rescued, screaming, from the lair of a monster. No other companion ever resonated with me the way she did. I had to admit I was also glad to see another small-boned brunette kicking galactic butt instead of the usual statuesque blonde who normally was cast in costume dramas alongside the gallant hero. Princess Leia had been a delight to me; here was another in my genotype.

I enjoyed many other companions throughout the series. For example, I couldn't help but love the savage Leela. Her forthright – if often unspoken – demand of "Can I kill him *now*, Doctor?" was an echo of the way I sometimes felt in my ordinary life but could not emulate, homicide laws being what they are.[2] I think we all felt a little sorry as well as thrilled for Andred when Leela chose to stay with him on Gallifrey at the end of "The Invasion of Time."

All of the companions in the new series, in my opinion, have been wonderful and received more comprehensive back stories than in the classic series. Rose Tyler and her turbulent home life; Martha Jones, the trainee doctor and her close-knit family; and the marvelous Donna Noble, who had gathered all those useful skills in dead-end jobs and always seemed to miss the important events going on around her – until

---

2. Leela even has a modern-day analog. Anyone who has watched the standout USA Network's program *Burn Notice* can't help but notice that Fiona, played by Gabrielle Anwar, is a lot like Leela; bloodthirsty, devoted and too good with weapons.

the Doctor came along. I loved Harriet Jones (ex-prime minister) and her ID folder. I thought it was kind of sweet that she had the insecurity of believing that no one would know who she was unless she identified herself, even after having gained – and lost – national office. (Even the Daleks said, "We know who you are!") She may have been wrong in the actions for which the Doctor saw her deposed from office, but she did them for the best of reasons. I was glad that the scriptwriters gave her a chance for redemption after she became drunk on power. Tom Baker once commented that he would have liked to have an older woman as a companion. The Big Finish audios have been graced with Evelyn Smythe, but I'm sorry the producers haven't yet done it during the televised series, Harriet being a prime example of what one could have been like.

Another thing that made *Doctor Who* more appealing to me than other shows was the accessibility of the people who made or performed in it. I attended the professional *Who* conventions in Chicago with my boyfriend, working as his still photographer. I would have found it impossible to approach these celebrities on my own, but at his shoulder I could get close to what turned out to be the very nice people who acted in my favorite show. Jon Pertwee and Elisabeth Sladen were the actors I met the most often, three or four times each. Pertwee's enormous personality embraced even the shyest of fans (me, for example). He told stories, made faces, sang snatches of songs for my friend's tape recorder, and posed for my lens. He could not have been more gracious or friendly.[3] Ms. Sladen couldn't have been nicer, talking to me as if I was a friend instead of a trembling fan. In my experience of the time, British actors displayed less "celebrity" behavior than their Hollywood counterparts, and were refreshingly casual about their contact with fans and reporters. I have a photograph of a press call at a convention that about 20 *Who* actors attended. There were not enough chairs, so everyone ended up sitting on the floor. (There was also, according to the actors, not nearly enough booze, so more drinks had to be sent for.)

Such open friendliness on the part of the actors made the fans even

---

3. Mr. Pertwee's lovely wife Inga and I sat together outside the recording studio of my college radio station in 1983 while he and Ms. Sladen were being interviewed on the air. I was about to go to Great Britain for the first time. Mrs. Pertwee most kindly advised me on places to shop in London, and gave me her address and phone number. During that trip, my zine-editing friend and I visited the *Doctor Who* studio in White City where a Peter Davison episode was being filmed. The story of how I nearly wandered into a live shot with a Dalek is a subject for another article.

more devoted to them and the show. I find myself nodding and smiling when I see one of the actors who played companions, villains or other parts turn up in other roles – or, indeed, other jobs. Louise Jameson played Eliza Doolittle in *My Fair Lady* in the West End not long after I met her in the 1980s. Anthony Ainley played in a Christmas pantomime in the West End. Nicholas Courtney took the role of the Narrator in the London production of *The Rocky Horror Show*. To my surprise and delight, in 2008 I was watching the Cruft's Dog Show from Westminster, I saw that one of the two on-air commentators was Peter Purves, who played Steven Taylor.

I may be in the minority among my fellow *Who* fans, but though I like what has been done with the current Doctors, I still preferred the character when he was not an obviously sexual being who became interested in his companions. In most of the earlier incarnations, he was a friendly – or not so friendly – uncle, or grandfather with whom it was safe to travel through the galaxy. Though most of us had a Doctor or two we fancied, we were all on equal footing – hoping but hopeless. After all, if he fell in love with one of his companions, what chance was there for the likes of the rest of us, who fantasized about being picked up and swept away in the TARDIS for points and times unknown? Not only would it be a very uncomfortable situation to be the third wheel over-looking a hot and heavy relationship with Rose Tyler (or Jo Grant, though in the case of the third Doctor, he didn't declare himself until Jo was just about to leave the TARDIS to be with her Earthbound professor beau), one worries about one's safety if the Doctor's concern is for a particular person at risk instead of perhaps the population of a planet. It's only human, after all, or in this case, Gallifreyan, but I worry it makes him less effective. I liked him better when he was a disinterested alien observer who couldn't help meddling on a galactic level. A true alien would no more be interested in mating with humans than we would with a plant.

The series has changed in tenor from a children's entertainment to a program aimed at adults or teenagers, with youngsters as very much a secondary audience. That's convenient for those of us who are the target market, but it provides less of a "gateway drug" to those viewers who would have become devotees as children. Russell T Davies refers to *Doctor Who* as "family entertainment," though the definition of that has changed greatly over the years. The spinoff series *Torchwood* is less acces-sible to – and unacceptable viewing for – the very young, who may end up watching it anyway alongside their parents or older siblings, and have nightmares afterwards. It was produced as a late-night show for adults, but post-watershed time-slots have been a poor fence to keep out young viewers since the coming of the time-shifting video tape machine, and are even less effective with the advent of digital video recorders and On Demand programming. Fortunately, the BBC has introduced a new series that is suitable for children to watch.

I collect slogan buttons: campaign buttons, joke buttons, picture buttons. *Doctor Who* fans in the 1980s were fortunate to have the talented Mississippi artist, Cheryl Whitfield Duval, who did beautiful little cartoons of characters from *Doctor Who*. She illustrated her own fanzine and contributed art to many others, but she probably made more money from selling individual cartoon buttons. One that I have cherished over the years read, "Bring back Sarah Jane!" Below it was a sketch of the character saying, "I'm still waiting." It seemed almost prescient when in 2006, Sarah Jane Smith returned in "School Reunion" (with K-9 in the boot of her car). Then, in 2007, she was given her own series, *The Sarah Jane Adventures*. I was absolutely delighted that my favorite companion has her own show, in which she is teaching another generation of fans to kick galactic butt.

Doctor Who, like its eponymous character, has died more than once and regenerated. I look forward to seeing what the next incarnation brings. I hope it's more of the same – but different. I've come to have high expectations of the man in the blue police box and those who travel gladly with him. Wish I could be one of them.

Two Generations of Fangirls in Middle America

Amy Fritsch is a high school English teacher in Chicago who lives with a wonderful husband, two wonderful children, a dog and three cats. She has been a *Doctor Who* fan since 1979 (when she was nine), and has been actively involved in fandom for over two decades as an avid viewer of many genre programs; an active participant in discussions of same; a costumer; and a reader, writer and editor of fan fiction.

One afternoon in 1979, at around 5:54 p.m., my brother and I were channel-surfing (which in this case meant actually turning the dial manually) and saw a minute and a half of the fourth Doctor and Sarah in Antarctica, the snow blowing madly, as a tiny miniature of a compound blew up. We didn't care that the model was clearly a model, or that the snow was clearly fake. We just knew that we had to watch again tomorrow to see what happened next in "The Seeds of Doom." My station, broadcasting out of the university just two miles from my house, aired the original segmented parts daily, Monday through Friday, at 5:30 p.m. We didn't know how lucky we were to see the show in its original format, with only a day's wait instead of a week.

I watched the credits with the eye of a practiced fan. By the time I saw episode six of "Seeds of Doom," I knew Terry Walsh's name. I thought that Elisabeth Sladen's name spelt with an 's' was especially pretty that way. I created a "Doctor Who Spelling List" that listed characters, actors, planets, gadgets, technobabble and important phrases or words to remember in that age of Before VCRs. My nine-year-old undiagnosed Asperger self did what any self-respecting, academically-oriented fourth grader would do: I wrote the words five times each.

My brother and I colluded together against our parents in our insistence that 5:30 to 5:56 p.m. was *Doctor Who* time, and thus sacrosanct. *Nothing* must disrupt our 25-ish minutes spent daily with the Doctor and his smart assistants. We banded together in a pact of *absolute silence* whilst watching, savoring every moment, sitting willingly in the same room and sharing rare camaraderie. My parents were shushed when they walked through our living room as we recorded the episode on three-for-a-dollar cassettes (purchased with my carefully-hoarded allowance money) in one of the old rectangular tape recorders with the centimeter square microphone propped against the television speaker. We would not come to the dinner table if the episode was not finished yet, and would stall for those extra two or seven or 15 minutes until it was over. My mother never quite forgave *Doctor Who* for consistently holding our attention better than a call to dinner.

Once our local PBS station stopped airing episodes, we were reduced to the occasional Sunday night when we had no school on Monday, trying to pull in the St. Louis station by doing the game of Twister that is Human Antenna ("A little farther to the right...and up...THERE! Don't move!") just to get a snowy, barely-audible, barely-visible picture. High school came, and my family adopted two more children. They were quickly indoctrinated into our sacred daily half hour of British SF with cardboard set walls. Yet, over time, the Doctor and his blue box and his magic slipped away, lost to university and jobs and other fandoms.

In 2000, I became a wife to a gamer husband with fannish tendencies. A year later, I became a mother. I named our beautiful daughter Elisabeth Louise. Her first name, obviously, I'd first seen with the lovely and talented actress who played Sarah Jane Smith, my first and favorite assistant. The middle name was actually from my husband's family's traditions, and only later did I realize that it is also from Louise Jameson, who followed Sarah Jane as the knife-wielding Leela. Perhaps my Elisabeth will inherit part of that legacy of standing up for herself: "There's nothing 'only' about being a girl," and "You will do as the Doctor instructs or I will cut out your heart," isn't a bad place to start for empowerment.

Not quite a year later, my son Benjamin was born. The kids cut their viewing teeth on *Sesame Street*, *Baby Einstein*, *Ranma 1/2*, *My Neighbor Totoro* and, when I was fed up with kids' stuff for a while, *Willow*. They saw remarkably scary stuff earlier than I could ever have handled. It's not much of a leap to show *Doctor Who* to a three year old who's seen *Willow*'s Bavmorda (played by Jean Marsh in "Battlefield" in exactly the same manner) turn everyone to pigs and try to sacrifice a crying baby.

Elisabeth liked classic *Doctor Who* right away. One afternoon when I was sick, the kids – who were about three and four years old at the time – watched along, enraptured, for four or five solid hours. A year or two later, when I had forgotten that they had seen those older episodes and tried to describe them, my fangirl daughter corrected me, telling me the stories of the Cybermat poisoning Sarah, the giant clam that almost broke Harry Sullivan's leg, the giant robot Sarah liked and the space bug that fell out of the cupboard and so forth, with crystal clarity and precision. I was surprised, but so very proud of my clever little fangirl's memory and enthusiasm.

That same year, *Doctor Who* was rebooted for BBC Wales. I figured that I'd just be disappointed if I hoped or watched. A friend of mine, Tara O'Shea, lured me in through a bulletproof weakness: "Elisabeth Sladen is appearing on *Doctor Who Confidential*... we can watch 'Rose,' and if you don't like it in ten minutes, we'll just watch Lis."

Christopher Eccleston and Russell T Davies had me at the grasp of a hand and, "Run!"

All my nine-year-old love was right there. The Doctor flying around the universe in a jury-rigged TARDIS – being wacky, serious, offbeat, and interfering, since it's what he's best at. He was accompanied by a companion who was smart and clever, used creative problem solving, and saved the Doctor at least as often as he saved her. The effects were disorientingly phenomenal, but still charming. A rubbish bin *ate Mickey* (which meant that this was proper *Doctor Who*, with adequate quantities of qualifying cheese). The dialogue was clever, witty and featured many quotable lines to share with friends. There were engaging guest characters like Clive, who has so many of the pieces and yet has it so wrong, and whose son refers to Rose as "another one of your nutters" with all the dismissive disdain of a kid embarrassed by a parent. The Doctor, with all his brilliance, not seeing the London Eye as a "huge transmitter, smack in the middle of London." This? This was my show. It had grown and changed, yet become new and fresh. I gulped it down, watched, rewatched, discussed and made notes, this time with the ease of a computer and the Internet, more friends old and new to glee with, and a joy none diminished by the passing of 26 years since I'd happened across it the first time.

I debated showing the new series to my four-year-old daughter. But she had, after all, seen *Willow*, so certainly "Rose" wouldn't be too scary. Elisabeth and I settled in and she watched from behind my arm and her blankie. She loved it. We stopped occasionally for her to ask questions, but she *loved* Rose. I withheld "The Empty Child" and "The Doctor Dances" for a while, concerned that the little masked boy Jamie was too scary. Then Elisabeth recited plot and details that proved that, yes, I'd slipped up, and my clever girl had already seen them when I'd re-watched them with her in the room, in my own enthusiasm.

How much do I *adore* that, on the first show my daughter watched fannishly with me, the highest compliment that can be paid someone is to deem them "clever"?

She was a bit sad, of course, at her loss of her first Doctor (the first one is always, always hard to lose), but had greater equanimity than she might otherwise because she remembered seeing Tom Baker and a bit of Peter Davison, and so had the idea going in that the Doctor does not always have the same face.

Lacking cable, I waited a couple of weeks into Tennant's first season before watching. One of the episodes was not to be missed – Sarah Jane, my first and favorite companion, the character central in the first quiet (and private) bits of pre-teen fanfic I tinkered at, and for whom I tried to record all the episodes and owned all the Target novelizations, was going to be on. "School Reunion" was well worth driving an hour out of my way to a friend's house in a busy part of the school year.

I watched my first David Tennant episode, hugging my not-quite-five-year-old daughter on my lap. It was three days after my 36th birthday, and what a gift, all the way from England. I got a new Doctor, who, for me, *became* the Doctor with the line, "I'm so old now. I used to have so much mercy," as he went toe-to-toe (in Converse high-tops) with Anthony Stewart Head (with his slicked-back hair and perfect shoes). My daughter's first and favorite companion was there, and she pointed delightedly, "That's Rose! She's my favorite!" I got to point and say, "That's Sarah Jane. She's *my* favorite!" My new generation fangirl said she was happy we each had our favorites together; there was not a dispute in sight, just mutual joy. That one time, I got to watch over *her* shoulder with our heads together so we could whisper about the episode. I couldn't stop grinning for days, just thinking about getting to catch up with Sarah Jane – finding out, nearly 30 years on, that it was Aberdeen where the Doctor had deposited her, and not South Croydon – and doing so with my daughter.

That moment, with Elisabeth on my lap, watching Rose and Sarah Jane together on *Doctor Who*, was the first time I understood the sentimentality of sports fans upon taking their children to a live game for the first time. *This* was my thing to pass down, my chance to watch the next generation fall in love with something that was such a part of my childhood.

I think even my mother finally forgave *Doctor Who* when she saw how much Elisabeth and I loved sharing it. "Good for you, Sarah Jane Smith," indeed.

In our home viewing, by the time we got to "The Impossible Planet" and "The Satan Pit," my son Ben – who inherited my autism spectrum disorder – was more communicative and had warmed a bit to the show (though he prefers *Star Wars* and its lightsaber battles, making sure to jump up on chairs and tables to add those levels so necessary to Jedi fighting). Elisabeth watched, cuddled next to me, hiding behind blankets and pillows (there wasn't room behind the sofa itself) like the proper English child I'd dreamt I could have been.

Elisabeth quickly surpassed my limited artistic efforts with regard to the show. In 8th grade ceramics class, I had designed, built, and carefully painted a clay TARDIS bank. That same year I crocheted (I didn't learn to knit for a few years after) two colorful scarves, one for me, one for my best friend. They didn't look right, of course, as crocheting comes out quite different from knitting. I had no pattern, but I was still proud of the attempt, though I have no idea where the scarf ultimately went. Elisabeth, at age five, drew a TARDIS with a brown Ten and a purple Rose, which we then hung on the fridge. While watching *The Sarah Jane Adventures* episode "Revenge of the Slitheen," she cowered from the scary monsters, and simultaneously drew quite a good approximation of said monster.

As the second season drew to a close, I found that I was more concerned about my daughter losing Rose, her first and favorite companion, the one who "has yellow hair like I do," than I had been about the transition from Eccleston to Tennant. She dealt fairly well, only crying a bit because she was sad that the Doctor and Rose couldn't "be together anymore since they miss each other." By this time, just like I could so many years ago, she could name episode titles and could tell within moments which episode it was – based on Rose's costume, just like I'd done with Sarah Jane – and knew the names of all the gadgets and how they worked, even if she didn't write the names five times each.

Elisabeth didn't take to Martha with the same fervor, nor Donna, but she continues to enjoy the show and snuggle with me to watch it, asking questions and, more often, explaining the plot to me. Even when watching other shows or movies, she understands time travel and body swapping and all manner of SF tropes. I paused once to explain something and she cut me off by explaining it to *me*, temporal paradoxes and all, then ended with saying, quite accurately, "It's like when Rose broke time and let the monsters in." Tara got to tell Paul Cornell at a convention that the first season episode *he* wrote was the favorite of a new five-year-old fangirl, and shared my daughter's succinct description of it. My little fangirl, however, ducked shyly behind me when I introduced her to Paul two years later.

For a local convention two years ago, a friend built a Clockdroid costume from "The Girl in the Fireplace" and sewed a pre-Revolutionary French dress for Elisabeth to wear as a mini-Reinette, and my daughter was in her first convention masquerade. She stayed up, patiently watching and waiting until the costume judging was done and is still very, very proud of her award (even though it's really an award to the designer and seamstress).

Last year, that same convention (Chicago TARDIS) had Elisabeth Sladen as a guest. It was not an option not to go, of course: it was local, Lis would be there, I'd never met her, and I could take my daughter! My Elisabeth handled all the waiting in line brilliantly; she was patient and well-behaved. She and other second and third generation Whovian children giggled over their sonic screwdriver and sonic laser battles, and watched in open-mouthed awe at the presence of a spookily believable Ten cos-player with his own Rose. Elisabeth declined to have her picture taken with those strangers (she hid in my skirt like she did with Paul Cornell), but she was perfect when there were photos with Lis Sladen. It's easier, I suspect, when it's someone with whom you've spent quality time from behind your living room cushions. After we were done with the photo line, I offered my Elisabeth the option to go out and do something less tedious, but she immediately requested to get *back* in line to get an autograph just for her, and beamed like a giddy thing when Lis praised her Reinette dress and said she'd never signed for "an Elisabeth with an 's' before." (I did confess how I chose my daughter's name.)

Soon, my clever girl and I will both be adjusting to a new Doctor together as David Tennant retires from the part. Even now, such a change can be hard. Fortunately, we can compare notes on which of Matt Smith's attributes and mannerisms and behaviors come from which of the Doctor's previous incarnations (whom Elisabeth can point to in photos and name by number). Perhaps if the new companion has "yellow hair" again, Elisabeth will fall more wholeheartedly back in love, or perhaps, now that she's eight, some other aspect will catch her fancy.

I am a fan, a wife and a mother. I write stories and share my shows. Best of all, my daughter and I share a love of storytelling and fantasy worlds to which we can travel together, sometimes courtesy of a blue box flown by the Doctor.

Mathematical Excellence:
A Documentary

Seanan McGuire is a science fiction and fantasy author and an award-winning singer/songwriter. DAW Books released her first novel, *Rosemary and Rue*, in 2009. Her first novel under the pseudonym Mira Grant, *Feed*, will be released by Orbit in 2010. She also produces an autobiographical web comic called "With Friends Like These..." available on her website. As a singer/songwriter, Seanan has released three albums (*Red Roses and Dead Things*, *Stars Fall Home* and *Pretty Little Dead Girl*). She won the Pegasus Award for Best Performer in 2007 and the Pegasus Award for Best Lyricist/Composer in 2008. http://www.seananmcguire.com/

People like to talk about when they "discovered" a show. Especially in *Who* fandom, it's practically become a game of one-upmanship:

"I discovered it during the McCoy era."

"Well, I discovered it during the Davison era."

"Well, I was watching it *in the womb*."

I guess that makes sense, when you're talking about a show based on time travel. I have no real memory of "discovering" *Doctor Who*; it's just something that's always been a part of my life, for as far back as my memory goes. In a world where most of the female icons offered for my consideration were pretty pink princesses and victims in waiting, the companions got to actually do things. Sure, they spent a lot of time screaming and running for their lives, but they had a *choice*. Sometimes they chose to wear impractical shoes and run around in quarries, and that was okay, too.

My devotion to this quirky serial from the United Kingdom made me a bit odd, even for the innately odd landscape of a Northern California elementary school playground. Being a geek was borderline okay if you were a boy and liked *Star Trek* or *Star Wars* (both of which redeemed themselves by being full of things that blew up), but even boys weren't supposed to be obsessed with shows that nobody else had ever heard of. If you were a girl, well... I could probably have committed a more efficient form of social suicide if I'd been willing to really work at it. I just didn't care enough to try. Playground politics were beneath future alumni of Gallifrey University.

It probably didn't help that I firmly believed *Doctor Who* was a documentary series.

See, in the San Francisco Bay Area, *Doctor Who* has traditionally been shown on public television stations ("supported by viewers like you"). Parents were still sorting out exactly how much television was safe for their kids to watch, and my mother found a unique way to combine the conservative "all TV is evil" approach with the liberal "they'll lose interest if we don't make it something forbidden" camp. She got me my own television, a small color set too old to have a remote control. She set it to PBS. And then she snapped off the knob, so that the channel could only be changed through use of pliers and the application of adult upper-body strength. My puny little seven-year-old arms didn't stand a chance.

"You can watch whatever you want, as long as it's on PBS," she said. Reasonable enough for a geek-in-training like myself; I definitely wasn't going to object to unlimited access to documentaries and educational programs. It was what came next that was the problem. See, PBS also showed educational fiction, like *Sesame Street* and *Reading Rainbow*. My mother decided to address this in the most direct way possible. Namely:

"They're going to use fake things to teach you real facts before twelve. So if it's on before noon, you should ask before you take it for true. But if it's on after noon, it's for real and for true and you can believe it."

Doctor Who came on at seven. The film quality of many episodes was similar to the film quality in many of the cheaper documentaries from the 1970s.

I'm sure you can see where this is going.

For years, I failed history tests and giggled behind my hand at history teachers who just didn't know the "real story" behind those events they were trying to explain to us. Since I was well-known to be a fan of science fiction, and to have an active imagination, nobody really tried to figure out *why* I was so determined to insert time travel, killer robots and the occasional alien invasion into world history. It was just sort of taken as a given that I would do something of the sort, and ignored in favor of kids with more obvious problems.

Now, I was a pretty smart kid, but let's hang on a second. One adult – my mother, who was supposed to know what she was talking about – basically told me that *Doctor Who* was a documentary series. None of my teachers ever bothered to contradict her, because none of them ever bothered to find out why I had an illogical fear of pepper shakers. And most of the other kids I knew were perfectly willing to agree that my logic made sense. After all, a world that contained dinosaurs and dodge ball (where the kids who took our lunch money were given an official mandate *from the teachers* to throw things at our heads) was definitely weird enough to contain a time-travel documentary series.

For years, I slept with a bag packed and waiting, just in case the Doctor showed up looking for a new companion. I watched the papers for signs of Cybermen, and avoided anything Dalek-shaped on general principle. After all, you never knew. My teachers eventually convinced me, through their ongoing unwillingness to discuss the truth, that I should just leave the actual, alien nature of reality out of my history papers. My GPA increased. My collection of *Doctor Who* tie-in novels increased. And I waited.

Jon Pertwee gave way to Tom Baker gave way to Peter Davison. I decided, regretfully, that I was probably not going to marry the Doctor – he was, after all, several hundred years too old for me – but that was okay, because I was going to marry Adric instead. Look, I was 12, okay? For a 12-year-old geek girl who really liked math, he was basically the perfect man. Also, he'd evolved from a totally parallel biology, and I figured that would give us plenty to talk about (again, weird kid). I had it all planned out. It was going to be perfect.

Once again, I'm sure you can see where this is going.

My mother came home one night to find me sitting in the living room with all the lights out and all the curtains drawn, crying piteously. I'd reached that point where there wasn't any sound, just tears and wracking sobs. Naturally, she freaked out, and started demanding to know what had happened. I managed to stammer out the terrible, tragic truth of my situation:

"Ah-Ah-ADRIC JUST DIED!"

Naturally, this freaked her out even more, since she didn't know the names of all my friends from school, and I went to school in California, where kids with names like "Arwen" and "October" were reasonably common. She asked if I had his parents' phone number, so she could call and see if there was anything they needed. I looked at her blankly. She asked if he was one of my friends from school. This was enough to make me a little more vocal, even if it wasn't enough to make me stop crying:

"No. He's from *Doctor Who*."

... right. My mother spent the next several hours trying to explain the difference between "reality" and "fantasy" to me – an explanation I found rather insulting, since I knew the difference between reality and fantasy, and more importantly, I *knew* that several adults had already confirmed which side of that divide *Doctor Who* was on. Hint: it wasn't "fantasy." In the end, I gave in more out of a desire to stop having an argument while I was in mourning than out of any real conviction that she was right. If she wanted to change her story, that was fine. I knew what was really real and true.

Years passed. I kept watching, fell in love with new Doctors, new companions. Sadly, my mother's recanting of her original confirmation of *Doctor Who*'s reality proved to be accurate; it was a television show, for real, and for true. But I'll always be the girl who believed with all her heart that one day, the Doctor would come for her, and one day, she'd see Gallifrey's skies with her own two eyes. I grew up believing that everything was possible, and part of me still does. Maybe that's why so much of my life has been lived doing things other people tell me can't be done. I believe there's a chance.

When I saw the first episode of the new series, I cried. More accurately, I started crying when the theme song started to play, and cried all the way through. We'd been good enough, and we'd been faithful enough, and the Doctor came back for us, all his most devoted companions, the ones who slept with backpacks next to their beds and learned to wake up in seconds when they heard the sound of the TARDIS. The ones who waited. Just in case.

I hope he never leaves us again. The girl I used to be hopes so, too. And sometimes, I still dream about a broken star for mathematical excellence... and I cry, because he never knew whether he was right.

You were right, Adric. Thank you so much. You were right.

The Fanzine Factor

Kathryn Sullivan is a writer of young adult science fiction and fantasy fiction for Amber Quill Press (*Talking to Trees*, *Agents and Adepts* and *The Crystal Throne*). She has also contributed short fiction to the Big Finish anthologies *Short Trips: Repercussions* and *Professor Bernice Summerfield and The Dead Men Diaries*, and to numerous *Doctor Who* charity anthologies. When she's not writing, Kathryn is the Distance Learning Librarian at Winona State University. She is owned by two birds (a cockatoo and a jenday), who graciously allow her to write about other animals. http://kathrynsullivan.com/

"Who is that ugly man?"

My sisters and I were visiting my father in Florida late in the 1990s, and I had happened to find *Doctor Who* on PBS. I was happily into the story when my younger sister asked the question. I looked at the TV screen, ready to explain the monster on display and realized she was actually asking about Tom Baker. I was shocked. "That's the Doctor!"

My sister was unimpressed and I paused just before launching into an explanation of the show, the Doctor, Tom Baker's fan following, etc. I knew I'd be wasting my breath. She just didn't understand. "I think his face has character," I said.

Nowadays, that same sister will call me about a week or so before Thanksgiving. "Are you going to be going to that convention thing? That *Doctor Who* thing? You going to stop for Thanksgiving with us on the way?"

"Sure, if it's not a problem," I reply.

"Of course it's not a problem. You're the only one who eats the drumsticks."

Doctor Who and Chicago TARDIS helps me stay connected with my family. But *Doctor Who* has connected me to a wider network of friends, and *kept* me connected. All thanks to a fanzine.

I got into *Doctor Who* fandom because of fanzines. I had discovered fanzines not long after I attended my first science fiction convention (WisCon) in 1980. I had been writing and sending out science fiction and fantasy stories for 12 years, but I didn't find out about fandom in general until I was 26 (information traveled a lot more slowly in the pre-computer days). I found a home for some of my original short stories in fanzines, and even tried writing a couple of fan stories – but those were based upon a book series I enjoyed, not a television series or movie. I enjoyed reading fan stories about *Star Trek* and *Star Wars*, but I didn't feel the need to write stories in those universes.

But one fanzine editor had other plans. MediaWest*Con I (May 22-25, 1981) was the first I heard of a fanzine con – there were no author guests or media guests; just a variety of fanzines, for more universes than I ever dreamed – and the place (I was told by other fanzine writers) to go to find new markets. It was held in Lansing, Michigan, which was ten hours' drive from where I lived in Winona, Minnesota. The plan, according to the editor – Paulie Gilmore – was for me to stop at her house in Kalamazoo, Michigan, on the way, and then follow her car the next day to the convention. She had accepted two of my fan stories for her book-based fanzine, and was waiting with an idea when I arrived: "I want you to write *Doctor Who* stories for my new zine," she announced.

"*Doctor Who*?" I had vague memories of two movies (*Dr. Who and the Daleks* and *Daleks' Invasion Earth: 2150 A.D.*) that had been shown on the then-brand new UHF channel in the Chicago area when I was in eighth grade, but I couldn't imagine writing any fan stories about those.

She sat me down in front of her television set and showed me "The Brain of Morbius." Now, those who remember that fourth Doctor story know that it has a mad scientist in search of a head for his creation into which he can transplant the brain of Morbius, a criminal Time Lord. Why would anyone start a newbie to the show on that? Ah, but she knew me. I saw the main storyline, but I also saw psi powers (which I tend to write about), a matriarchal society that was as powerful as the Doctor's people, and Sarah Jane Smith rescuing the Doctor. I was hooked.

At the convention, I hunted down any zine that contained a *Doctor Who* story. (Most of the *Doctor Who* fanzines, unfortunately, didn't start to appear until a few months later. This was the early days of *Doctor Who* fandom, when independent stations around the US had begun to air the Tom Baker episodes.)

MediaWest*Con also had a panel on *Doctor Who* as well as one on British science fiction shows in general (plus a few video showings at room parties), so I was able to learn about more than just "The Brain of Morbius." It wasn't enough for me to spark any ideas about a story to write, so I kept trying to find out more. The Target novelizations were starting to reach the US, and that gave even more details about the various Doctors. I had picked up a number of flyers about upcoming *Doctor Who* fanzines at that first Media*West Con and ordered them, so I had reading material to keep me busy until *Doctor Who* finally appeared on my TV.

As it turned out, I had just missed being able to watch the show. Channel 5 KSTP in St. Paul had been airing some Tom Baker episodes during the afternoons, but since I worked during the day and didn't get my first VCR until late in 1981, I didn't find out about that until *after* they had stopped carrying the show. Channel 2 KTCA, the public television station in St. Paul, began carrying the episodes in January 1982, and that is when I finally began to watch *Doctor Who* on television.

There were a wide variety of fanzines in their heyday. Newszines were usually published by clubs, such as DWIN (*Contact*), the North American Doctor Who Appreciation Society, the Doctor Who Fan Club of America (*Whovian Times*) and Friends of Doctor Who. Multi-universe fanzines (*Time Distort, Shadowstar, Rerun, Everything But the Kitchen Sink,* and *Warped Space*) included stories about series such as *Star Trek, Star Wars, Starsky and Hutch, Robin Hood* and *Blake's 7,* and often had *Doctor Who* stories as well.

Doctor Who-specific fanzines had ratings levels ranging from G to R. As an example of how much women had gotten interested in the Doctor, *Doctor Who* fanzines which had women publishers/editors and/or women authors and illustrators included *Gallifrey Chronicles* (1980-1981), *The Gallifreyan Dispatches* (1981-1983), *Jelly Baby Chronicles* (Paulie Gilmore's zine) (1981-1985), *Zeta Minor* (1981-1984), *Timelog* (1981-1986), *Dimension 4* (1982-1984), *Faces of Time* (1982-1984), *Traveling Companion* (1983-1984), *Time Winds* (1983-1984), *Rassilon's Star* (1983-1986, 1991), *Gateway to Time* (1984), *Castrovalva* (1985), *The Gallifrey Gazette* (1985) and *The Black Scrolls of Rassilon* (1985). There were also the Sarah Jane Smith spin-offs, *From the Notebook of Sarah Jane Smith* (1983-1985) and *Roving Reporter* (1991-1995). Some zines focused specifically on the fourth Doctor and some on the fifth (*Dimension 4, Castrovalva*), while others had stories with each of the Doctors, and included the sixth Doctor almost as soon as his first story debuted. Fan authors whose work I read that have since gone on to careers with their own universes include Jody Lynn Nye, Susan Sizemore and Rie Sheridan.

There were also many different types of fanzine stories. Parodies abounded, but there were also adventure stories or character-driven stories that would have worked perfectly well as televised *Doctor Who*, and short vignettes that filled in the gaps between stories or gave a bit of character background. There were alternative universe stories: some with recognizable *Doctor Who* characters (the fourth Doctor meeting Tom Baker) and some with people with the characters' names and descriptions – but behaving so differently from those in the show, I often wondered why the author bothered.

I quickly discovered writing fan stories for a media-based universe was quite different than writing fan stories for a book-based universe. Television and movie fans not only got what the writer of the script put into the story, but also what the actor contributed (consciously or unconsciously). Until I saw the episodes with Doctors other than the fourth, I had to rely on the Target novelizations and fanzine stories to get an idea of what those Doctors were like. There were some fanzine authors (and Target novelizations) that got them wrong, but others filled in the characterizations extremely well. Close detail was paid to faint smiles, the lift of an eyebrow or almost undetectable glances between characters. There were also clichéd descriptions and mannerisms – grasping the labels of a jacket, widening bulging eyes, repeating phrases ("Hm? What?") – that could be used rather than referring to a Doctor by number.

A vital piece of equipment needed in order to notice those details, though, was a VCR, which was not cheap back then. Video stores did rent out VCRs at that time, but the rental periods didn't always fit into any sort of writing schedule. I finally gave in and bought my first VCR late in 1981 (and thereby got into many more fandoms because of it – V'ger and I both did a lot of traveling).

Cross-universe stories were popular: the Doctor in *WKRP in Cincinnati*, the Doctor and *Star Trek*, the Doctor and *Hill Street Blues*, *Hitch-Hiker's Guide to the Galaxy* (with the fourth Doctor), the Doctor meets hobbits, the Doctor and *Star Wars*, *Remington Steele*, *M*A*S*H*, *Time Tunnel*, *Wizards and Warriors*, etc. As a time and space traveler, the Doctor was able to appear anywhere, and writers took advantage of it.

I succumbed to the siren call as well, by writing a story crossing the Doctor with *The Omega Factor* (Louise Jameson appeared in that program) and a music video that people were certain Tom Baker had appeared in (he denied doing so at several conventions, but the resemblance was there, and it triggered a story).

The appeal of the *Doctor Who* universe for me was that, unlike *Star Trek* (where practically every week had a new love interest for the main characters), the stories focused on the Doctor and his friends traveling together and having adventures in time and space. This isn't too dissimilar from the fourth series of the new show, with Donna and the Doctor traveling together as "just mates." The fourth Doctor constantly referred to his companions (and K-9) as his best friends, and a careful viewer could spot that friendship and affection. Fans did write stories, though, where the Doctor found romance, either with a particular existing companion or a new character that often could be seen as a Mary-Sue.

Hurt / comfort stories abounded; and, while some researchers on fanzines (such as Camille Bacon-Smith in *Enterprising Women*, University of Pennsylvania Press, 1992) analyzed the erotic aspects of such stories, those from backgrounds or cultures where one did not easily express affection realized that some characters couldn't say that they cared unless the person was unconscious, in a hospital bed or both. Then it was okay, but only because the person couldn't hear you. One could argue that this was a result of 60s and 70s culture, but it's a technique that is still used in television today, and I just heard it used in the *Torchwood* audio play "The Dead Line."

Fandom and early conventions

In 1980 through 1982, the local conventions I attended only featured a few media panels. *Doctor Who* conventions began in my part of the country in 1983, starting with Tom Baker's appearances (through Creation and the North American Doctor Who Appreciation Society) and Jon Pertwee and Lis Sladen's trip across the United States. Suddenly, *Doctor Who* and media conventions were sprouting up everywhere – Panopticon West in Columbus, the Ultimate Celebration / TARDIS 20 in Chicago, and, for other media, BlooMN'con in Minneapolis-St. Paul, and Scorpio in the Chicago area.

On July 16 to 17, 1983, Tom Baker was in Chicago for a two-day convention run by Creation and NADWAS. Marilyn Pulley and I carpooled down to attend on Saturday. Tom had two "talk" sessions, separated by a "meet the fans" session outdoors by the pool. July in Chicago is often hot, and the hotel's air-conditioning wasn't working too well. Outside by the pool was warm, but cooler than inside. The pictures I have of the crowds gathered in lines by the pool to see Tom Baker show many more women than men or boys.

While waiting in line by the pool to greet Tom, Marilyn and I decided we would be calm and polite and not frighten the poor man, who had a lot of fans to meet. Finally he reached our spot in line. We got out a "hi" and "welcome to Chicago," then, before either of us could think of anything else to say (I remember seeing Marilyn lift her camera), he had moved on to greet the group of four squealing women behind us. Marilyn and I glanced at each other and realized that, in this case, it didn't pay to be "Minnesota nice."

There was another question and answer session indoors, and then we had to return to Minnesota. On the drive back, one of us commented, "The Doctor would have known to wait." After that, I never confused an actor with the character again.

Marilyn did get a picture with Tom Baker in November 1983 at the Ultimate Celebration (also known as TARDIS 20 or "the convention right after 'The Five Doctors' aired in the US two days before it aired in the UK"). She took many more pictures of him as well as pictures of Patrick Troughton, Jon Pertwee, Peter Davison and the other companions and guests. (It helps to have a friend with a good camera.) She's also the reason I have many pictures of Colin Baker from Panopticon West 1984. We watched "The Twin Dilemma" before carpooling to Columbus, Ohio, and met the very charming Colin, who was much nicer than the sixth Doctor had been portrayed.

Scorpio II in August 1984 was a *Blake's 7* convention, but I counted it as *Doctor Who* because Terry Nation was a guest. The high point of that convention to me was winning the bid at the charity auction to have brunch with him Sunday morning, which was all Paul Darrow's fault. The bidding on a belt he wore as Avon went so well, he subsequently offered breakfast with him as another auction item. Terry Nation followed his lead – and I won. We talked about writing, naturally. I remember him being very gracious to a young writer.

Fandom and clubs

Doctor Who connections turned up everywhere. I found out that two of my colleagues at Winona State University already knew about *Doctor Who* because they had been to the UK. One, a psychology professor, had been at university in the UK in the 1960s and had fond memories of the first Doctor. The other was a fellow librarian and had been in the UK in a study abroad program in 1976 (he also had a fourth Doctor scarf). Those two helped form the nucleus of Winona State University's *Doctor Who* student club, which started out meeting in my apartment at some point in 1981. We sent petitions to two local PBS stations, asking them to carry *Doctor Who*. The timing must have been right, because both stations did so within a year. The meetings became monthly, but then attendance grew so large I had to find a bigger place, which turned out to be the Winona State student commons. By 1984, it had turned into a student club: "The Companions of Doctor Who," with myself as faculty advisor. We had both students and non-students (adults and children) as members. Most of the time, the monthly meetings entailed announcements of the latest news from newszines and *Doctor Who Monthly*, and viewings of episodes not shown on the local PBS stations (or related movies and television shows featuring the *Doctor Who* stars). But the club also volunteered to man the phones at KTCA pledge drives along with other *Doctor Who* clubs in the state, and members carpooled to *DW* conventions in Chicago.

Because of the time periods that the local PBS stations aired *Doctor Who*, I was able to observe how the age groups varied in willingness to express interest in the Doctor. KTCA, at the beginning of its run in 1982, aired the Doctor at 5 p.m. Monday through Friday, then changed to 5:30 p.m., then in 1983 showed just the compiled versions at 10:30 p.m. Friday night, then *both* Friday and Saturday nights before changing to Saturday nights at 10 p.m. in 1986. Meanwhile, WHLA in La Crosse showed *Doctor Who* at noon on Sundays. The correlation I noticed of age to gender amongst the viewership could be broken down as follows...

Pre-high school: both boys and girls came to the club meetings.

High school age: only boys.

College age: only women.

After college: both women and men, both with kids and without. (There were also several university employees in this group.)

By 1985, the club had become a local chapter (TARDIS) of the national Companions of Doctor Who club: Vortex Rift TARDIS (since Winona is on the border between Wisconsin and Minnesota). The official confirmation of the chapter took place at Panopticon West 1985 in New Orleans, in a wonderful ceremony with the chapter heads (Cardinals) dressed in Time Lord robes. Colin Baker, John Nathan-Turner, Nicholas Courtney and Gary Downie, guests at that convention, were presented with Time Lord robes and collars for the ceremony. Colin's robes and collar were polka-dotted, while JN-T's had a Hawaiian shirt pattern. Nicholas Courtney (as befitting the Brigadier) had olive green robes with gold trim on the collar.

Creation had two Doctor Who Festivals in Minneapolis in 1986, bringing Peter Davison in on May 23 and Colin Baker and Patrick Troughton to the Minneapolis Armory on October 4, and club members carpooled to meet them. The same occurred when Creation brought Louise Jameson (Leela) to Minneapolis on July 5, 1987. When the *DW* Tour came to the Twin Cities to introduce Sylvester McCoy on July 12, 1987, club members were there to help with the concession stand (as well as meet the new Doctor). The Winona group – working alongside some of the other *Doctor Who* clubs in the state – organized activities besides PBS pledge drives, including a Halloween party in Winona. One of the options at the party was group-writing a fan story ("The Bat in the Stone" which finally found a home in the British fanzine *Eye of Orion* in 2001). By 1988, with both PBS stations showing so much of the Doctor's episodes, interest began to die down in the club. The last activity the club sponsored was in 1995, when it funded bringing Paul Cornell (who was visiting America) over from the east coast for a book signing at Uncle Hugo's on August 12.

A Changing Fandom

I had cut back my attendance at conventions to mainly media conventions and then later to basically only *Doctor Who* conventions. Because I had volunteered at several of those conventions (usually in registration, art show, and security) for a number of years, the con committees of conventions in the 90s such as Visions knew me, and knew I could be trusted not to drool on guests. In that way I became guest escort (or a "minder," if you will) for *Doctor Who* guests such as Terry Nation, Colin Baker, Peter Davison and Sylvester McCoy.

But the community attending the conventions was changing. I no longer saw a number of people I knew from the 80s at conventions. Some had moved on to other fandoms, some had dropped out of fandom altogether, and real life had just proved too intrusive for others. As the years passed, the number of *Doctor Who* conventions dwindled to two.

I had been in the UK in 1986 for a semester class in Oxford. (The trip had two *Doctor Who* highlights: going to the BBC in Shepherds Bush and seeing Colin Baker and Nabil Shaban – who played Sil – rehearsing a scene from "Mindwarp," and seeing Janet Fielding in a performance in Oxford.) So, after hearing about how wonderful the UK conventions were, I decided in 1994 to visit a friend who was on sabbatical in the UK and then go to Manchester and attend Manopticon 3.

I had heard that *Doctor Who* fans in the UK were mainly male, but it was still a shock, after all the *Doctor Who* conventions I had attended in the US, to see an auditorium filled with men and boys. There were a few females – a dealer in the huskers room, a presenter doing a Vanna White impersonation during one of the game show segments, and a few girl-friend/wives scattered about – but not many others that I could see.

The high point of Manopticon 3 for me, though, was attending a small panel where Virgin gave out submission guidelines for their line of New Adventures books. My only problem was that I couldn't think of any storyline for the seventh Doctor, who at the time was the incum-bent. Virgin came out later that year with their Missing Adventures line with previous Doctors, but it turned out that I couldn't think of a book-length adventure for any of the previous incarnations either.

I still wrote a few fan fiction pieces in the 1990s. I was asked to con-tribute *Doctor Who* stories for charity anthologies, such as *Perfect Timing* (I and II), *The Cat Who Walked Through Time*, *Missing Pieces* and *Walking in Eternity*. That gave me the chance to write for several different Doctors. In 1996, Tom Beck, editor of the Friends of Doctor Who news-letter, asked me to write reviews of fan videos. I had a column in that newsletter from 1996-2001 where I wrote reviews about fan videos, the McGann TV movie, and then later the BBV videos and audios and Big Finish audios.

Doctor Who wasn't the only fandom I followed: *Star Trek* in its vari-ous forms, *Star Wars, Scarecrow and Mrs. King, MacGyver, Blake's 7, Remington Steele, The Avengers, Sapphire & Steel, Adderly, Robin of Sherwood, Beauty and the Beast, Babylon 5, Stargate SG-1* – as well as oth-ers. Many of those fandoms vanished as soon as the shows went off the air. Others lingered for awhile before their fans moved on. I stayed a *Doctor Who* fan because the fandom continued to exist even after the show didn't. Thanks to the Internet, I could find like-minded fans to discuss stories and themes. I could still attend conventions (even if there were just the two). I could find books and audio dramas (and there was always the dream of writing for one or the other, if I could think of a good idea).

In time, I didn't attend *Doctor Who* conventions because a particular star or stars would be there (since I had already heard most of their stories before), but because it was a chance to visit with friends I only saw once a year. Which was fun, and a much-needed sanity break from work. But then the conventions started inviting "people behind the scenes," such as the writers, and that caught my interest.

The change in guests wasn't really all that new. Visions 90 had invited John Freeman, editor of *Doctor Who Magazine*, John Peel and Jean Marc L'Officier. Visions 91 brought back John Peel as well as Jeremy Bentham.

Visions 95 started the recognition of the New Adventures book series with authors Kate Orman and Paul Cornell, followed the next year with Gary Russell, who was the new editor of *DWM* as well as an author. A few months later, Gallifrey 1997 brought Gary Russell and David McIntee to the West Coast. And then the New Adventures (and BBC books) authors began turning up at Gallifrey. These were the guests I came to see!

Thanks to a review in the DWIN newszine, I found out about the AudioVisuals (fan audios), which was the start of my correspondence with Gary Russell around 1988. Robert Franks and I put together a website for Gary (we up and decided he needed one) for his birthday in 1997. A few months later, Gary – now a producer for the newly born Big Finish – asked me to help put together a website for the company. At that time, the webpages were still on Gary's website, so I helped him get the pages set up and tweaked while interviews and casting for Benny Summerfield began. In 1998, the first of the Big Finish's Bernice Summerfield audios was released. Then in July 1999, Gary was a guest at CONvergence in Minneapolis; "The Sirens of Time," the first of Big Finish's monthly *Doctor Who* audios, was released later that month. I continued to help with the Big Finish webpages for both the Benny stories and the *Doctor Who* productions until August 1999, when Shaun Lyon took over the Big Finish website.

At Gallifrey 2000, Gary approached me with those fatal words, "I'd like to commission you to write a short story..." It was intended for a Bernice Summerfield anthology, *The Dead Man Diaries*, with Paul Cornell serving as editor. Plans were underway to relocate Bernice to the Braxiatel Collection, and the set-up was fascinating to behold, full of little post-it notes from the various characters. I had less than four months to write 5,000 words, and I had a great time doing so. The collection was released in September 2000, just a few months before my first book (a non-*DW* one) was released.

Gary approached me again about writing a story for his *Short Trips* collection, *Repercussions*, in 2004, and this time I was able to write for the sixth Doctor and Evelyn with "The Diplomat's Story." I pitched for some of the other *Short Trips* collections, but I have a hard time writing story pitches. Unfortunately, the editor often wants to know how the story *ends*, but I never know how that's going to happen until I finish writing it.

2005 and beyond

Through the years people have predicted the end of *Doctor Who* fandom – when Tom Baker left, when Sylvester McCoy began or left, when the McGann movie aired, when The New Adventures ceased publication and so on. Each and every time, they've got it wrong. As some fans left, new fans joined. Looking at conventions, I can see the impact of the new series. There are more fans attending Chicago TARDIS and Gallifrey, the two main US conventions. There are more *Doctor Who* panels – discussing both the new series and the old – at media conventions. There are new forums on the Internet as well as Facebook groups. The new popularity is wonderful – it's great to see *Doctor Who* nominated for and winning Hugo awards, to see new products such as audio books and animated adventures and listen to those marvelous soundtracks. It's a wonderful time to be a fan and I'm enjoying being swept up in the exciting adventures through time and space again, never knowing (except for spoilers) where the Doctor will appear next and how he will react. I've had a fan-made TARDIS key on my key ring since I first got into *Doctor Who* fandom. I keep it, because you just never know...

An Interview
with Laura Doddington

Laura Doddington has worked extensively on stage and on radio in the UK, notably with acclaimed playwright/director Sir Alan Ayckbourn, and on television as PC Wood in *Prime Suspect: The Final Act*. She plays the villainous Zara in the "Key 2 Time" mini-series from Big Finish, and also in the related *Companion Chronicles* audio, "The Prisoner's Dilemma."

Q. What is your background as an actor?

A. None of my immediate family are in the business; I simply had a passion for acting from a very young age, and I was lucky enough that my parents encouraged it. They didn't send me to a young kids' drama school, as they wanted me to be as grounded as possible. At the time I hated them for it, but now I'm very grateful!

I went to Drama school in Edinburgh at age 18; when I graduated at 21, I was given an amazing opportunity – I won the Carlton Hobbs Award, which includes a six-month contract with the company which produces all of Radio 4's drama. It was an amazing learning experience which I really enjoyed, and it was wonderful to come out of college with a job lined up!

Then I had nine months of on and off "resting," which was really hard. I went traveling, got two "normal" jobs and seriously considered giving up on acting. Then I had the audition which changed my life: I got a job at Stephen Joseph Theatre in Scarborough. I ended up doing two summer seasons and two Christmas shows back to back, and worked on five shows with the great Sir Alan Ayckbourn, who has taught me so much. Then my life as a jobbing actor ensued.

Q. How many full-cast radio plays did you wind up doing before working with Big Finish?

A. I did about 20 full-cast radio shows with the radio repertory. The most exciting was probably Phillip Pullman's *Northern Lights, Subtle Knife* and *The Amber Spyglass*. The Radio 4 set up, however, is very different to the one Big Finish uses!

Q. How so?

A. With the Radio 4 dramas, the cast is all in a room together, gathered around a stereo mic, and you have to make your own sound effects. With the Big Finish dramas, everything is added [in post production], and you get your own booth. Trust me, it's very hard, when you're standing in a small booth wearing massive headphones, to not do a "Do They Know It's Christmas Time" impression.

Q. How familiar were you with Doctor Who or Big Finish, before you got the part of Zara?

A. I have to admit that I hadn't heard of Big Finish before I auditioned with them. I had, obviously, heard of *Doctor Who*, and Sylvester McCoy and Sophie Aldred were "my" era. As a child, I would probably manage to watch about an eighth of the show – the rest of the time was spent *not* looking at the telly, through fear! I was a very sensitive child.

Anyway, my ignorance is going to show here, but until the first day of recording, I had no idea that there were TV episodes featuring the Key to Time. It was amazing holding the original prop for the photo shoot though!

Q. When you read the character breakdown and audition sides for Zara, what were your first impressions?

A. I have only ever played "evil" once before, and loved doing it. You get to have so much fun! I also loved the concept of Zara and [her sister] Amy – not just the "yin and yang" aspect, but the journey the characters undertake.

Q. What were the greatest challenges in playing Zara, who's a living embodiment of a Key to Time tracer device? It's not often you get asked to play a newborn consciousness in an artificially constructed body, who develops autonomy and a sense of self based upon the people around her.

A. The part was written so well, it came quite organically through the text. That sounds so "actor speak," but it really is so true. The hardest was probably in "The Prisoner's Dilemma," as I was switching back and forth between different parts of the story. But it wasn't that difficult for me to embody Zara; with audio dramas, you can really go inside the character's head. The most difficult part of it was probably the complex "sci-fi" talk!

Q. What sort of rapport did you have with directors Lisa Bowerman and Jason Haigh-Ellery?

A. I had known Lisa – and got on very well with her – through a corporate job we did together, so we sort of picked up right where we left off. She's an amazing director. I didn't know Jason at all, but he knew a lot of the cast, so at first it was a bit like trying to fit in on the first day of school. But he was a great director and made me feel included, which was lovely.

Q. Were you able to meet Sophie Aldred, Peter Davison or Ciara Janson [who plays Amy] before recording?

A. Kind of... when you arrive in the morning, you have informal introductions in the green room. But unlike Radio 4, there's no full-cast read through of the script, so I only got to know the actors you've mentioned throughout the day's recording. Clara and I got on really well straightaway. Peter was a real source of energy in the green room, and Sophie was also great – it was amazing to meet an acting hero from my childhood. I couldn't believe that even now, she doesn't look all that different from Ace.

Q. What was it like, the first time you heard the finished product, all the performances edited together with all the music and sound effects?

A. I find hearing my own voice very difficult. I haven't listened to "The Prisoner's Dilemma" yet, but I have listened to "The Judgement of Isskar" [the first "Key 2 Time" installment] and really enjoyed it. It sounds great with all the sound effects. Without sounding like an old bugger, it's amazing what you can do nowadays with editing and post production.

Q. Did you have any idea what conventions were like before you were a guest at Chicago TARDIS and Gallifrey One in Los Angeles? Or was it old hat, given your stage experience?

A. The convention signings were lovely, and I loved talking to people on a one-on-one basis when there wasn't any pressure. The panels, however, were very scary – especially at the Chicago show, as it seemed that no one there had heard the audios! [Editor's note: Doddington appeared at Chicago TARDIS 2008, two months before her Big Finish stories were released.] I'm not great at being in the spotlight as myself; I'm used to being on stage in front of hundreds of people while playing a character, which allows me to hide behind someone else's words.

I was even more nervous at Gallifrey One, because it was bigger and more intimidating than the Chicago show. Unlike Chicago, though, some people had heard my CD stories – so they could have told me that they were rubbish, but no one did!

Q. What surprised you the most about conventions, and Doctor Who fandom?

A. *Doctor Who* has been going a loooong time in the UK, but I had no idea that it even had a following in the States. The social aspect of it was a surprise, too – it was so nice to get to know some of the fans, and I got the feeling that conventions are kind of like a reunion, but one you actually want to go to because everyone has something in common. I loved talking to people in the bar and lobby, and I've made some real friends through this experience.

Renaissance of the Fandom

LM Myles was born and raised in the rural backwater of Scotland. She went to Edinburgh University and got a law degree. She's been writing fan fiction since 2000 and currently runs the main *Doctor Who* fan fiction archive, *A Teaspoon and An Open Mind*. In 2007, she had a *Doctor Who* short story published in the Big Finish collection *How The Doctor Changed My Life*.

For almost as long as I can remember, I've loved *Doctor Who*. It's my Mum's fault – she started watching the show in 1963, from the very first episode. As time went on, while her younger brothers hid behind cushions from Cybermen and Ice Warriors, she kept watching – thrilled by the adventures of this strange man and his mysterious blue spacecraft. Twenty years later, she was *still* watching, and thought the show had never been better (she's a bit of a Peter Davison fan, my Mum). So, although *Doctor Who* had been cancelled when I was but a wee nipper of five, she wasn't going to have her children miss out on such fantastic stories. She made sure that my sister and I were brought up on a steady diet of the nineties VHS releases. It wasn't a complete success: my sister thought all this space and time adventuring was a lot of daft nonsense (though that didn't stop her flailing in terror at the Haemovores in "The Curse of Fenric"), but I was convinced that *Doctor Who* was surely the most brilliant and exciting story ever told.

When I finally got online in 1998 or thereabouts and discovered other people who loved it with the same mad passion, I was overjoyed (and somewhat relieved). I had discovered *Doctor Who* fandom, a magical place where people were happy to talk about the magnificence of Patrick Troughton's acting and why "The Curse of Fenric" was a brilliant piece of television, and to spend an absurd number of hours playing silly games replete with jokes that required a terrifyingly intimate knowledge of the show. For the next few years, I considered the Outpost Gallifrey forum (which is, sadly, no longer active) to be my online home and whiled away many an evening discussing terribly important issues, like whether the Kandy Man is a creation of diabolical genius or just a bit daft. (The answer is, of course, the former.)

Elsewhere on the Internet, at fanfiction.net to be precise, I delved into the cache of *Doctor Who* fan fiction. It was a relatively small section at the time – there were only a few hundred submissions – but it seemed a vast treasure trove of stories that could or would *never* have been told on screen. Eventually, I managed to screw up the courage to post stories of my own – dreadful ones of course (as virtually everyone's first fan fiction is), but it was awfully good fun. So much so, I'm still writing fic nearly a decade later although it has, I very much hope, improved a bit.

In 2003, I received an e-mail telling me about the opening of *A Teaspoon and An Open Mind*, a brand new *Doctor Who* fan fiction archive (created to replace the previous one, *The Panatropic*, which had gone down in 2002) and a link there led me to LiveJournal, where I began to blog and found a corner of *Doctor Who* fandom whose creativity and humour I adored. Here there was less interest in the show's continuity and more in the characters, their facets and their relationships with each other. Daft special effects were considered more a part of the show's charm than something to be embarrassed about. It was a small community but fun, friendly and seemingly content to trundle on quietly while the new BBC Books and Big Finish releases made sure that its numbers, while modest, were never in decline.

Then along came 2005 and the new series, and the landscape of *Doctor Who* fandom transformed as though some sort of ultra-fast glacier had just whooshed across it. Suddenly, there were hundreds and hundreds of new fans interacting online and the previously male-dominated fandom found itself a lot closer to gender parity as most of the new fans appeared to be girls. They brought with them a great tsunami of squee and creativity and experiences in other online fandoms. It was an amazing time to be a fan, with an amazing new series, a new Doctor, a new companion and so much excitement and enthusiasm from the fans, new and old!

Within a matter of weeks, *thousands* had joined communities dedicated to the new series. LiveJournal went from being a quiet little corner of *Who* fandom to a great hub of fannish activity for the new series.

But, for me, the really, *really* fantastic part came a little later, when the first season of the new series had finished, the Christmas special was months away, the next season even further, and the new fans were eager for more of the show *right now*. With so long to wait, many of them became interested in seeing where this fantastic hero had come from. Now at this point, barring the Paul McGann TV movie in 1996, *Doctor*

Who had been off the air for 16 years. Most of the classic series was older than most of the new fans. So, given the absence of the nostalgia factor and that they were used to seeing *Doctor Who* (and television generally) with an actual budget and state of the art special effects, I can honestly say I didn't really expect anyone to watch the classic series with much enthusiasm. As it turned out, I was incredibly wrong. Many loved it; some even decided that *this* was their *Doctor Who* series, preferring it over the new incarnation. Suddenly, I didn't feel quite so alone in my love of "The Time Monster" – a story that is admittedly pretty dreadful, but also ridiculously good fun and I adore it for that.

In fact, there were fresh new perspectives on dozens of the classic series stories, ones that tended to be a lot more aware of social equality and diversity. The new fans tended to be a lot less forgiving of racist and sexist elements in the stories – "The Talons of Weng Chiang," with its "yellow-facing" of the actors, would never win any popularity polls here – but a lot more forgiving of daft special effects, continuity errors and bad acting. They wanted to have a good story, good characters and *fun*, and if a giant clam turned up in the middle of a very serious World War II allegory and Harry Sullivan went and stuck his foot in it, then that was okay.

There was a whole new perspective on the companions too; they were just as interested in the companions as the Doctors. They were often delighted and amazed that the "ankle-twisting screamer" stereotype was, in fact, complete rubbish and there were actually dozens of female characters that were just as strong and interesting as Rose had been in the new series. All the companions were looked at with fresh eyes and often judged to be pretty darn good actually: even poor forgotten Dodo had her admirers! Barbara, Romana, Liz, Ace, Zoe... characters decades old found themselves new fans and new popularity, and even the companions that had the worst reputations in classic *Who* fandom gained defenders. Jo may have been a bit of a ditz at times, but she was still an expert escapologist and did save the universe that one time. Polly may have screamed a lot, but she also came up with an effective weapon to fight the Cybermen, and was more often than not the one doing the rescuing rather than needing to be rescued.

And then there was the fan fiction – the lovely, lovely fan fiction! Not only was there a whole lot more (which was dead nice in and of itself), but the new fans brought with them the tendency to "ship" – that is, a type of story where a romantic relationship between two characters is explored – that had been more commonly seen in other fandoms, but not so much with classic *Who*. Previously, *Doctor Who* fanfic was mostly concerned with big adventure stories and original Doctors and companions and virtual seasons (mostly written by male fans), while there was a small amount of stories that focused more on the characters (mostly by female fans) and a very little shipping.

Now, instead of the odd bit of tentative shipping between the fifth Doctor and Tegan or the eighth Doctor and Fitz, no pairing was off limits. Encouraged by the new series playing on the possibility of a romantic relationship between the Doctor and Rose, classic *Who* fans and new series fans applied the new rules of How To Interpret The Show to the classic series and suddenly, there were a ridiculous amount of characters and relationships to play with. A touch or glance, a shared smile or a desperate handholding run was now more than enough subtext to prompt a ship fic.

Prior to 2005, I'd written fanfic shipping Tegan and the fifth Doctor and Grace and the eighth Doctor. By 2006, there were dozens of pairings I'd happily read and write, from the many that had obvious on-screen chemistry (such as Jamie and the second Doctor – seriously, pick a story, any story, and count how many times they cling to each other) to the many more who'd never even met on screen. (If Big Finish ever get the chance, might I suggest a Donna Noble and sixth Doctor adventure? Romance need not be included, though it would be rather awesome.) With the sheer volume of new fans embracing the idea of a Doctor who was capable of both sex and romance, the old idea of the asexual Doctor was cast aside. Everything, from how sweet the romance between the first Doctor and Cameca was in "The Aztecs" to "Isn't it a bit dodgy the way the fifth Doctor looks at Susan in 'The Five Doctors'?", was being discussed. Every Doctor got to see a bit of action in fanfic and the fandom became a much busier, more vibrant and exciting place. Awesomeness.

It wasn't just the companions who benefitted. The villainy of the Doctor's nemesis, the Master, and his inability to actually get around to killing the Doctor was no longer seen as incompetence on his part or evidence of cartoon villainy, but was far more satisfyingly reinterpreted as the Master's obsessive, rather twisted, need for the Doctor's approval and respect, often seen in the context of an epic and incredibly messed-up lovers' quarrel. After the end of the third season of New *Who*, this previously niche view became very popular and there was a surge in interest in classic *Doctor Who* stories featuring the Master, creating a second wave of new series fans whose interest was with primarily for this character and his relationship with the Doctor, rather than the companions. This meant a whole new round of increased creativity and discussion.

With all these new fans came many new friendships, and I became more involved in the fandom than ever before. I ended up taking over the *Teaspoon* as it expanded from a small website of less than a thousand stories to a vast archive of over 20,000 today. Each week I spent hours moderating various communities on LiveJournal, most of which would never have existed without New *Who* prompting the renewed interest in the classic series.

The two major *Doctor Who* conventions in the United States are now regular holidays for me, and have been ever since one of these New *Who* fans (very easily) managed to persuade me to go to Chicago for my very first *Doctor Who* convention, Chicago TARDIS, almost three years ago now. It was a little terrifying – I'd never travelled abroad by myself before, and I was going to be meeting people that, though I was terribly fond of them, had only known online. It was also ridiculously exciting, and I loved the people and the experience so much that I went back the next year and plan on attending a third; sharing fannish glee online is quite, quite marvellous, but sharing fannish glee in person is a bit like magic.

Now, yet again, there's a whole new Doctor in Matt Smith, a new companion and a new producer at the helm of the series. I hope that with all the new adventures they'll be having, there'll be yet another influx of new fans. Maybe some of them will become curious about where this extraordinary hero has come from, and will go on to discover the classic series, and add their own layer of ideas and creativity to this most awesome of fandoms.

If I Can't Squee, I Don't Want to be Part of Your Revolution: Crone-ology of an Ageing Fangirl

Kate Orman, one of the most acclaimed authors of *Doctor Who* tie-in fiction, has written or co-written 13 original *Doctor Who* novels. She authored *The Left-Handed Hummingbird, Set Piece, SLEEPY, Return of the Living Dad* and *The Room with No Doors* – plus co-wrote *So Vile a Sin* with Ben Aaronovitch – for the Virgin New Adventures. For BBC Books, Kate co-wrote, along with husband Jonathan Blum, the Eighth Doctor Adventures *Vampire Science, Seeing I* and *Unnatural History*. She also wrote the EDA *The Year of Intelligent Tigers* and the Past Doctor Adventure *Blue Box*. Along with her *Doctor Who* novel work, Kate has written numerous short stories and the Bernice Summerfield novel *Walking to Babylon*. Kate and Jon's *Doctor Who* novella *Fallen Gods* (Telos Publishing) won the prestigious Aurealis Award (given to the best Australian SF writers) for Best Science Fiction Novel in 2003. It is the only piece of *Doctor Who* tie-in fiction to ever win a major SF award. http://kateorman.livejournal.com/

My first certain memory of *Doctor Who* is of "Spearhead From Space": the Doctor escaping in the wheelchair. *Doctor Who* was a staple of Australian television through my childhood – usually sandwiched between *The Goodies* and the seven o'clock news. With constant repeats, it seemed as though the Doctor was always there, and that everyone watched the show: kids, parents, teachers.

But real life inevitably began to dent this happy routine. I lost every fourth episode of "The Key to Time" to piano lessons. In mid-1980, we moved to the United States for two years – then returned just as the end of Season Nineteen was repeated.

Two key things happened at this time. One was that, in the US, I'd discovered the concept of fandom, reading books such as *The Making of the Trek Conventions* and the anthology *Star Trek: The New Voyages 2*, which prompted my first-ever attempt at fanfic – although sadly *The Mitosis Effect* only got as far as a rough outline and some drawings of the aliens involved. Plus, returning to Australia via the UK, I'd discovered the *Blake's 7* magazine and spent my pocket money on my first-ever issue of *Doctor Who Monthly* (#69, October 1982). I now understood that there was a whole world behind the TV screen.

Also, my proclivity for hurt/comfort was making itself known. When Peter Davison's Doctor was zapped into unconsciousness at the end of "Arc of Infinity" Part One, I spent the wait for Part Two in a bit of a state, worried to death about him. You know, I never wanted to bed the boy, but I very quickly understood that watching him suffer was mysteriously, profoundly thrilling. (The opening chapters of *Set Piece* began life, at least in my mind, as the fulfilment of Davros' threat to kill the fifth Doctor slowly and painfully.)

This brings us up to 1984. I was hanging out in high school with friends who also watched the show, but it wouldn't be until my first year at university that I really became involved with fandom. But blimey, I was a stereotypical fangirl in the making. I was gifted, a top student, a target for bullies. I had a few close female friends, but no social life to speak of; I generally preferred my own company. I was a bookworm. I wrote poetry (lots) and prose (little), I drew and painted, I wrote elaborate stories inside my head. I had no interest in real-life boys, but I had deeply felt (and deeply sublimated) crushes on imaginary ones. Nor was I interested in clothes (to this day I seldom bother to wear anything other than jeans and a shirt or T-shirt) or makeup. Instead, I tended to share my two younger brothers' interests: superhero comics, action movies, video games, computers and role-playing. The three of us found refuge from the continual harassment of the playground in a recess and lunchtime chess club. (If there was another girl in the club, I can't remember her.)

I wasn't a tomboy (zero interest in sports, tree-climbing, etc) or transgender (I knew quite firmly that I was a girl). I was, quietly and unintentionally, *gender non-conforming*. I had no awareness of this, but the bullies certainly did: the topic of ridicule and abuse switched from my hair color to my supposed lesbianism. (Years later, work colleagues, other fans and at least one relative would all make the same assumption.)

As I would later discover, many other fangirls and geek girls report the same kinds of experiences growing up. In *Enterprising Women*, Camille Bacon-Smith recounts how many female fans have experienced "scorn" for their "masculine" interests. She describes *Star Trek* fangirls growing up during a time when, as teenagers, they were expected to give up any tomboy inclinations and defer to and flatter boys. "Many women in fandom, however, did not make this transition." Some were outcasts because of their physical appearance; some refused to mask their intelligence. But even in fandom, some suffered ostracism or harassment from male fans – sometimes precisely because of their "feminine" interest in relationships and romance.

Now, "fangirl" is a word with a slippery meaning. I polled people in my LiveJournal for their definitions, which ranged from "silly screeching teenager" through "a self-deprecating term used by female fans to refer to themselves" through simply "a fan who is a girl." In this essay, I use the word with the lattermost meaning in mind. But many female fans are keen to dissociate themselves from "fangirl" behavior, and not just because they see it as adolescent. In *Cyberspace of Their Own: Female Fandoms Online*, Rhiannon Bury writes that members of the David Duchovny Estrogen Brigade would play down their association with the group to avoid ridicule and to be "taken seriously" – by male fans.

* * *

In 1987, my best mate Steven Caldwell persuaded me to join him at a "Doctor Who Party" held at Sydney University, a sort of one-day mini-convention run by the Australasian Doctor Who Fan Club. There were dealers and fanzines, toasted sandwiches, and, most importantly, a pirate copy of "The War Games." We sat rapt through all ten episodes of dodgy picture and sound. And then, to top it all off, there was a sneak preview of the first ten minutes or so of "Time and the Rani." We were berserk with excitement. Hooked!

Steven and I had met through the university's gaming and specfic club. (We're to blame for the club's still current name, SUtekh.) Then, as now, the small group was predominantly – though certainly not exclusively – male. The same was true of Australian *Doctor Who* fandom: I was a rare fangirl in a sea of fanboys.

Australasian *Doctor Who* Fan Club survey respondents:
1985: 79% male
1986: 85% male
1988: 80% male
1989: 80% male
1990: 81% male

You get the picture. British *Doctor Who* fandom, too, was and is majority male; the Doctor Who Appreciation Society estimates its membership to be about four-fifths male. In the most recent *Doctor Who Magazine* survey, 71% of respondents were male. This was not the fandom I'd read about – seventies *Star Trek* fandom, largely run by women for women – nor the fandom I was going read about when I encountered academic accounts. I did know that US *Doctor Who* fandom was more female than male, but in those days I had next to no contact with it. I'd meet plenty of female fans, but it wouldn't be until I joined LiveJournal in 2004 that I'd encounter majority-female fandom.

I became increasingly involved in Australian fandom. This was my first real social life: meetings to get the newsletter *Data Extract* ready for mailing, weekend get-togethers of the small local clubs, more parties, conventions and interstate trips to visit fannish friends. I made friends I still have today (I still miss our cutthroat games of *Doctor Who* Charades!). I helped organize Console 88, began to produce my own fanzine, *The Question Mark*.

I wrote fanfic. Mountains of the stuff. Not lengthy epics, but lots of short stories, rarely longer than four thousand words, and almost invariably hurt/comfort. Which is interesting, because I was writing much more fanfic than I was reading; this was almost but not quite spontaneous (but not quite, because I had encountered a little of it in those *Star Trek* books). I think I was more influenced by my adolescent reading of SF anthologies than by fanfic.

I also wrote a lot of articles and opinion pieces. My ambition was to get something published in every fanzine in Australia. (You might think this would be an easy task, but there were a lot of zines in those pre-Web days; I can think of four off the top of my head that I never cracked.) Eventually, Simon Moore and I began to produce a magazine for the Australian Doctor Who Fan Club: *Dark Circus* complemented the newsletter *Data Extract*. When long-time ADWFC president Dallas Jones decided to take a break, I took over editing *Data Extract* – which meant I also inherited the presidency, such as it was. (I changed the club's name; the thriving New Zealand fandom had never been too happy about that "Australasian.")

Virgin announced their line of original *Doctor Who* novels in 1990, and I jumped at the chance this gave so many budding writers. *Writing For Pleasure and Profit* by Michael Legat was my heavily-highlighted bible, full of useful advice, like having a regular time for writing (one hour every night after dinner!). More importantly than how to write, though, it explained how publishing works. My plan was simple: read The New Adventures as they came out, follow the guidelines and keep sending in novel proposals until they accepted one. Expect only rejection letters; but aim for encouraging ones. It worked a lot faster than I had expected. My first New Adventure, *The Left-Handed Hummingbird*, was published in November 1993.

Counting co-writes, 12 more novels followed. In my second New Adventure, *Set Piece*, I had the privilege (and the problem) of writing Ace out of the series. In the books, the troubled teen we'd seen on TV had grown up into a hard-assed space soldier in a body-hugging combat suit. This was not the easiest character to write for, but on the whole I adored the characters created by the other authors: Ben Aaronovitch's Kadiatu Lethbridge-Stewart (whom I brought back in *Set Piece*), Paul Cornell's Bernice Summerfield (who got her own spin-off series of books, including my effort, *Walking to Babylon*), and Andy Lane's future cops Roz Forrester (the story of whose heroic death Ben started and I finished in *So Vile A Sin*) and Chris Cwej.

* * *

I've often been asked how my gender affects my writing – in particular, how my *Doctor Who* novels were different from the boys'. It's a question I've never been able to give a really satisfying answer. Rummaging through books about gender and writing at the local library, I found that feminists have been trying to define that difference too. "The most common answer," wrote English professor Judith Kegan Gardiner in the early eighties, "is that women's experiences differ from men's in profound and regular ways. Critics using this approach find recurrent imagery and distinctive content in writing by women, for example, imagery of confinement and unsentimental descriptions of childcare. The other main explanation... posits a 'female consciousness' that produces styles and structures innately different from those of the 'masculine mind'." (Gardiner isn't satisfied with either explanation and gives her own one, based in psychoanalysis and therefore beyond my ken.)

On the other hand, Joyce Carol Oates dismisses the question: "Content is simply raw material. Women's problems – women's insights – women's very special adventures: these are material: and what matters in serious art is ultimately the skill of execution and the uniqueness of vision... individual style... is sexless." I think Oates' goal here is to resist the lumping together of "women's writing" into a ghetto; but the idea that a writers' style is "sexless" is hard to swallow. I've got an anthology on my shelf called *Rotten English* – postcolonial writers deliberately using non-standard English, often to remarkable and beautiful stylistic effect. Clearly, their style is not "colorless."

Is there some analogous style in writing by women? If there is, I don't think we're going to find it in my *Doctor Who* novels. Although each author in the range has their own personal style, and the books have varied hugely in tone and genre, we're all recounting adventure stories and that constrains our style. What about content, then, informed by typically female experiences? Here there's a problem: I simply haven't had the life experiences that so many other women have had, positive and negative: pregnancy, abortion, childbirth, child rearing... On the other hand, there are plenty of experiences I share with other women: street harassment, fear of rape, dieting, running a household, worrying about contraception. I got married in a huge meringue dress. I may be gender non-conforming, but that doesn't mean I can opt out of having a gender: as Susan Stryker writes in *Transgender History*, in this culture, you must have a gender, you must have just one gender, and it must be immediately clear which one. Nor does it make me a man – whether you reject the strict man/woman binary, in which case "not woman" doesn't equal "man"; or whether you accept it, in which case I'm just a rather unfeminine woman.

As always with *Doctor Who*, the companions are central and almost always female; but in a novel as opposed to a TV story, there's plenty of room to involve them in the plot and develop their characters. By the time I arrived, male writers had already introduced remarkable creations such as Benny and Kadiatu. This is not to say that the novels were flawlessly feminist – off the top of my head, I can think of a half a dozen examples of dodginess, which I'll spare you – but it does further cloud any difference between my books and the rest.

The demographics of *Doctor Who* fandom help to explain why The New Adventures were almost entirely written by men. Especially from a US perspective, this must have looked odd, even suspicious, even after Rebecca Levene took over as editor of the range in 1993. I don't know what proportion of proposed novels came from outside the UK and/or were written by women. But only a tiny, tiny number of submissions ever escape a publisher's slush pile. Figures are hard to come by, but out of more than two thousand total submissions in 2006, *Realms of Fantasy* magazine published just two from their slush pile. If female writers submitted, say, around a fifth of all manuscripts – the figure suggested by club memberships and surveys – then simple mathematics would make NAs by women rare.

* * *

Overlapping with all this was my arrival on Usenet in 1993, thanks to a spare computer at work which I could use after hours. I've often credited Usenet with having turned me into a feminist, as I began doing research to counter 90s backlash lies about violence against women. Looking back now, my feminism is inchoate but definite: one of my earliest postings in rec.arts.drwho is a request for articles for *Bog Off!*, a feminist fanzine Sarah Groenewegen and I edited.

Usenet fandom was overwhelmingly male, and sometimes hostile to female fans. For example, in "Uncertain Utopias," Andrea McDonald recounts how female *Quantum Leap* fans were effectively driven off the rec.arts.tv newsgroup for being "too silly" – and then off a mailing list where male fans continued to tease them for discussing the characters' relationships, their own lives and "Scott Bakula's cute butt."

Within a month, my signature files (appended to each posting) announced that I was an Associate Member of the splendidly named Star Fleet Ladies Auxiliary and Embroidery/Baking Society. The SFLAaE/BS mailing list provided a haven for female fans, away from immature fanboys ("We were sick of the wasteful postings that were bandied back and forth on the Net, contemplating whose breasts held more worth, Troi's or Crusher's") and from more serious problems such as harassment. By now I was used to being surrounded by boys, but this was the first time I'd had a whole group of girls to hang out with. It was my first real-life contact with the overwhelmingly female fandom which, up until that point, I'd only read about.

My earliest postings in the *Star Trek* newsgroups are a mix of terribly sincere politics, punchlines and very silly remarks about the characters I fancy. This sort of thing:

"One cannot be dignified when one has Julian in one hand, Data in the other, a bottle of maple syrup clutched in one's teeth and a gibbon twaddler gripped between the toes."

(Don't ask me what a gibbon twaddler is supposed to be.)

As daft as those postings were, they were also a reaction to the fanboys' adolescent sexuality – an assertion of heterosexual female lust, as was the Siddig El Fadil Estrogen Brigade (the first in a long line of Estrogen Brigades: "An enclave of female fans within a traditionally male-dominated fandom"). The Auxiliary also stuck up for each other in feminist debates – why wives in the 24th century take their husband's surnames, the double standard when it comes to actor's looks, Captain Janeway, etc.

Despite this feminine refuge, I absorbed the communication style of the testosterone-drenched environment of Usenet. In *Women, Men, and Politeness*, feminist and linguist Janet Holmes describes broad differences between how men and women talk. Women tend to use language to maintain relationships and to address the "face needs" of others – the need to be liked, and not to be imposed on. Men tend to use language as a tool – for exchanging information, for making decisions, etc. "Men's reasons for talking often focus on the content of the talk or its outcome, rather than on how it affects the feelings of others," notes Holmes. "It is women who rather emphasize this aspect of talk. Women compliment others more often than men do, and they apologize more often than men do too." Plus: "Men's greater social power allows them to define and control situations, and male norms predominate in interaction." Similarly, feminist and linguist Susan C. Herring studied two academic mailing lists, counting responses which agreed, praised, and called for further discussion: women were all over these, while men barely posted any. The opposite was true for responses which disagreed and called for the subject to be dropped.

So it's not hard to see why so much Internet discussion was (and is) "masculine" in nature: confrontational, brusque, concerned with winning the argument rather than with group bonding or soothing ruffled feathers. In turn, that helps to explain the grinding of gears that's happened so often when I've interacted with majority-female fandom: my learned "masculine" style of bluntly disagreeing and baldly arguing sends others into "face-saving" defensiveness. Rhiannon Bury observed exactly that pattern on the David Duchovny Estrogen Brigade mailing list, whose members "worked to avoid, minimize or mitigate disagreement." When bald assertions led to bad feelings, work had to be done to restore the community's coherence – not always successfully, with members quietly leaving, or avoiding discussion. So my bluntness shuts down discussion; it's something about myself I want to change. At the same time, I worry that an exaggeratedly "feminine" style of discussion can also impede discussion – by making dissent itself unacceptable.

* * *

Wind forward to May 1996, and the US premiere of the *Doctor Who* television movie. The TVM, pitched at female viewers as well as male ("From the moment she saw him, she knew he was her destiny!" boomed one ad), meant an influx of new fangirls. Within two weeks, female fans had formed the Paul McGann Estrogen Brigade – by this time, one in a long line of EBs and majority-female mailing lists.

With the novels, there had always been a great deal of resistance from some fanboys to the inclusion of "adult" material, especially sex, which was seen as the sort of thing *Doctor Who* by definition didn't include. Even the Doctor's granddaughter, Susan, was explained away by saying that "grandfather" was just her affectionate nickname for him.

Some of this stemmed from the comfort gay fans took from being able to watch a hero who never got the girl and didn't care; if he wasn't explicitly gay, at least he wasn't explicitly straight, and the lack of romance in the show was a refuge from the media message of compulsory heterosexuality. (Happily, rather than destroying that refuge, The New Adventures soon included gay authors and characters.) For the most part, though, the resistance was simply a sort of playground squeamishness in which violence and horror were fine but girl germs weren't. (And it continues to this day, with "Planet of the Dead" prompting one disgruntled fanboy to protest: "Timelords(sic) do not do sex.")

The TVM featured the Doctor's first on-screen kiss (not to mention his second and third) and re-ignited the debate. There was a marked difference in the typical reactions of female and male *Doctor Who* fans. "I personally thought that the addition of romance to *DW* was long overdue," wrote one fangirl on rec.arts.drwho. "I don't see how the Doctor becoming romantically (or sexually) involved with a woman of *any* race 'corrupts and demeans' him... I mean, if we think that, then that gives you the general opinion of sex in the general population... a nasty, dirty thing that 'higher beings' do not demean themselves to." She concluded: "The Doc's been lonely for many years... let the poor man have some life."

The TVM triggered a landmark change in the books: a new Doctor, and also a new publisher, as the BBC allowed Virgin's contract to lapse and took on the novels themselves. Jon Blum and I worked together on four of these Eighth Doctor Adventures (*Vampire Science, Seeing I, Unnatural History, The Year of Intelligent Tigers*) and I fulfilled a long-standing ambition by writing a sixth Doctor novel, *Blue Box*, in which Peri wore normal clothes and at one point wielded a flamethrower. Our books had always been well-received by fandom online and off, but in 2003, Jon and I were bowled over to win the Aurealis Award for best Australian SF novel for *Fallen Gods*, an eighth Doctor novella we co-wrote for Telos Publishing.

In The New Adventures, the Doctor's own sexuality remained largely unaddressed, although *Lungbarrow* established that Time Tots are made, not born. Perhaps partly due to the influence of female fans, the arrival of the eighth Doctor prompted something new in the novels: sexual subtext. Suddenly, everyone was falling in love with the Doctor, from companion Sam Jones to real-life programmer Alan Turing. The lovestruck character of Karl in *Tigers* was inspired by a fanboy's voluble revulsion at the thought of the Doctor having a relationship. In 2001 and 2002, other female authors began to appear in the range, starting with Lloyd Rose's novel *The City of the Dead* – in which the subtext erupted into text in the otherworldly boudoir of Mrs. Flood. (Books from Kelly Hale and Mags Halliday followed shortly, although a proposal from Rebecca Levene fell through due to time commitments.)

1999 saw the publication of *Warm Gallifreyan Nights*, a substantial fanzine collection of erotic fiction, poetry and art, mostly created by women. For at least a few male *Doctor Who* fans online, this female intrusion was too much. "Jokes about McGann with his nob (sic) out are perfectly acceptable," one explained. "What scares me is that this woman is genuinely doing it for the porn value."

Women (men, too) defended the zine with spirit and humor. But eventually, another fanboy linked to a story by the zine's editor, remarking: "... if you go to check it out, be sure to have a box of tissues handy (in my case, for tears of laughter)." There followed the posting of quotes from the story, accompanied by giggling and mockery. It's still one of the nastiest moments I can recall from online fandom, and I've seen some beauties. For at least some fanboys, the only comfortable *Doctor Who* sexuality was schoolboy smut; for a grown woman to fantasize about the Doctor was funny or sick or both.

The new *Doctor Who* must have given them one *hell* of a shock.

* * *

We're up to the present, pinching ourselves to see if the smash hit success of the new *Doctor Who* is just a wet dream. Head writer Russell T Davies set out to attract women to the series, making romance and family central to the stories, and succeeded outrageously, turning *Doctor Who* into the BBC's flagship show (and David Tennant into the fantasy of a million British women, with *Times* columnist Caitlin Moran leading the cheers).

A side effect of this success was the demise of the *Doctor Who* novels as we knew them: no more cheap paperbacks for grownups churned out by a large staff of freelancers, but a smaller number of hardbacks, with a younger audience in mind. These are mostly written in-house, so as to tie in with the show, rather than farmed out to freelancers like me. I'm not a *Doctor Who* novelist anymore; I'm back to being just one of the fans. Which is not a bad thing to be. Mostly.

Fanboys wage epic battles over the most amazing trivia (the shape of the TARDIS windows!) and can carry a grudge against some member of the production team for decades. As I discovered, fangirldom has its own version of these spats. The shipwar, or "relationship war," is a squabble over true love: Harry Potter, or the Doctor, or whomever, should find true love with the right female character (i.e., the one they personally happen to identify with). Plus – often in tandem with the shipwar – there's harsh criticism of female characters (Rose, Gwen) who seem to get too much approval from the showmakers or from the male characters.

Girls are trained to hide our aggression, not to get it into the open and deal with it. So when girls get nasty, it's often through indirect means, such as malicious gossip, spreading rumors, attacking reputations – with the excuse that "she asked for it." Online fandom has dedicated forums for this kind of bullying, including one specifically for humiliating fans who openly express anger. The bullies' identities are protected, while their targets may have no way to defend themselves from being pilloried in front of thousands of strangers. Fans who think this cyberbullying is harmless fun haven't been reading the headlines.

Of course, as we've already seen, fanboys can be bullies too. Some years ago I stumbled across a male fanzine editor's hate site dedicated to the New Adventures' authors. (Fortunately, his ISP took it down in a heartbeat.) But it breaks my heart to see girls and women squabbling over imaginary men, and turning on each other for not being suffi-ciently "feminine."

But of course, this ugliness is only part of the picture. What keeps me coming back to fandom are the jokes and references everyone gets, the delightful shared crushes, the general camaraderie: knowing that *it's not just me*. Thousands of other people watch the show with the same inten-sity I do. There's something more to *Doctor Who* than just a television series, some deep mythological thing that has woven it into the fabric of the culture and into so many individual hearts.

Let me leave you with a mention of a part of fandom I'm very proud of: the LiveJournal community ihasatardis, dedicated to the fine art of adding silly captions to pictures from the show. It's a profoundly good-natured place, with thousands of members, its own repertoire of traditions and in-jokes, and very little in the way of controversy and nastiness. And that really has little to do with my moderation: the communication is light-hearted and friendly because that's what its members want it to be.

Cites

Bacon-Smith, Camille. *Enterprising Women: Television Fandom and the Creation of Popular Myth.* University of Philadelphia Press, 1992.

Bury, Rhiannon. *Cyberspaces of Their Own: Female Fandoms Online.* New York, Peter Lang, 2005.

Gardiner, Judith Kegan. "On Female Identity and Writing By Women." in Elizabeth Abel (ed). *Writing and Sexual Difference.* University of Chicago Press, Chicago, 1982.

MacDonald, Andrea. "Uncertain Utopia." in Harris, Cheryl and Alison Alexander (eds). *Theorizing Fandom: Fans, Subculture and Identity.* Cresskill, NJ, Hampton Press, 1998.

Oates, Joyce Carol. "Is There A Female Voice?" in Janet Todd (ed). *Gender and Literary Voice.* Holmes and Meier, New York, 1980.

Stryker, Susan. *Transgender History.* Seal Press, Berkeley, CA, 2008.

Holmes, Janet. *Women, Men and Politeness.* London, Longman, 1995.

S. C. Herring, "Two Variants of an Electronic Message Schema." In S. Herring (ed). *Computer-Mediated Communication: Linguistic, Social and Cross-Cultural Perspectives.* John Benjamins, Amsterdam, 1996, pp. 81-106.

Acknowledgments Many thanks to Paul Winter of the Doctor Who Appreciation Society, David Lane of Sutekh and Tony Cooke of the Doctor Who Club of Australia for their assistance with demographics.

Two Steps Forward, One Step Back: Have We Really Come That Far?

Shoshana Magnet is an assistant professor in the Institute of Women's Studies at the University of Ottawa. She is currently working on a book entitled *When Biometrics Fail: Culture, Technology and the Business of Identity*. **Robert Smith?** is a professor of biomathematics at the University of Ottawa who researches eradication of diseases such as HIV, malaria and human papillomavirus. In his spare time, he writes a column for *Enlightenment*, the Canadian *Doctor Who* fanzine, runs the online *Doctor Who Ratings Guide* and is co-editor on three volumes of *Time, Unincorporated: The Doctor Who Fanzine Archives*. Oh, and he's also the braaaaaiiiiinnnnnnnssssss behind the recent academic paper on mathematical modelling of zombies that achieved worldwide fame and massive media attention by combining two incredibly geeky things in his life. Trust us, he was as surprised by this as anyone.

When the new *Doctor Who* works, it really works. From a populist perspective, it's been a massive success, with out-of-this-world viewing figures, merchandising, *Radio Times* covers and, thus far, an extremely effective changeover in at least one of the main cast every season. The special effects are finally special, the stories are tighter and faster, the sets are more believable and the theme tune is zippier.

What's most impressive, perhaps, is just how much attention is paid to the companions. They serve a magnificent purpose: they broaden the appeal of *Doctor Who* beyond the 14-year-old boy to give the 14-year-old girls in the audience role models as well.

But how do the new series companions rate in terms of social equality? How much forward progress have we really made in terms of gender, race and sexuality? In the 16 years since the old show went off the air, have we really come that far? Rose, Jack, Martha and Donna each

---

1. Intersectional feminist theory tells us that we can't consider gender separately from race, class, sexuality and disability. The components of our identities are like cake ingredients; once you've added them all to the mix and baked the cake, you can't pull out the flour and study it separately from the rest. In examining the progress made by *Doctor Who*, we need to think about the ways that sexism intersects with other forms of oppression.

represent a step forward in terms of gender, race and/or sexuality.[1] But each of the new series companions also has a limiting factor that dilutes that forward progress. All too often, the new series has given us role models that take two steps forward while taking one step back.

In this essay, we examine each of the new companions' strengths and weaknesses through the lens of progress as it pertains to gender, race and sexuality, as well as offering suggestions for the future on what a truly progressive companion might look like.

Rose: the Doctor's compassion

The first entry into the ranks of new series companions is the compassionate figure of Rose. She's the one who humanises the damaged ninth Doctor, who helps him to make his way toward a healthy emotional state. She's the one who has compassion for the lone Dalek when no one else does – the Doctor included. Her value to the Doctor is as his emotional core, the reminder of his "humanity," the embodied force of compassion that keeps him from tipping over into homicidal lunacy.[2]

Rose is the Doctor's compassion, in human form. This is crucial in *Doctor Who*, a show in which compassion is a central theme. Rose gets to play two of the female archetypes: maiden and mother.[3] She's both desirable and nurturing, and fulfils this role with very little variation on the script.

Although allotted a pretty traditionally gendered role, Rose in Series One rises above her humble beginnings to match and even exceed the Doctor's abilities, saving the day in "The Parting of the Ways" because she was brave enough to stand up and say no. There's no way in which you could call her inferior to the ninth Doctor in that moment, which marks a dramatic step forward for the show and a magnificent year of television.

However, in Series Two, the undercurrent of romance takes over Rose's character. It's no longer just there as subtext, and Tennant's first season consequently sees Rose almost completely de-clawed. The Rose of Series One would have stood up to the Sycorax, even if she failed; the

---

2. This point is made very clearly in "School Reunion," where Sarah Jane observes that the Doctor needs someone to stop him from going too far; "The Runaway Bride," where Donna makes basically the same observation about the fresh-off-"Doomsday" Doctor; and "The Waters of Mars," where a companion-less Doctor finally veers off into God-complex land.

3. The third of the female archetypes is the crone, but Rose is far too young to adequately venture into crone-hood.

Rose of "The Christmas Invasion" is weepy and inept, reduced to the damsel that the Doctor must rescue. The narrative builds up the Doctor's value by proportionally decreasing Rose's, and it does irreparable damage to the forward progress of the character.

Jack: acceptable and non-acceptable queerness

In some ways, Jack represents a massive step forward in terms of sexuality. He's put forth as the future of the human race, an emissary from a time and place where gender is no longer a limiting factor on human sexuality. He becomes a kind of queer hero, someone who flirts shamelessly with male and female, alien and human, companion and Doctor alike. The way in which the Doctor responds to Jack's advances, however, demonstrates the show's tenuous level of comfort with "nonstandard" sexuality.

New *Who* is careful to keep the Doctor's repartee with Jack to the same level of homosocial banter that you'd find in any male sports team. Even when the Doctor and Jack do briefly kiss, a) it's never repeated, b) we're given no semiotic indication that the Doctor felt the same way, unlike his (multiple) kisses with all his female companions, and c) the next thing the Doctor does is run far away, expending a great deal of energy avoiding having the subsequent awkward conversation. And when he and Jack finally do have a proper talk, two years later in "Utopia," they're separated by thick metal doors and framed in the context of a near-death situation, because, as the producer says in the associated episode of *Doctor Who Confidential*, that's just how "men" relate.

In fact, the Doctor veers profoundly towards heterosexuality in his relationships with the new companions. We've replaced the asexual hero of the old series Doctor with not just a sexualised hero, but a specifically heterosexualised one. The issue here isn't just that the Doctor sometimes likes to kiss the girls, it's that he puts his quasi-romantic relationships with his female companions on a higher level, vowing to hunt down anyone who so much as harms a hair on his girl's head, but callously leaving other people to die. The net effect is to continually remind us that heterosexual love is the highest love of all: it beats friendship, it beats random kindness and it beats compassion. This is an enormous change for the series, but unfortunately it represents a step backwards.

Jack's pansexuality is allowed on *Doctor Who*, but only because he's from the (very) distant future. People exactly like him exist in the 21st century – but you'd never know it from Rose's reactions in "The Doctor Dances." Here, the series uses a classic science fiction allegory to examine issues of today... except that it doesn't need to, because these aren't actually issues. Queerness and polyamoury aren't fantastical imaginings from the 51st century, they're something that happens every Friday night down at Club Babylon.

Torchwood attempts to counteract this (initially at least) by giving us a range of bisexual heroes. Of course, Gwen has one token kiss and Owen's only moment of non-strict heterosexuality is as part of an incredibly troubling date-rape threesome. But Jack and Ianto's relationship in the second and third series gives us actual gay action heroes, which are long overdue on TV.[4] Whatever its faults in consistent characterisation, *Torchwood* manages to think outside the heterosexual norm – which is delightful to see on television.

Martha: unrequited love, unforgivable blackness

Back on *Doctor Who*, Rose is followed by Martha – the first female companion in decades to have an actual profession. It's still one of the stereotypically feminine "nurturing professions," but it's marvellous to see them attempting to give us an accomplished woman with an actual career path.[5]

The main trouble with Martha is that, like Rose, she's completely defanged by the love story with which she's saddled. Although she's established as a doctor and even gets to use her medical skills beyond her first episode, her character is completely subsumed beneath the puppy-dog-eyes arc she's given. It's hard to be taken seriously as an empowered 21st century career woman when you're forced to spend all your time pining for the male hero.

Martha is the first female companion of colour (in the TV series, at least) and only the second racialized companion.[6] While it's great to see a woman of colour in such a prominent position, we wish the show

---

4. However, something both shows consistently lack is good-old-fashioned girl-on-girl action. Why aren't Donna and Martha shagging when they're travelling in the TARDIS in Series Four? The answer is that they undoubtedly are – but only in slash fiction. Which clearly still has an important place, since the main fiction steadfastly refuses to go there.

5. The most recent TV companion with a profession was journalist Sarah Jane Smith, way back in 1974. Peri sort of counts, as a botany student, and there is Mel and her computer programming, but they did nothing whatsoever with it and her profession isn't even mentioned on screen. Tegan and her gendered airline stewardess uniform, on the other hand, is far too stereotypical to count.

wouldn't have been so terrified of tackling the issue head-on in historical stories such as "The Shakespeare Code." Rather than directly deal
with her racialized identity, they sidestep the issue.

Race is a thorny issue for *Doctor Who*, and it always has been. In some
ways, it's a pity they didn't cast Carla Henry (Nathan's friend in the
British *Queer as Folk*) as the first companion, as the rumours suggested,
thus setting the scene from the start. Instead, the new *Who* debuted in
2005 with two white leads. There were rumours that the eleventh
Doctor might see the first casting of a non-white Doctor, but instead it
was back to yet another white guy in a very long series of white guys.

Torchwood handles the issue of race a little more successfully: without
the historical albatross that *Doctor Who* carries around its neck, it can
deal with a non-white cast member with no textual hang-ups. Of
course, they do take a Japanese character explicitly established as a
medical doctor in "Aliens of London" and retcon her as being a nerd-
girl. (She's good at computers, you say? No kidding! And she spends the
rest of her time making doe eyes at an obnoxious, hegemonic male
character who keeps emotionally beating her into the ground? No way!)

Donna: free will is an illusion after all

Then there's Donna. She's initially – and again in "Turn Left" –
defined as the person who stops the Doctor; like Rose, she represents
the Doctor's sense of compassion. She's also no shrinking violet, and she
overturns a huge limitation that the series has never overcome: she
doesn't have the body of a model.

This is actually quite remarkable, because no previous medium has
dealt with this: not the comics, not the books, not the audios. Donna,
gloriously, cuts right through that, giving young female viewers a role
model that isn't emaciated for once.[7] It's a much-needed step forward
in the arena of sexist beauty standards.

However, Donna's actualisation as a person also has limitations. The
Doctor keeps proclaiming that she's the most important person in the

6. Remember Mickey? The guy who started off as the person of colour we're all supposed to laugh at and whose interracial relationship is so dull that Rose has no hesita-
tion leaving him for the Doctor? He did eventually manage some character growth,
mainly because expectations for him were so low to start with.

7. Of course, you wonder if that would have been the case had Catherine Tate not
already been a celebrity. It's also probably a coincidence that the only new series
companion the Doctor doesn't seem to be attracted to is the one who *doesn't* look
anorexic, but you've got to wonder. That said, what works so well about their dynamic is that she's so clearly *not* attracted to him.

universe, but this turns out to be due to a freak accident, not because of her resourcefulness, intelligence or even her compassion. And when she becomes his equal at the end of Series Four, it's something that must immediately be taken away from her, against her will. Worse, the price she pays for this is a horrific one: she's returned to her previous life with no memory of her abilities.

What's bizarre is that, at the conclusion of "Journey's End," Donna isn't given a choice; the Doctor makes this decision for her. The Doctor – the man who always finds a solution where none appears to exist, who always finds a third way – gives up entirely and bundles her home, removing her from the decision process entirely. Donna succeeds brilliantly in many respects as a companion, but when it comes to her ultimate fate, she has no agency over her own decisions.

Looking back: what's past is prologue

While there's much to admire about Rose, Jack, Martha and Donna, each of them inevitably goes only so far. The new *Who* has made strides towards gender equality, though it makes several backward steps as well. It struggles with race, giving us several racialized companions, but in commodified and tokenized form. Sexuality is hugely successful in the form of Captain Jack and his Torchwood employees, but the Doctor's female companions (and to some degree, the Doctor himself) are resolutely hetero. The new series has tried to have its cake and eat it too, but it commits a crucial dramatic sin: it's too timid. We may have made some progress, but we still have a long way to go.

The irony here is that we're not asking for something that *Doctor Who* hasn't already accomplished. Can anyone accuse Ace of being too girly, or subservient to the Doctor? She's not; she's independent, has useful skills and has commendably crafted her own identity despite a less-than-ideal home life. Leela is another excellent example, despite the savage pin-up-girl outfit. She's in no way the Doctor's equal, explicitly having less education and knowledge than not just the Time Lord she travels with, but almost everyone she encounters. And yet, she's intelligent, resourceful and autonomous. She reasons, she learns. Then there's Romana: a Time Lord who starts out as the Doctor's equal (his better, even) in terms of sheer technical skill, but who noticeably lacks his wealth of experience. By the time Lalla Ward takes over the part, the character has learned a lot from her adventures; for the first time, it's as if the two *Doctor Who* leads are entirely on par with one another.

We might think the new series has made great progress by recruiting so many female viewers, but much of this owes to its "soaping" up the character's relationships, not actually breaking free of stereotypes. While romance isn't bad in and of itself, there's a whiff of contempt in the direction New *Who* has taken: namely, that women will tune in if the series includes more (straight) relationships and tones down the technobabble. The approach seems to be that female viewers will be so obsessed by the will-they/won't-they nature of the Doctor and Rose's relationship, they won't need any actual character to go with it. We're betting that the modern-day audience can handle both just fine.

If New *Who* needs inspiration on this point beyond the classic-series companions we've mentioned, it could do worse than to look to *Doctor Who* in the 90s. After the TV show expired in 1989, the seventh Doctor and Ace's adventures continued in The New Adventures – a book range with strong female characters who had actual professions and credible libidos, such as archaeologist Bernice Summerfield and police officer (and woman of colour) Roz Forrester. The Doctor's novel companions freely exercised their sexualities (Chris Cwej had a fling with a guy in *Damaged Goods*, a book written by Russell T Davies; Samantha Jones was involved with a woman in *Seeing I*). There was even pansexuality in the form of Jason Kane, who became Bernice's husband.[8]

The New Adventures also addressed racism in the form of Chris Cwej. Though white, he was marked by genetic difference, his genetic line oddly intact despite centuries of everyone else mixing races. And they dealt with the historical problem head-on by making it about character: when Roz was transported in the past, she had to learn that she was oppressed, which nicely holds up a mirror to our own society.

Then there were the new companions from the visual media: Grace is especially interesting because she's Martha, only without the puppy-dog eyes. Yes, she kisses the Doctor, but she makes her own choices at the end and even decides not to go with him because she knows who she is. There's also Ace becoming a Time Lord in "Death Comes to Time," or Sophie Okonedo's character from "Scream of the Shalka." These are women who aren't there simply to hang off the Doctor's arm, who have actual, non-gender-stereotyped careers and whose strengths lie in their resourcefulness, wit and intelligence, not in freak moments of science fiction wackiness to make them important.

Within New *Who*, there actually is one female companion who falls

---

8. Jason in many regards was a precursor to Jack; he even made a fortune writing erotica based upon his own numerous and varied sexual escapades. But unlike the far-future Jack, Jason was a contemporary hero, born in 1983.

along the lines of what we're describing; she's a consistently good role model, she strives to think things through and she has an actual career. Unfortunately, Sarah Jane only properly appeared in three New *Who* episodes. Instead, in her spin-off show for children, she's a better role model today than any new-series companion.[9] Even though Sarah Jane was invented back in the early 70s, she's demonstrated the robustness of the character, decades on from her "Women's Lib" origins.

Looking forward: a role model for success

Partly, this is about balance. Had even one or two of the ninth and tenth Doctors' companions been more akin to the novel companions or Sarah Jane, we might not be having this discussion. Part of it is about experience: Rose is a 19-year-old shop girl, whereas Sarah Jane has been doing this for decades (although she was capable to begin with, of course).

Doctor Who is fundamentally about a man who knows more than any mere human can. This means that if you aren't actively working to overcome it, the female companion can easily fall into the role of subservient girl, asking the stupid questions and existing only to be impressed by the Doctor's brilliance. However, this doesn't have to be a problem; it can also be an opportunity.

Knowing that the Doctor can be such an overpowering character, it's vital that the show-makers craft companions who can keep up with him. This can be done either by giving them a wealth of experience (Sarah Jane, River Song), making them more than human (Romana), or bestowing them with enough sheer force of personality to compensate (Ace, Bernice).

So does every companion have to be another Romana, the Doctor's female equal, in order to avoid being stereotyped? Not at all. We've seen excellent examples in Bernice, Roz, Ace, Leela and Sarah Jane Smith. Female characters with flaws and imperfections, who nevertheless are defined by their brain, not their ability to simper or make doe eyes at the Doctor. Characters who can be police officers, tomboys, warriors or journalists, not shop assistants and temps or a bit of totty for the

---

9. What's interesting is that *The Sarah Jane Adventures* are basically the Pertwee UNIT years in action. The lead character once travelled throughout time and space, but is now stuck on Earth, uses a sonic device and has a "family" of assistants to help fight a series of weekly alien invasions. She does this through mostly nonviolent means, and is heroic and nurturing at the same time. Even better, the supporting cast features multiple people of colour, who largely aren't playing tokenized characters.

Doctor. In short, we need less Jo Grant, more Bernice Summerfield.

In this regard, the future of *Doctor Who* looks surprisingly promising. Steven Moffat is taking over, and he's been responsible for a number of strong female characters in his television work. Some of his creations (River Song, Nancy from "The Empty Child," Sally Sparrow and Madame de Pompadour) are all excellent pseudo-companions with strong characters. They overcome inherent limitations – such as living in the 17th century – to provide surprising insights and clever deductions.[10] And characters such as River Song are precisely the kind of capable, professional woman we should have seen all along. With the Moffat era on the horizon, *Doctor Who*'s feminist future is suddenly looking very bright indeed...

---

10. Madame de Pompadour even manages a credible love story with the Doctor, yet she does it as an equal, despite being light years behind Rose in terms of her setting. And yet, that one-episode love story is more powerful than Rose, Martha and Kylie Minogue put together.

Traveling with the Doctor

Mary Robinette Kowal is an award-winning puppeteer and science fiction and fantasy author. As a puppeteer, she has performed for the children's show *LazyTown*, Jim Henson Pictures (*Elmo in Grouchland*) and the Center for Puppetry Art. She founded Other Hand Productions and has won two UNIMA-USA Citations of Excellence (the highest award for American puppetry) for her design work. As an SF author, Mary won the John W. Campbell Award for Best New Writer in 2008. Her short story "Evil Robot Monkey" was nominated for the 2009 Hugo Award for Best Short Story. Tor Books will release her first novel, *Shades of Milk and Honey*, in 2010. Subterranean Press released her first short story collection, *Scenting the Dark and Other Stories*, in 2009. Mary contributed a story to the Big Finish *Doctor Who* anthology *Short Trips: Destination Prague*, and also serves as Secretary to the Science Fiction and Fantasy Writers of America (SFWA). http://www.maryrobinettekowal.com/

My history with *Doctor Who* starts far younger than it really should. Ironically you can even say that the good Doctor taught me about time. In this memory, I can tell that I'm very young because I had to reach up to turn on the television. I wanted to watch *Mister Rogers* and when I turned on the TV, there was a shiny silver tube that seemed to stretch away from me. It writhed back and forth and beckoned me to fall into it. I didn't understand what I was seeing, but thought it might be the tunnel that the trolley on *Mister Rogers* went through. Fascinated, I stared at it, waiting for something familiar to appear. Drums pulsed and something wailed like my dad's musical saw, but with a strange electronic edge. Without warning, it all vanished.

What remained was a dark gaping hole in a wall, and a monster.

Yelping, I slapped the button to the television off and ran upstairs to tell my mother about the terrible thing in *Mister Rogers' Neighborhood*. I still remember how my heart raced and the weak feeling in my knees.

She looked puzzled and explained to me that this was Saturday. *Mister Rogers* only came on during the weekdays at 2:00. Time had never really occurred to me before.

Fast forward 11 or so years to high school. At a friend's house after school, we were flipping through channels looking for something inter-esting and there was that same silver tube. I had the same instant shock of terror that I'd had when I was little, followed immediately by curiosity.

Before my friend could skip to the next channel, I said, "Hang on. Stay here for a minute."

"What?"

"I saw this when I was little and it scared me. I want to see what it is."

Words slipped down the writhing tunnel. *Doctor Who*. Clearly that was the title of the show, but it was as much of a question as an answer. Again, the curiosity. What was this? I braced myself for seeing the dark hole and the monster again.

But when the tunnel vanished, the monster wasn't there. Instead I met a curious man with a floppy hat and a ridiculously long scarf. We watched the whole episode. I don't remember what that first episode was, but we were, as they say, hooked.

Later on, when I finally saw that gaping hole in the wall again and the monster, I thought, "Wait. I was frightened of... bubble wrap?" But the thing is, I still got the same electric terror. And this is what makes *Doctor Who* so brilliant: even with the cheesy sets and the cardboard special effects, you couldn't help but be caught up in the stories and the sheer grand adventure of it all.

So what was it that captivated us?

To start with, it wasn't like anything else on the television at the time. It could be a historical costume drama one day and a science fiction epic the next. The sheer variety of experiences you could have by following the Doctor were staggering. Other heroes might cover vast quantities of space, but almost no one else on television had a time machine.

And oh, how I wanted a TARDIS. Some of it was the sheer magic quality of something that was bigger on the inside than the outside. But most of the allure was the time travel. The TARDIS took me places I'd never get to go on my own.

But the real hook to the show, though I didn't realize it the time, were the Doctor's companions. For the most part, they were ordinary people, not super-gifted or bizarre aliens. Discounting the odd robotic dog, a companion could be *someone like me*. You understand the allure, don't you? I don't think there's a single teen who gets through high school without feeling like a misfit at some point. Watching the Doctor travel across time and space with his companions meant that I could imagine myself in early Rome, or on Mars, or Gallifrey.

That was magic.

I mean think about it. If the TARDIS materialized and any one of the Doctor's incarnations offered to take you on a spin around the universe and have you back in time for dinner, wouldn't you go? If you could have a chance to see other worlds, to meet Shakespeare, to save galaxies, well, who wouldn't want to do that?

My sophomore year of high school, we went to London and while we were walking down the street, I saw a blue English police box. It was the first time I'd seen one in real life. That electric feeling washed over me, even though I knew better, but still, there was a *chance*, wasn't there? There was a chance that it might be bigger on the inside than on the outside. I've still got the picture of me standing outside the police box, grinning as if I was about to go time-traveling with the Doctor.

As an adult, I have gotten to travel with the Doctor in a manner of speaking. It's simple and yet so amazing, it seems as magic as seeing a police box for the first time. See, Big Finish puts out a series of *Doctor Who* short stories and they hired me to write one. On the one hand, this makes complete professional sense and shouldn't be out of the ordinary. On the other hand, I was a squeeing fangirl who was able to imagine an adventure for my hero and have it enter the canon. It's almost like that blue box in London really had opened up.

I watch the new series avidly and have gotten my husband hooked on it as well. What makes me love the new *Doctor Who*? Pretty much exactly the same things excite me now that did when I was a teen. To be sure, the production values are much, much higher. Bubble wrap won't suffice to scare the modern audience and the range of tentacled, slimy or robotic menaces that the Doctor faces seem unending. But, as with the original series, the stories that really excite me are the ones in which the Doctor can examine the human condition by being an out-sider.

The real difference for me as an adult is that I associate more with the Doctor than his companions. I love the notion that this 900-year-old man retains a boyish enthusiasm and curiosity. It's a reminder to me to never stop learning and trying new things. I still wish I could pick up and travel with him.

In New York, we live in an apartment and my office faces out on the airshaft. Unlike the TARDIS my office is *smaller* on the inside than it is on the outside. When I write here, the noises from the airshaft always tug at my attention.

And then one day, I heard the TARDIS materialize in the airshaft. My heart froze and that prickle of possibility woke on my skin. Sure, I knew it was the neighbor's television but still... what if it wasn't?

Wouldn't you look out the window, too?

Martha Jones: Fangirl Blues

K. Tempest Bradford is a writer and editor of interstitial, science fiction, and fantasy literature. Her work has appeared in numerous magazines and anthologies, including *Interfictions* and *Federations*. Tempest is a well-known blogger on issues of gender, race, sexuality, and politics at *The Angry Black Woman*, *Feminist SF*, Carl Brandon and Tor.com blogs. http://tempest.fluidartist.com/

When you're a fan of *Doctor Who*, there are two discussions you're bound to have with other fans, no matter what the setting: "Who is your favorite Doctor?" and "Who is your favorite companion?" Most people don't make assumptions about my choice in the first category (Nine, by the way), but almost always assume that my choice for the second is Martha Jones. They assume this because I'm a black woman. I find that annoying for reasons you may well imagine. The main one being that Martha *is* my favorite, but not just because she's black.

When the announcement came that Freema Agyeman would be the next companion, I was happy that there would be another companion who was also a person of color. Unlike some fans, I do count Mickey as a companion and I also count Chang Lee from the (admittedly horrible) American *Doctor Who* movie. But Freema would be the first on-screen "main" companion of color.

This kind of thing means a lot to me, but it didn't mean that I'd automatically like the character or even prefer her over others. It remained to be seen if Martha Jones was made of awesome or just another stereotype.

The answer turned out to be a complex mix of both, with much of the blame lying with the show's creators and writers, and much of the success attributable to the actress.

Made of Awesome...

The writers did many things right in introducing Martha. The character was impressive in her very first episode, but it was a bit of dialogue in the second that sealed the deal for me. In "The Shakespeare Code,"

Martha steps out of the TARDIS and into the past. The Doctor is going on about similarities between Elizabethan London and her own when Martha asks a question that I'm sure many black fans had in the back of their mind:

> Martha: "Am I all right? I'm not going to get carted off as a slave, am I?"
> The Doctor (look of utter bewilderment on his face): "Why would they do that?"
> Martha: "Not exactly white, 'case you haven't noticed."
> The Doctor: "I'm not even human. Just walk about like you own the place. Works for me."

Though the Doctor blows off the question, I believe my first reaction to that line was *thank you*. If I was traveling in the past, that would have been one of my chief concerns, too.

This is indicative of everything that made me love Martha from the beginning. When her hospital gets transferred to the moon in "Smith and Jones," Martha doesn't panic, logically deduces that the windows can be opened, and, when asked by the Doctor who she thinks is responsible for transporting the hospital, she immediately answers: extra-terrestrials. This was a very pointed way for the show's creators to indicate that Martha was a companion worthy of the Doctor.[1]

Another thing I liked about Martha was her willingness to stand up to the Doctor and tell him off when it was clear he needed it. Badly. At the end of "Gridlock," she forces him to stop being oblique about himself. As things began to go south in "The Sound of Drums," she refuses to simply follow his orders and puts her concern for her family over his priorities. In "The Sontaran Stratagem," she won't let him make her feel guilty for being part of UNIT operations that involve guns (as if there are any other kind).

I love that even *before* Martha met the Doctor, she was already clever and competent and doing something with her life. She didn't need him to help her escape from a mediocre existence, she didn't need him to blossom into an extraordinary person. That she did grow due to their travels is a bonus, but because she came from a solid foundation, she was better able to walk away from the Doctor when she needed to. The

---

1. Compare her to Donna in "The Runaway Bride" (who was always away on vacation when major alien events happened and was therefore ignorant – or just in denial – of them), and Gwen in the *Torchwood* episode "Everything Changes" (who knows about the incidents but denies that any of them were real).

scene where Martha left the TARDIS was the perfect end to that season, especially given all the crap she had to endure while inside it.

Just Another Stereotype...

Though Martha is a great character, there were several choices the show's creators made that diminished my enjoyment of the episodes where she appeared. Some have to do with her interactions with the Doctor, but most have to do with some troubling attitudes toward race and the introduction of a heinous stereotype.

Within the show's continuity, Martha meets the Doctor a short while after Rose was accidentally sucked into an alternate dimension and trapped there. The Doctor is still mourning Rose, which is natural, and he constantly reminds Martha that she is not as good as Rose, which is a punk move. I often bemoan the fact that the Doctor is a huge jerk, despite being the hero of the show.[2] In Series Three, this quality is often on display when he interacts with Martha.

He screams at her ("Utopia"), treats her like second best ("The Shakespeare Code"), hides important information from her ("The Sound of Drums"), lies to her ("Gridlock") and strings her along as regards how long she can travel with him ("The Lazarus Experiment"). This can be explained away by the whole Jerk thing – it's part of canon, after all, that the Doctor can be nasty and mean just as easily as he is heroic and kind – but what *cannot* be explained away is why he treats her so differently than almost every female companion he's come across since his ninth incarnation.

Though it can be infuriating and infantilizing, the Doctor tends to treat his female companions as damsels in distress. Rose gained some agency by the end, but there was only one time[3] in her tenure on the show when the Doctor blithely disregarded her safety and well-being in favor of whatever dangers were going on around them or other people. Donna, abrasive as she is, still gets the damsel treatment, though she often chafes against it. Astrid ("Voyage of the Damned") definitely fits into the damsel profile.

Martha gets to play a different stereotype: that of the Mammy.

In her July 2, 2007 post in the LiveJournal community lifeonmartha,[4]

---

2. See my essay "The Lonely God is a Jerk" at *Fantasy Magazine*;
http://darkfantasy.org/fantasy/?p=721

3. "The Girl in the Fireplace." The Doctor essentially abandons Rose in the future in order to save Reinette, which makes no sense given the history of the characters.

blogger Karnythia laid out many of the problematic racial and sexist elements that cropped up during Series Three. She noted that the damsel stereotype is more often applied to white, female characters and that, "Damsels are always desirable, no matter how much ass they kick (or don't) and nothing they do makes them unworthy of love or protection." However, black women on television are often only given three choices: Mammy, Jezebel or Sapphire (a "nagging shrew constantly emasculating a weak black man," as defined in the post). Martha flirts or pines after a couple of men, including the Doctor, but she isn't wantonly sexual, so she doesn't fit Jezebel. But she most certainly fits the Mammy stereotype, which is also closely associated with the Strong Black Woman stereotype. Karnythia laid it out perfectly by saying, "[Martha] is supposed to be willing to sacrifice everything to protect the ones that can actually do some good."

The first, and probably most annoying, example of this is in "Human Nature/ The Family of Blood," wherein Martha literally works as a maid for the Doctor – who is disguised as a human in 1913 England. What I find most interesting about this episode is that it's based on a *Doctor Who* novel, *Human Nature*, which was originally written with the seventh Doctor and a white companion. In the novel, the companion poses as the Doctor's niece. Obviously, in the adaptation to television, this detail needed to be changed. But the nature of that change is troubling, especially for a black, female viewer such as myself.

From an in-series perspective, one wonders why the TARDIS chose an era which necessitated Martha having to play the part of a maid surrounded by people who would most certainly be horribly prejudiced toward her. Or why the Doctor didn't offer it some guidance for eras of history perhaps best left alone. Imagine if they'd ended up in the American South just before the Civil War. From an outside perspective, one wonders why the show's creators didn't see this as a real problem. Of course, the disparity between Martha's situation in 1913 and what she can achieve and be in 2007 is acknowledged within the script. That doesn't absolve the creators of a sketchy thought process, though. I wish that they had waited to produce this episode with a different companion. Beyond this aspect, it's one of the best in the series.

We again see Martha playing Mammy in "Blink," where it's revealed that she has to work in a shop in order to support the Doctor while he, supposedly, works on getting them home. The burden of being the care-

---

4. http:/ / community.livejournal.com/ lifeonmartha/ 268192.html

taker falls on her again. Why the Doctor can't also get a job is never explained. Nor why a highly educated person such as Martha would end up in a shop, a career path often held up in the Whoniverse as being highly undesirable and something to escape from ("Rose," "World War Three," "The Parting of the Ways"). It may be that Martha couldn't get anything else due to her race or gender. If so, we have another instance of the creators putting Martha in a setting where she's not allowed the same level of respect and autonomy, for no good reason. Then in "The Sound of Drums," Martha is the one who has to brave being caught by the police to get food for the Doctor and Jack while they're on the run. I also have to wonder if the Doctor would have asked Rose to wander the world, spreading the gospel about him, as he did Martha ("The Sound of Drums/Last of the Time Lords").

It's a troubling trend, both seen within the context of the show and from without. This is the kind of thing that people of color often fear when one of us is included on mainstream television – there's a community called deadbrowalking on LiveJournal for a reason. For all that is awesome about Martha Jones, my enjoyment of her tenure on *Doctor Who* was marred by the subtle current of racism and sexism that runs throughout.

I know from watching episodes of *Doctor Who Confidential* that the producers and directors are very impressed with Freema and call her a great leading lady for her ability to exude and give energy to everyone around her. She infuses Martha with this energy, plus confidence and intelligence. Though obviously the character was written with this intention, the wrong actress or the wrong attitude could have ruined it all. She wasn't given the greatest material to work with, but she always appeared to approach episodes with an eye toward squeezing the best out of them. In the *Confidential* episode "Alter Ego" (companion to "Human Nature"), Freema talks about how the script touches on issues of racism and how great it is to play a character that overall doesn't have limitations due to race or gender.

In many ways, she's right. In another time, Freema would have been given the part of a maid as a matter of course instead of an ironic, if problematic, twist. Her recognition of this lends weight to her performance, not just in this pair of episodes but all of them.

The elements of Martha's character, both positive and negative, could so easily have slipped into triteness. The unrequited love thread throughout Series Three annoyed me to the point of distraction in nearly every episode. A lesser actress would have allowed that aspect to overwhelm everything else about the character – who doesn't love a love story? But Martha is more than just a woman in love with a man who doesn't love back. Freema worked hard to bring out all the other, deeper things that make Martha who she is.

Forever Fangirl...

This is why, despite all of the issues I have with the show and the creators, I still love Martha. Hell, I still love *Doctor Who*. After all that, many might quite rightly ask: why? The troubling race stuff doesn't begin or end with Martha. I'm not even an old school legacy fan – the first episode of *Doctor Who* I ever watched was "Rose." So, why?

There's no easy answer.

The very basic one is that I just love the show. I love it down to the bottom of my toes. The SF geek in me loves all the cool aliens and different cultures and new planets and fantastic ideas. And the running. The running is awesome. I still love adventure stories, and stories about good people triumphing over the badness in the universe.

Doctor Who is a complex show, especially when compared to most television. Even when it's being an adventure or good vs. evil and all that, the core of the story isn't necessarily simple or straightforward. The Doctor is a flawed, damaged, brilliant, dangerous alien. He's also the hero. How can any show with such a character at the center of it be simple or straightforward?

Yes, the show's creators make thoughtless mistakes and probably don't understand why many of the issues I raised are problematic. They aren't completely clueless, though. And they *are* trying – note the number of interracial couples on *Doctor Who* and *Torchwood*.[5] There does appear to be an effort to show the future as multiracial, and to give characters of color a range of personalities from hero/ heroine to villain/ villainess and the many, many shades in between.

I love the universe that *Doctor Who* often shows me. I love the other companions – Rose and Mickey and Jack and Donna – and I even love the Doctor. Whatever the faults of the show's creators, they obviously love Martha, too. And it helps that Freema is a great actress that breathed life into her. Good acting is often able to make up for defects in writing and execution.

So I keep watching. And hoping.

---

5. I do realize this is a contentious issue on its own. Even allowing that Martha and Mickey wound up married, somehow, many fans of color often wondered if the show creators knew that people of color sometimes dated and even married each other.

Hoping that the writers do away with both the damsel and the Mammy stereotype. Hoping that they will stop under-utilizing Martha so criminally. Hoping that they will, by some miracle, begin to Get It.

Because, yes, Martha Jones is my favorite companion. She's clever and brilliant and brave and amazing. She's less needy and more independent than Rose and more faceted and less abrasive than Donna. I want to see her treated better by all involved. She deserves to be only awesome and more than just another stereotype.

In Defense of Smut

Christa Dickson is the co-author of *Dusted* and *Redeemed* – respectively the largest unauthorized guides to *Buffy the Vampire Slayer* and *Angel*. When she's not pondering the intricacies of the vampire invitation rule or wondering how fast Spike's hair grows, she soothes her damaged neurons by practicing yoga, whipping grass, reading OT3 fanfic and cooking things that contain no meat. She has the good fortune to be married to a man who's sweeter than Ten and looks better shirtless than either Nine or Jack.

People get into *Doctor Who* for lots of different reasons. Me? I'm in it for the smut.

I've been around *Doctor Who* for a long time. I remember it being on television as a child, and my high school boyfriend showed me a few episodes from his treasured VHS collection. I'm married to someone who makes a substantial part of his living off *Doctor Who*. For years, I appreciated the show, albeit in sort of a distant, removed way. I understood why people loved it so much; it just wasn't *my* thing.

When the new series started in 2005, I enjoyed watching it. It surprised me, hooked me in a way I hadn't expected. But even though I was willingly sitting down to watch it each week, I still wouldn't have called myself a fan. A supportive onlooker, perhaps. A casual dabbler. But not a *fan*.

Then along came Jack.

They say you never forget your first Doctor. I've seen Doctors come and go. It took a pansexual ex-Time Agent to get me on board.

I liked Jack, and not just because he was pretty. There was something gleefully dirty about him, a sort of cheerful smuttiness that resonated my concrete walls. Even better, he brought out the dirty in everyone else. His presence brought new undertones to the mostly innocent flirtation between Rose and the Doctor. Sly glances, innuendos, hints of depravity. This was something I could get my hooks into. This was *my show*. All of a sudden, my casual interest in *Who* took a sharp spike. I made a few inquiries, received a few gentle nudges from fellow fans, and before I knew it, I'd fallen headlong down the rabbit hole of smutty fan fiction. The posted word took me places that the show couldn't. It fulfilled my urges to get between the lines, flesh out those sly looks between the characters in all their glorious potential.

My husband was confused, to say the least. I was suddenly spending more time in *Who* headspace than seemed entirely natural. I spent my nights devouring fan fiction in spades, the filthier the better. (Ah, for that glorious happy story-gap between "The Doctor Dances" and "Boom Town.") I learned ridiculous amounts of detail about the TARDIS and its various (ahem) nooks and crannies. He really started to get curious when I'd innocently ask him to verify details about the TARDIS' inner workings... such as, for instance, the precise conditions under which the central column would pulse, or if your standard-issue timeship came with, say, a giant hot tub. ("Why do you ask?" he'd reply, his eyebrows climbing into his hairline. "No reason!" I'd chirp back glee-fully.)

He adopted a smile-and-nod approach. He didn't get it, exactly, but he was thrilled that we finally shared a *Who*-based enthusiasm. Whatever it took to get me interested was fine by him. And hoo boy, was I interested. Smut got me into *Doctor Who* in a way that nothing else could have done. I was surprised to learn that by supplementing my weekly watching with online fiction, I actually felt more invested in the characters and the setting. The world felt richer, deeper, more full of detail. I spent so much time exploring the characters' vices that they started to feel like old friends.

When David Tennant was cast, fanfic writers spent the summer of 2005 theorizing about what would make this new Doctor tick. What would thrill him? Repulse him? What would turn him on? We watched Tennant's performances in *Blackpool* and *Casanova* and made wild, inti-mate speculations. By the time Ten debuted in "The Christmas Invasion," I felt like I already knew him. That scene in the wardrobe room, where he's picking out his new duds, felt like reading back over those months of stories. We'd already peeked behind all those wardrobe doors, explored a hundred what-ifs. Now it was up to the show to carry that torch forward.

When I went to my next *Who* convention, I bounded in like a happy puppy. I was so eager to share my newfound fandom with other people, in the flesh. I'd always enjoyed watching fans banter points of discussion back and forth, but now I could play, too. Thanks to the power of smut, I was now a full-fledged fan.

So it came as a bit of a surprise when I learned that not everyone was as gung-ho about the new influx of squeeing fangirls. For the most part, the people I've encountered in *Who* fandom have been enthusiastic about my back-door entry into fandom... at worst, they're pleasantly bemused. But there's a definite contingent of folks who, while they're pleased to see new blood coming into fandom, are not entirely comfortable with the route by which we got there. The fact that I'm in it for the smut unsettles some people. It's... unseemly. Embarrassing. Not something that really belongs at the table of "serious" fandom. I occasionally get the sense such people wish we would either grow up and stop fixating on the peurile, or go off somewhere where our squees can't be heard by the "real" fans.

The people who are uneasy about smut tend to fall into two general camps. First, there's the old-school *Who* fans who love the classic show because the Doctor *isn't* your typical leading man. He's not human; he's quirky, verging on asexual. He's not concerned with petty diversions such as skirt chasing. Many of these fans find the notion of a romantic relationship between the Doctor and Rose sort of mortifying, because they feel like it cheapens the Doctor's character to have a 900-year-old Time Lord fall for a 19-year-old shop girl. (This is a familiar argument for *Buffy* fans, some of whom don't quite get why a 200-year-old vampire would go all googly over a high school cheerleader.) Many of these folks were even more disgusted by the seemingly casual sexual excesses of *Torchwood*. (I had one disgruntled fan explain it to me in these terms: every other show on television has tawdry sex. *Doctor Who* had been an exception to that. *Torchwood* seemed like an attempt to pander to the lowest common denominator.)

Then there's the feminist smut naysayers. They're insulted by the new series' attempts to "appeal to women" by "making it about relationships," because the presumption seems to be that women are only interested in love and romance. They feel that the smut-peddlers and the rabid dirty fanfic writers just reinforce that stereotype, by making female *Doctor Who* fans seem like a bunch of giggling hormonal teenagers who are only interested in how many settings the sonic screwdriver has (and what, exactly, they do). The question becomes: how can women in fandom be taken seriously if we constantly fixate on sex? How are we any better than the overgrown manchild that drools over Peri's bikini?

In both cases, the overarching concern is that the inclusion of sex in fandom cheapens it, makes it tawdry or common. *Doctor Who* is a faceted, intellectual show. It's unlike anything else on television. If we open the door to the floodgates of smutty fanfic, the fear is that we're dragging *Doctor Who* down to a frat-boy level.

But just because something's sexual doesn't necessarily mean that it's cheap. For that matter, just because fiction is written by a fan doesn't necessarily make it bad. Just like everything in existence (particularly when it's on the Internet), roughly 95% of fan fiction is terrible. But some of that remaining five percent is very good indeed. Even if (and I'd venture *particularly* if) it includes sex, fan fiction at its best can be gloriously speculative. It can deepen the reader's appreciation of the source material. It doesn't replace the canon, but it can supplement it in a way that no other form of fannishness can really replace.

As I see it, people write fan fiction for two fundamentally different reasons. Some people write fan stories as "missing episodes," an extension of what you see on screen. The goal for this kind of fan fiction is to replicate what's seen on screen as closely as possible. They write it to feed their hunger for more of the same, to tide themselves over during the gap year (or when seven days between episodes just seems like *too damn long*).

Then there's fan fiction that exists for nearly precisely opposite reasons, what I like to call "variations on a theme." The goal is *not* to give you more of what you see each week; instead, it's to show you things that you would *never* see on screen. It's the "elseworlds" stories, the exploration of "what if," the infinite possibilities that we'll never get in canon.

While the former certainly has its place, I'm much more interested in the latter. When you venture out of canon, when you tell stories that television wouldn't touch, you get a deeper understanding of the characters and the world. Almost every science fiction property features an alternate universe story at some point. What would our characters do if circumstances were different? Fan fiction gives us the opportunity to do this on a grand scale. The question isn't simply "How do the Doctor and Rose and Jack relate to each other in a purely non-platonic way commensurate with what we see on screen?" Instead, it's "What if the Doctor and Rose and Jack had an orgy in the Zero Room?"

While that particular example might sound silly, I firmly believe that sex is a vital and necessary way of understanding the way a person or (character) ticks. How someone expresses themselves sexually can be the most raw embodiment of their personality. It's the most distilled form of the conflicts that make us human (or alien, as the case might be). It's a window into character that nothing else can quite touch. And at its heart, good science fiction (or any good fiction *period*, actually) is about character. If we were only interested in the technical nuts and bolts of the universe, we could spend hours poring over fictional technical manuals. Instead, we watch people interact with each other. And where else can we really see people's inner workings laid bare (ahem) than when they're naked and sweaty?

There are those out there who believe – as one of my friends puts it – that the Doctor has no willy, that it's just *wrong* to make the Doctor the star of your sordid little fantasies. If you're more comfortable with seeing the Doctor as verging on asexual – or somehow "above" sexuality – you're welcome to that opinion. (Although I'm not really sure how you can watch episodes like "The Girl in the Fireplace" or "Human Nature" and not conclude that the Doctor must have *some* kind of sexuality.) Again, though… part of the reason that exploring the idea of the Doctor as a sexual being is interesting is because it's *not* the obvious choice. You learn more about a character when you put them in a non-obvious situation than if you stick to the tried and true. Would the Doctor be uncomfortable if Jack dragged him into a New Orleans brothel on Mardi Gras? Quite possibly. And *that's* what makes it interesting.

In fact, I often find stories more exciting and interesting further they deviate from traditional expectations. If you can take characters who are unlikely to get together on screen – what I like to call, in *Buffy* terms, the Spike/Xander phenomenon – *and* somehow make it believable, that's fascinating. It's one thing to write about established couples such as Doctor/Rose or Jack/Ianto. We've seen that on screen; it's predictable. It's entirely another thing to take an unconventional pairing and make it convincing. I want to be challenged. Give me Jack/Owen, or Jack/Master, or Doctor/Jack/Rose, or Jack/Sarah Jane. Turn my world upside down. Make me believe the impossible. Bring on the orgies; just keep it interesting.

To those who feel that fixating on sex somehow cheapens or degrades fandom, I'd gently suggest that you're capitulating to a general sex-negative attitude in our culture. In an era where advertising and media scream sex from every corner, we still hear that sex is dirty, cheap, wrong. We hear it from pulpits and academic institutions alike, from people who think sex is somehow the worst of sins to those who believe it's a tool of the patriarchy. Our culture consistently bombards us with constant access to sexual material while simultaneously shaming anyone who displays overt interest in it.

Those who say that smut has no place in fandom because it's cheap and dirty are echoing that, even if they're not intending to. Part of our power as human beings lies in reclaiming our sexuality, not being afraid of it. To believe that sex equals shame is just buying into those age-old systems of oppression. There's absolutely nothing wrong with enjoying stuff that turns you on.

I understand that my unabashed enthusiasm for all things smutty is not for everyone. But I firmly believe that smut has a place at this table. It's not just a silly diversion. It's a vital and necessary component of a mature fandom. I propose that not only is smut a valid extension of all things fannish, it's actually good for *Doctor Who*.

As far as I'm concerned, this fandom is big enough for all of us. Just because I like it dirty and non-canonical doesn't mean that there isn't plenty of room for those of you who would rather believe that the Doctor has no willy. Part of liberation is being free to do your own thing and letting everyone else be free to do theirs. There's room for all of us in this TARDIS (it's bigger on the inside, after all). You'll find me in the Zero Room, with my laptop open and my sonic screwdriver on setting number three.

Regeneration X

Catherynne M. Valente is one of the most acclaimed fantasy writers of the last five years. She has published numerous poems, short stories, and novels (including *The Labyrinth, Yume no Hon: The Book of Dreams* and *The Grass-Cutting Sword*). Her poem "The Seven Devils of Central California" won the Rhysling Award in 2008. Cat's novel duology *The Orphan's Tales* (*In the Night Garden* and *In the Cities of Coin and Spice*) won the prestigious Mythopoeic Award for adult literature in 2008. The first volume also won the James Triptree Jr. Award for the expansion of gender and sexuality in speculative fiction in 2006. Bantam Spectra released her most recent novel, *Palimpsest*, in 2009. PS Publishing will be releasing her first short story collection in late 2010. Cat is also currently serializing her children's novel *The Girl Who Circumnavigated Fairyland in a Ship of Her Own Making* on her website. She makes her home off the coast of Maine with her partner, two dogs and a cat. http://www.catherynnemvalente.com/

The funny thing about real life is how much it's like a television show. If you look, you can find every one of us in that strange, hyper-colored world. Reflected, distorted, blown up, writ large, but we are all there. We cannot help but find ourselves there – and not just find but seek. We live a dozen lives a day that are not our own, through books and movies and television, and we need so desperately to believe that it is not wasted time, that it means something more than the deepening of the couch cushions. We want to believe that life can be as circular, as karmic, as rich and deep as art. That in life, too, themes repeat poetically, and sorrow ends. That is, in the end, what fan activity is: seeking ourselves, seeking meaning in stories. We choose our idols out of dozens, hundreds, and clothe ourselves in the appropriate vestments and icons. We buy, say, an absurdly long scarf, or Converse shoes, to identify ourselves as these acolytes. In a very real way, television is the new mythos. It defines the world, reinterprets it. The seasons do not change because Persephone goes underground. They change because new episodes air, because sweeps week demands conflagrations and ritual deaths. The television series rises slowly, arcs, descends into hiatus, and rises again with the bright, burning autumn.

To some this might seem horrific, the destruction of serious thought. I don't think so – and I am a classicist by training. Persephone is my co-pilot. But part of what classicists do is to see how old stories take on new shapes, how they remain the same despite the constant warping influence of technology. Television has become something new, has grown up and grown more serious, shrinking to a standard of thirteen (talismanic thirteen!) episodes rather than a rambling twenty-two, twenty-four, thirty-nine. It breaks myth into bites small enough to chew. It has become the best way to tell a long story on screen.

And *Doctor Who* is a very long story.

I'm a New *Who* girl. I never watched the old show – having been born in 1979, I just missed it on multiple levels. I was only peripherally aware of *Doctor Who* at all, despite moving in science fiction circles for most of my adult life. But I lived in southern Virginia for awhile, and there just isn't much to do down there. I saw a little blue box – the new Series One DVD set – at the video store and decided to take it home and see what the fuss was all about. And it seized my heart like few other shows. I don't think *Doctor Who* has ever touched the heights of the ninth Doctor arc again, but it was enough to grab me like a hook to the heart, and keep me going through less ambitious cycles. There is an ache to the first season, an urgency and a mythic spread most shows don't even try for. And then there was the little detail that, at least in that first season, we were all allowed to have stories: women and queer and polyamorous and every sort of freak. We were right there, on the screen of the world, next to the straight white heroes, and we weren't less than they.

I bought a scarf. I bought a brown coat, and it wasn't because of *Firefly*.

Yet it's always been hard for me to express what I see in *Doctor Who*. After all, even in its new incarnation, it is often silly, nonsensical, and emotionally stunted. The writing is uneven, the plots preposterous, the aliens range from sublime to infantile. A love of *Buffy* or *Farscape* is comparatively easier to defend. The *Doctor Who* fan must forgive so much. And yet, what is there, behind it all, is so primal that all the wobbling styrofoam costumes in the world cannot hide it. Because that delicate viewer-identification dance that moves back and forth through all television shows is peculiarly expressed in *Doctor Who* – perhaps even perfectly so. Because if this Doctor or that companion is not a mirror held up to your soul, well, wait a few seasons. Everything changes.

Though I understand that the regeneration theme began as a necessity of casting, the grace of it is occasionally breathtaking. We say: *My Doctor. Your Doctor.* Because among the eleven of them, one is always us. Nine is mine – his sadness, his weird intensity, his guilt, his desperation for connection. Maybe Ten is yours – his nerdy ebullience, his enthusiasm, his endless apologizing, his acceptance of fate. The Doctor is all of us, he lives and dies as all of us, and we need him to – because, no matter the anvil-imagery of the Doctor as Christ, this is actually a far older, and far simpler, story than that. Everything changes.

We all regenerate. I am not the same woman who first saw Rose ascend. Years go by and I become someone new, with the same memories, but a new face, a new self. When I first watched the Doctor dance I was a Navy wife, unhappy and stuck and reaching for something, anything, that connected me to the world. Now I am on the verge of marrying again, living on an island in the sea, writing books and adventuring in an unobtrusive little box. I am bigger on the inside than I am on the outside. Who knows who I will be when the twelfth Doctor rolls around? The Doctor and I change together, evolve, learn, grow. Sometimes our lovers, our friends, our enemies, our companions will stay with us for awhile. Sometimes they will come and go so fast, with such flashes of light and love that you flounder in their wake. You can set your internal clock by the cycles of the Doctor. Because it wouldn't be mythology if it weren't played out in large and small in every sphere of our lives, in ugly military divorces and post-collegiate ennui and lost jobs and pirated BBC shows – and thus in the stories we tell. We are born, we fight our battles, we make terrible mistakes, we lose our companions, we die in vain and otherwise, and are reborn to do it all over again. It's the old sacrificial king rag, in which Christ is just a first-chair flautist – but oh, how sweet it plays on the Gallifreyan pipes.

And then there's the companion, whose face changes, too. The new incarnation of the Doctor insists on playing out a male Doctor / female companion dyad (Jack was always his own man, just stopping by for an arc or two, and that is sad, because no woman is given the same autonomy when faced with the Doctor). This is deceptive – it makes it look like the story of the Doctor and the companion is always one of a tempting trickster, a Hades, beckoning Persephone down into the dark, infinite otherworld of the TARDIS. The amoral alien ever in control, offering riches and adventure and awful beauty to an innocent young girl. And on that level, it works for a subset of viewers, who are either innocent and young and want to be tempted, or older know-it-alls who want to dazzle a nubile maid. And if we watch that story, we can change with her, from a shop girl to a doctor to a lost soul to a Doctor again. The companions are always ascending, always, moving upward, around on their own wheels. But there is another story going on underneath it.

The companion is not innocent, she is not agog. She pulls the Doctor out of grief and into another cycle of living, she is, ineffably, the life force, pushing him through the hero's cycle again and again. Even though he wants to rest. Even though the moment he sees her he knows he will die in her arms, if not this specific girl, one like her, when she has changed her face the way he changes his. She is Hades, literally, his death come to take him on one – or two, or three – final rides before it's down into the dark again, and the painful rising towards light. His wheel turns down as hers turns up, looking into the vortex of time and becoming the light of the world, the goddess of terrible, awful light – and when their wheels touch (and they always touch, once a season, ever so briefly: cheeks pressed to the same wall, caressing the same watch, sharing the same mind) and she passes it to him, it drags him back into shadow, into change, into the momentary oblivion of death. In some sense, perhaps, the seasons only exist to move these two icons, the Queen of Life and the King of Death, or the Lord of Light and the Queen of Air and Darkness, towards each other, to merge for just a moment, and inevitably part – which is the core of every tale ever told. There is no he or she in that. There is only a binary system, seeking itself, repulsing, destroying, creating and seeking again. I look, have always looked, at the Doctor and seen not fathers, husbands, brothers, men moving and shaking, but myself, the brainy post-traumatic girl moving so bright and fast through the lives of others, appearing and disappearing like magic as I moved through three countries and five states in the space of a few years, writing and re-writing stories until they came out right, offering to take people with me, over and over, until someone said yes, talking constantly so that no one knew how afraid I could be, how lonely I was. Apologizing, always apologizing. I always looked at him and saw me, looked at the companions and saw my mates in life.

And yet I can't help but remember an old girlfriend, miserable, eyes streaked with tears, insisting: *All I ever wanted was to be someone's companion. I'm not like you. I'm not a Doctor.* And being horrified, because her wheel was spinning nowhere near mine, and I didn't want a girl to stay in the TARDIS and make cookies, and I couldn't see how the wheel that started with a lost shop girl could ever end with golden light spilling grace out into every cell. Letting her go because I couldn't love her in anything like a normal way. Because if this stuff wasn't universal there'd be no sense in writing silly space stories where it happens over and over. Everything repeats. Everything changes. It all depends on which wheel you're on. Sometimes you're on your way up, into the heavens all full of angry robots you can turn to stardust with a wave of your hand. Sometimes you're on your way down into hell, with demons turning and turning in the dark, just waiting for you to come within reach. Life consists mainly of jumping from one wheel to the other. The Doctor does it, roughly every thirteen episodes. And so do we. Life moves like that, in patterns, in shapes familiar and strange, and at no point does the curtain close and the screen fade to black while lurid nebulae keep on bleeding into the black. Sometimes ratings are low and viewers miss the old flash and crackle. Sometimes our demons are ridiculous and ugly, sometimes they are boring and keep showing up no matter how far beyond them we think we have grown. Sometimes the jokes fall flat and a plotline that should have been profound runs smack into a wall of tragedy and failure and mindwiping because Life and Death cannot live in the same body but *ye gods* how we wish they could. More than we wish for there to be a perfect world where we can have our impossible lover, we wish for this world to be one where we can be both human and divine, Light and Dark, Donna and the Doctor, both wheels spinning together. Sometimes everything seems stupid and tawdry. Sometimes the sonic screwdriver is a beeping piece of light-up plastic. Sometimes it can do anything. Everything changes.

The Doctors and the companions are push-pins on a map. They regenerate constantly, every year, winter into spring. Our reactions to them, our identification with or repulsion by them, our need for them, our rejections of them tell us how far we have come, how far we have to go. They are silly, and unsightly, and self-indulgent, sublime, and glorious, and utterly necessary for the sacred acts of self-mythology.

And they tell us that there is always next season, when ratings will be up, and the smiles will return, and everyone will be reunited. We'll ride a blue box into the sunset, the tale finally illuminated by two wheels, one falling down into the past, one rising upward, eternally, into the future.

Acknowledgements

Books like this don't happen without a lot of moral and material support from our friends and colleagues. The editors would like to thank, in alphabetical order: Elizabeth Bear, Abbie Bernstein, Lee Binding, Graeme Burk, Paul Cornell, Susan M. Garrett, Javier Grillo-Marxuach, Jason Haigh-Ellery, Jennifer Adams Kelley, Susie Liggat, James Moran, Sean M. Murphy, Helen Raynor, Gary Russell, Rob Shearman, Gene Smith, Robert Smith?, Ruth Ann Stern and Mark Waid. Also, Tara's mum.

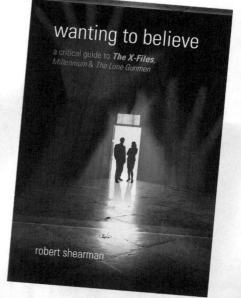

OUT NOW... In Whedonistas, a host of award-winning female writers and fans come together to celebrate the works of Joss Whedon (Buffy the Vampire Slayer, Angel, Firefly, Dollhouse, Doctor Horrible's Sing-Along Blog).

Contributors include Sharon Shinn ("Samaria" series), Emma Bull (Territory), Jeanne Stein (the Anna Strong Chronicles), Nancy Holder (October Rain), Elizabeth Bear (Chill), Seanan McGuire (October Daye series), Catherynne M. Valente (Palimpsest), Maria Lima (Blood Lines), Jackie Kessler (Black and White), Sarah Monette (Corambis), Mariah Huehner (IDW Comics) and Lyda Morehouse (AngeLINK Series). Also featured is an exclusive interview with television writer and producer Jane Espenson, and Juliet Landau ("Drusilla").

ISBN: 978-1935234104
MSRP: 14.95

WHEDONISTAS

WHEDON, J.
48 - 152342

A CELEBRATION OF THE WORLDS OF
JOSS WHEDON BY THE
WOMEN WHO LOVE THEM

mad norwegian press

Credits

Publisher / Editor-in-Chief
Lars Pearson

Design Manager / Senior Editor
Christa Dickson

Associate Editor (Chicks)
Michael D. Thomas

Associate Editor (MNP)
Joshua Wilson

The publisher wishes to thank...
All of the show-runners, guests and attendees of Chicago TARDIS
– the convention that in one way or another was the genesis of
this book.

A special thank-you to Tara, for providing the raw inspiration for
Chicks Dig Time Lords, and to Lynne, for providing the raw blood
and sweat needed to pull it off. Also, thanks are due to Sophie
Aldred, Jeremy Bement, Lisa Bowerman, Graeme Burk, Christa
Dickson (my favorite chick who digs Gallifreyans), Laura
Doddington, India Fisher, Tammy Garrison, Shawne Kleckner,
Shoshana Magnet, Robert Smith?, Katy Shuttleworth, Michael D.
Thomas and that nice lady who sends me newspaper articles.

mad norwegian press

1150 46th Street
Des Moines, Iowa 50311
madnorwegian@gmail.com
www.madnorwegian.com

And please join the Mad Norwegian Press group on Facebook!